CITIES OF THE PLAIN

CITIES OF THE PLAIN

Cormac McCarthy

Volume Three
The Border Trilogy

Alfred A. Knopf New York 1998

THIS IS A BORZOI BOOK
PUBLISHED BY ALFRED A. KNOPF, INC.

www.randomhouse.com

Library of Congress
Cataloging-in-Publication Data

McCarthy, Cormac.
    Cities of the plain / Cormac McCarthy.
        p.   cm. — (Border trilogy ; v. 3)
    ISBN 0-679-42390-7 (alk. paper)
    I. Title   II. Series: McCarthy, Cormac, [date]
Border trilogy ; v. 3.
PS3563.C337C58   1998
813'.54—dc21   98-11583
                                                      CIP

A limited signed edition of this book has been published by B. E. Trice Publishing, New Orleans.

Manufactured in the United States of America
First Edition

CITIES OF THE PLAIN

I

THEY STOOD in the doorway and stomped the rain
from their boots and swung their hats and wiped the
water from their faces. Out in the street the rain
slashed through the standing water driving the gaudy red and
green colors of the neon signs to wander and seethe and rain
danced on the steel tops of the cars parked along the curb.

Damned if I aint half drowned, Billy said. He swung his dripping hat. Where's the all-american cowboy at?

He's done inside.

Let's go. He'll have all them good fat ones picked out for
hisself.

The whores in their shabby deshabille looked up from the
shabby sofas where they sat. The place was all but empty. They
stomped their boots again and crossed to the bar and stood and
thumbed back their hats and propped their boots on the rail
above the tiled drainway while the barman poured their
whiskies. In the bloodred barlight and the drifting smoke they
raised their glasses briefly and nodded as if to salute some
fourth companion now lost to them and they tilted back the
shots and set the empty glasses on the bar again and wiped their
mouths with the backs of their hands. Troy jutted his chin at
the barman and made a circling gesture with one finger at the
empty glasses. The barman nodded.

John Grady you look like a goddamned wharf rat.

I feel like one.

The barman poured their whiskies.

I never seen it rain no harder. You want a beer back? Give us
three beers.

You got one of them little darlins picked out?

The boy shook his head.

Which one you like, Troy?

I'm like you. I come down here for a fat woman and that's what I'm havin. I'm goin to tell you right now cousin, when the mood comes on you for a fat woman they just wont nothin else satisfy.

I know the feelin well. You better pick you one out, John Grady.

The boy turned and looked across the room at the whores.

How about that old big'n in the green pajamas?

Dont be puttin him on my gal, said Troy. You'll be the cause of a fight breakin out here in a minute.

Go on. She's lookin over here.

They're all lookin over here.

Go on. I can tell she likes you.

She'd bounce John Grady off the ceilin.

Not the all-american cowboy she wouldnt. The cowboy'd stick like a cocklebur. What about the one with the blue windercurtain wrapped around her?

Dont pay no attention to him, John Grady. She looks like her face caught fire and they beat it out with a rake. I'm goin to say that blond on the end is more your style.

Billy shook his head and reached for his whiskey. They aint no reasonin with the man. He just aint got no taste in women and that's a mathematical fact.

You stick with your old dad, said Troy. He'll get you onto somethin with some substance to it. Parham yonder actually claimed that a man ought not to date anything he couldnt lift. Said what if the house caught fire.

Or the barn.

Or the barn.

You remember the time we brought Clyde Stapp down here?

I do and he was a man of judgment. Picked him out a gal with some genuine heft to her.

JC and them slipped the old woman a couple of dollars to let em go back there and peek. They was goin to take his picture but they got to laughin and blew the deal.

We told Clyde he looked like a monkey fuckin a football. I thought we was goin to have him to whip. What about that one in the red yonder?

Dont listen to him, John Grady.

Value per pound on a dollar basis. He dont even want to consider a thing like that.

You all go on, said John Grady.

Pick you one out.

That's all right.

You see there Troy? All you done is got the boy confused.

JC told everbody that Clyde fell in love with the old gal and wanted to take her back with him but all they had was the pickup and they'd of had to send for the flatbed. By then Clyde had done sobered up and fell out of love and JC said he wasnt takin him to no more whorehouses. Said he hadnt acted in a manly and responsible fashion.

You all go on, said John Grady.

From the rear of the premises he could hear the rain rattling on a metal roof. He ordered another shot of whiskey and stood turning the glass slowly on the polished wood and watching the room behind him in the yellowing glass of the old Brunswick backbar. One of the whores crossed the room and took him by the arm and asked him to buy her a drink but he said he was only waiting for his friends. After a while Troy came back and sat on the barstool and ordered another whiskey. He sat with his hands folded on the bar before him like a man at church. He took a cigarette from his shirtpocket.

I dont know, John Grady.

What dont you know?

I dont know.

The barman poured his whiskey.

Pour him anothern.

The barman poured.

Another whore had come up to take John Grady's arm. The powder on her face had cracked like sizing.

Tell her you got the clap, said Troy.

John Grady was speaking to her in spanish. She tugged at his arm.

Billy told that to one down here one time. She said that was all right she had it too.

He lit the cigarette with a Third Infantry Zippo lighter and laid the lighter on top of his cigarettes and blew smoke down along the polished wood and looked at John Grady. The whore had gone back to the sofa and John Grady was studying something in the backbar glass. Troy turned and followed his gaze. A young girl of no more than seventeen and perhaps younger was sitting on the arm of the sofa with her hands cupped in her lap and her eyes cast down. She fussed with the hem of her gaudy dress like a schoolgirl. She looked up and looked toward them. Her long black hair fell across her shoulder and she swept it slowly away with the back of her hand.

She's a goodlookin thing, aint she? Troy said.

John Grady nodded.

Go on and get her.

That's all right.

Hell, go on.

Here he comes.

Billy stepped up to the bar and adjusted his hat.

You want me to go get her? said Troy.

I can get her if I want her.

Otra vez, said Billy. He turned and looked across the room.

Go on, said Troy. Hell, we'll wait on you.

That little girl the one you're lookin at? I bet she aint fifteen.

I bet she aint either, said Troy.

Get that one I had. She's five gaited or I never rode.

The barman poured their whiskies.

She'll be back over there directly.

That's all right.

Billy looked at Troy. He turned and picked up his glass and contemplated the reddish liquor welling at the brim and raised and drank it and took his money from his shirtpocket and jerked his chin at the watching barkeep.

You all ready? he said.

Yeah.

Let's go get somethin to eat. I think it's fixin to quit rainin. I dont hear it no more.

They walked up Ignacio Mejía to Juárez Avenue. The gutters ran with a grayish water and the lights of the bars and cafes and curioshops bled slowly in the wet black street. Shopowners called to them and streetvendors with jewelry and serapes sallied forth to attend them at either side. They crossed Juárez Avenue and went up Mejía to the Napoleón and sat at a table by the front window. A liveried waiter came and swept the stained white tablecloth with a handbroom.

Caballeros, he said.

They ate steaks and drank coffee and listened to Troy's war stories and smoked and watched the ancient yellow taxicabs ford the water in the streets. They walked up Juárez Avenue to the bridge.

The trolleys had quit running and the streets were all but empty of trade and traffic. The tracks shining in the wet lamplight ran on toward the gateshack and beyond to where they lay embedded in the bridge like great surgical clamps binding those disparate and fragile worlds and the cloudcover had moved off down from the Franklins and south toward the dark shapes of the mountains of Mexico standing against the starlit sky. They crossed the bridge and pushed through the turnstile each in turn, their hats cocked slightly, slightly drunk, and walked up south El Paso Street.

IT WAS STILL DARK when John Grady woke him. He was up and dressed and had already been to the kitchen and back and had spoken to the horses and he stood in the doorway of Billy's bunkroom with the canvas curtain pushed back against the jamb and a cup of coffee in one hand. Hey cowboy, he said.

Billy groaned.

Let's go. You can sleep in the winter.

Damn.

Let's go. You been layin there damn near four hours.

Billy sat up and swung his feet onto the floor and sat with his head in his hands.

I dont see how you can lay there like that.

Damn if you aint a cheerful son of a bitch in the mornin. Where's my by god coffee at?

I aint carryin you no coffee. Get your ass up from there. Grub's on the table.

Billy reached up and took his hat from a wallpeg over the bed and put the hat on and squared it. Okay, he said. I'm up.

John Grady walked back out up the barn bay toward the house. The horses nickered at him from their stalls as he passed. I know what time it is, he told them. At the end of the barn a length of hayrope hung from the loft overhead and he drained the last of his coffee and slung the dregs from the cup and leaped up and batted the rope and set it swinging and went out.

They were all at the table eating when Billy pushed open the door and came in. Socorro came and took the plate of biscuits and carried them to the oven and dumped them into a pan and put the pan in the warmer and took hot biscuits from the warmer and put them on the plate and carried the plate back to the table. On the table was a bowl of scrambled eggs and one of grits and there was a plate of sausage and a boat of gravy and bowls of preserves and pico de gallo and butter and honey. Billy washed his face at the sink and Socorro handed him the towel and he dried his face and laid the towel on the counter and came to the table and stepped over the back of the empty chair and sat and reached for the eggs. Oren glanced at him over the top of his paper and continued reading.

Billy spooned the eggs and set the bowl down and reached for the sausage. Mornin Oren, he said. Mornin JC.

JC looked up from his plate. I guess you been fightin that bear all night too.

Fightin that bear, said Billy. He reached and took a biscuit and refolded the cloth back over the plate and reached for the butter.

Let's see them eyes again, said JC.

Aint nothin wrong with these eyes. Pass the salsa yonder.

He spooned the hot sauce over his eggs. Fight fire with fire. Aint that right John Grady?

An old man had come into the kitchen with his braces hanging. He wore an oldfashioned shirt of the kind the collar buttoned to and it was open at the neck and no collar to it. He had just shaved and there was shaving cream on his neck and on the lobe of one ear. John Grady pushed back his chair.

Here Mr Johnson, he said. Set here. I'm all done.

He rose with his plate to take it to the sink but the old man waved him down and went on toward the stove. Set down, he said, set down. I'm just gettin me some coffee.

Socorro unhooked one of the white porcelain mugs from the underside of the cabinet shelf and poured it and turned the handle facing out and handed it to the old man and he took it and nodded and went back across the kitchen. He stopped at the table and spooned two huge scoops of sugar out of the bowl into his cup and left the room taking the sugarspoon with him. John Grady put his cup and plate on the sideboard and got his lunchbucket off the counter and went out.

What's wrong with him? said JC.

Aint nothin wrong with him, said Billy.

I meant John Grady.

I know who you meant.

Oren folded the paper and laid it on the table. Dont you all even start, he said. Troy, you ready?

I'm ready.

They pushed back from the table and rose and went out. Billy sat picking his teeth. He looked at JC. What are you doin this mornin?

I'm goin into town with the old man.

He nodded. Out in the yard the truck started. Well, he said. It's light enough to see, I reckon.

He rose and crossed the kitchen and got his lunchpail from the counter and went out. JC reached across the table and got the paper.

John Grady was sitting behind the wheel of the idling truck. Billy got in and set the lunchpail on the floor and shut the door and looked at him.

Well, he said. You ready to put in a day's work for a day's wages?

John Grady put the truck in gear and they pulled away down the drive.

Daybreak to backbreak for a godgiven dollar, said Billy. I love this life. You love this life, son? I love this life. You do love this life dont you? Cause by god I love it. Just love it.

He reached into his shirtpocket and shook out a cigarette from the pack there and lit it with his lighter and sat smoking while they rolled down the drive through the long morning shadows of fence and post and oaktree. The sun was blinding white on the dusty windshield glass. Cattle standing along the fence called after the truck and Billy studied them. Cows, he said.

They nooned on a grassy rise on the red clay ranges ten miles south of the ranch house. Billy lay with his rolled jacket under his head and his hat over his eyes. He squinted out at the gray headlands of the Guadalupes eighty miles to the west. I hate comin out here, he said. Goddamn ground wont even hold a fencepost.

John Grady sat crosslegged chewing a weedstem. Twenty miles to the south a live belt of green ran down the Rio Grande valley. In the foreground fenced gray fields. Gray dust follow-

ing a tractor and cultivator down the gray furrows of a fall cot-
tonfield.

Mr Johnson says the army sent people out here with orders
to survey seven states in the southwest and find the sorriest
land they could find and report back. And Mac's ranch was settin right in the middle of it.

Billy looked at John Grady and looked back at the mountains.

You think that's true? said John Grady.

Hell, who knows.

JC says the old man is gettin crazier and crazier.

Well he's still got more sense crazy than JC's got sane so
what does that make JC?

I dont know.

There aint nothin wrong with him. He's just old is all.

JC says he aint been right since his daughter died.

Well. There aint no reason why he should be. He thought
the world of her.

Yeah.

Maybe we ought to ask Delbert. Get Delbert's view of
things.

Delbert aint as dumb as he looks.

I hope to God he aint. Anyway the old man always had a few
things peculiar about him and he's still got em. This place aint
the same. It never will be. Maybe we've all got a little crazy. I
guess if everbody went crazy together nobody would notice,
what do you think?

John Grady leaned and spat between his teeth and put the
stem back in his mouth. You liked her, didnt you?

Awful well. She was as nice to me as anybody I ever knew.

A coyote came out of the brush and trotted along the crest of
a rise a quarter mile to the east. I want you to look at that son
of a bitch, said Billy.

Let me get the rifle.

He'll be gone before you get done standin up.

The coyote trotted out along the ridge and stopped and looked back and then dropped off down the ridge into the brush again.

What do you reckon he's doin out here in the middle of the day?

He probably wonders the same about you.

You think he seen us?

Well I didnt see him walkin head first into them nopal bushes yonder so I dont expect he was completely blind.

John Grady watched for the coyote to reappear but the coyote didnt.

Funny thing, said Billy, is I was fixin to quit about the time she took sick. I was ready to move on. After she died I had a lot less reason to stay on but I stayed anyways.

I guess maybe you figured Mac needed you.

Horseshit.

How old was she?

I dont know. Late thirties. Forty maybe. You'd never of knowed it though.

You think he's gettin over it?

Mac?

Yeah.

No. You dont get over a woman like that. He aint gettin over nothin. He never will.

He sat and put his hat on and adjusted it. You ready, cousin?

Yeah.

He rose stiffly and reached down and got his lunchpail and he swiped at the seat of his trousers with one hand and then bent and got his jacket. He looked at John Grady.

There was a old waddy told me one time he never knowed a woman raised on indoor plumbin to ever turn out worth a damn. She come up the hard way. Old man Johnson was never nothin but a cowboy and you know what that pays. Mac met her at a church supper in Las Cruces when she was seventeen years old and that was all she wrote. He aint goin to be gettin over it. Not now, not soon, not never.

It was dark when they got back. Billy rolled up the window of the truck and sat looking toward the house. I'm a wore-out sumbuck, he said.

You want to just leave the gear in the truck?

Let's bring in the come-along. It might rain. Might. And that box of staples. They'll rust up.

I'll get em.

He got the stuff from the bed of the truck. The lights came on in the barn bay. Billy was standing there shaking his hand up and down.

Ever time I reach for that son of a bitch I get shocked.

It's the nails in them boots.

Then why dont it shock my feet?

I dont know.

He hung the come-along on a nail and set the box of staples on a framing crossbrace just inside the door. The horses whinnied from their stalls.

He went on down the barn bay and at the last stall pounded the flat of his hand against the stall door. There was an instant explosion against the boards on the other side. Dust drifted in the light. He looked back at Billy and grinned. Egg it on, said Billy. He'll put a foot through that son of a bitch.

JOAQUÍN STEPPED BACK with both hands atop the board he was leaning on and lowered his head as if he'd seen something in the corral too awful to watch. But he was only stepping back to spit and he did so in his slow and contemplative way and then stepped forward and looked through the boards again. Caballo, he said. The shadow of the trotting horse passed across the boards and across his face and passed on. He shook his head.

They walked on down to where some two by twelves were nailed and braced along the top of the corral and climbed up and sat with their bootheels wedged in the board below and smoked and watched John Grady work the colt.

What does he want with that owlheaded son of a bitch anyway?

Billy shook his head. Maybe it's like Mac says. Ever man winds up with the horse that suits him.

What is that thing he's got on its head?

It's called a cavesson halter.

What's wrong with a plain hackamore?

You'd have to ask the cowboy.

Troy leaned and spat. He looked at Joaquín. Qué piensas? he said.

Joaquín shrugged. He watched the horse circle the corral at the end of the longeline.

That horse has been broke with a bit, Troy said.

Yeah.

I guess he aims to break it and start over.

Well, Billy said, I got a suspicion that whatever it is he aims to do he'll most likely get it done.

They watched the horse circle.

He aint trainin it for the circus is he?

No. We had the circus yesterday evenin when he forked up on it.

How many times did he get thowed?

Four.

How many times did he get back up on it?

You know how many times.

Is he supposed to be some sort of specialist in spoiled horses?

Let's go, Billy said. He's liable to walk that son of a bitch all afternoon.

They went on toward the house.

Ask Joaquín yonder, Billy said.

Ask me what?

If the cowboy knows horses.

The cowboy says he dont know nothin.

I know it.

He claims he just likes it and works hard at it.

What do you think? said Billy.

Joaquín shook his head.

Joaquín thinks his methods is unorthodox.

So does Mac.

Joaquín didnt answer till they reached the gate. Then he stopped and looked back at the corral. Finally he said that it didnt make much difference if you liked horses or not if they didnt like you. He said the best trainers he ever knew, horses couldnt stay away from them. He said horses would follow Billy Sánchez to the outhouse and stand there and wait for him.

WHEN HE GOT BACK from town John Grady was not in the barn and when he walked up to the house to get his supper he was not there either. Troy was sitting at the table picking his teeth. He sat down with his plate and reached for the salt and pepper. Where's everbody at? he said.

Oren just left. JC's gone out with his girl. John Grady I reckon is laid up in the bed.

No he aint.

Well maybe he's gone off somewheres to think things over.

What happened?

That horse fell backwards on him. Like to broke his foot.

Is he all right?

I reckon. They carried him in to the doctor, him cussin and carryin on. Doctor wrapped it up and give him a pair of crutches and told him to stay off of it.

He's on crutches?

Yep. Supposed to be.

All this happened this afternoon?

Yep. It was lively as you could ever wish for here for a while. Joaquín come and got Oren and he went down there and told him to come on and he wouldnt do it. Oren said he thought he was goin to have to whip him. Hobblin around after the damned horse wantin to get up on it again. Finally got him to take his boot off. Oren said another two minutes and they'd of had to cut it off of him.

Billy nodded his head and bit thoughtfully into a biscuit.

He was ready to fight Oren?

Yep.

Billy chewed. He shook his head.

How bad is his foot?

He's sprained his ankle.

What did Mac say?

Nothin. He's the one carried him in to the doctor's.

I guess he cant do no wrong where Mac's concerned.

You got that right.

Billy shook his head again. He reached for the salsa. I miss ever show that comes to town, he said. I guess this might whittle down his reputation as a pure D peeler some though, mightnt it?

I dont know if it will or not. Joaquín says he stood in one stirrup and rode the son of a bitch down like a tree.

What for?

I dont know. I reckon he just dont like to quit a horse.

He'd been asleep maybe an hour when the commotion in the dark of the barn bay woke him. He lay listening a minute and then he rose and reached for the cord and pulled on the overhead light and put on his hat and stepped to the door and pushed back the curtain and looked out. The horse hove past a foot from his face and went hammering down the bay and turned and stood breathing and stamping in the dark.

Damn, he said. Bud?

John Grady went limping past.

What the hell are you doin?

He hobbled on out of the lightfall. Billy stepped into the bay.

You are a goddamned idjit, aint you? What in the hell is wrong with you?

The horse began to run again. He heard it coming and knew it was coming but he'd no more than just got back inside the doorframe before it exploded into the space of light from the single bulb in his cubicle, running with its mouth open and its eyes like eggs in its head.

Goddamn it, he said. He got his pants off of the iron footrail of his cot and pulled them on and squared his hat and stepped out again.

The horse had started down the bay again. He flattened himself against the stall door next to his bunkroom. The horse went by as if the barn were afire and slammed up against the door at the end of the bay and turned and stood shrieking.

Goddamn it will you leave that squirrelheaded son of a bitch alone? What the hell's got into you?

John Grady came limping past into the dusty light again trailing a loop of rope and limped on out the other side.

You cant even see to rope the son of a bitch, Billy called.

The horse came pounding down the far side of the bay. It was saddled and the stirrups were kicking out. One of them must have caught on a board toward the far end where it turned in the thin slats of light from the yardlamp because there was a crack of breaking wood and a clattering in the dark and then the horse stood on its forefeet and jackslammed the boards at the end of the barn. A minute later the lights came on at the house. The dust in the barn drifted like smoke.

There you go, called Billy. The whole damn house is up.

The dark shape of the horse shifted in the barred light. It leaned its long neck and screamed. The door opened at the end of the barn.

John Grady limped past again with the rope.

Someone threw the lightswitch. Oren was standing there flapping his hand about. Goddamn it, he said. Why dont somebody fix that thing.

The crazed horse stood blinking at him ten feet away. He looked at the horse and he looked at John Grady standing in the middle of the barn bay with the catchrope.

What in hell's thunder is goin on out here? he said.

Go on, said Billy. Tell him somethin. I sure as hell dont have no answer for him.

The horse turned and trotted partway down the bay and stopped and stood.

Put the damn horse up, said Oren.

Let me have the rope, said Billy.

John Grady looked back at him. You think I cant even catch him?

Go on then. Catch him. I hope the son of a bitch runs over you.

One of you all catch him, said Oren, and lets quit this damn nonsense.

The door opened behind Oren and Mr Johnson stood there in his hat and boots and nightshirt. Shut the door, Mr Johnson, said Oren. Come in if you want.

John Grady dropped the loop over the horse's neck and walked the horse down along the rope and reached up through the loop and took hold of the trailing bridlereins and threw the rope off.

Dont get on that horse, said Oren.

It's my horse.

Well you can tell that to Mac then. He'll be out here in a minute.

Go on bud, said Billy. Put the damn horse up like the man asked you.

John Grady looked at him and he looked at Oren and then he turned and led the horse back down the barn bay and put it up in the stall.

Bunch of damned ignorance, said Oren. Come on, Mr Johnson. Damn.

The old man turned and went out and Oren followed and pulled the door shut behind him. When John Grady came limping out of the stall he was carrying the saddle by the horn, the stirrups dragging in the dirt. He crossed the bay toward the tackroom. Billy leaned against the jamb watching him. When he came out of the tackroom he passed Billy without looking at him.

You're really somethin, said Billy. You know that?

John Grady turned at the door of his bunkroom and he looked at Billy and he looked down the hall of the lit barn and spat quietly in the dirt and looked at Billy again. It wasnt any of your business, he said. Was it.

Billy shook his head. I will be damned, he said.

IN THE MOUNTAINS they saw deer in the headlights and in the headlights the deer were pale as ghosts and as soundless. They turned their red eyes toward this unreckoned sun and sidled and grouped and leapt the bar ditch by ones and twos. A small doe lost her footing on the macadam and scrabbled wildly and sank onto her hindquarters and rose again and vanished with the others into the chaparral beyond the roadside. Troy held the whiskey up to the dashlights to check the level in the bottle and unscrewed the cap and drank and screwed the cap back on and passed the bottle to Billy. Be no lack of deer to hunt down here it looks like.

Billy unscrewed the cap from the bottle and drank and sat watching the white line down the dark road. I dont doubt but what it's good country.

You dont want to leave Mac.

I dont know. Not without some cause to.

Loyal to the outfit.

It aint just that. You need to find you a hole at some point. Hell, I'm twenty-eight years old.

You dont look it.

Yeah?

You look forty-eight. Pass the whiskey.

Billy peered out at the high desert. The bellied lightwires raced against the night.

They wont care for us drinkin?

She dont particularly like it. But there aint much she can do about it. Anyway it aint like we was goin to show up down there kneewalkin drunk.

Will your brother take a drink?

Troy nodded solemnly. Quicker than a minnow can swim a dipper.

Billy drank and handed over the bottle.

What was the kid goin to do? said Troy.

I dont know.

Did you and him have a fallin out?

No. He's all right. He just said he had somethin he needed to do.

He can flat ride a horse. I'll say that.

Yes he can.

He's a salty little booger.

He's all right. He's just got his own notions about things.

That horse he thinks so much of is just a damned outlaw if you want my opinion.

Billy nodded. Yep.

So what's he want with it?

I guess that's what he wants with it.

You still think he's going to have it follerin him around like a dog?

Yeah. I think it.

I'll believe it when I see it.

You want to lay some money?

Troy shook a cigarette from the pack on the dash and put it in his mouth and pushed in the lighter. I dont want to take your money.

Hell, dont be backwards about takin my money.

I think I'll pass. He aint goin to like them crutches.

Not even a little bit.

How long is he supposed to be on em?

I dont know. A couple of weeks. Doctor told him a sprain could be worse than a break.

I'll bet he aint on em a week.

I'll bet he aint either.

A jackrabbit froze in the road. Its red eye shone.

Go on dumb-ass, Billy said.

The rabbit made a soft thud under the truck. Troy took the

lighter from the dashboard and lit his cigarette with it and put the lighter back in the receptacle.

When I got out of the army I went up to Amarillo with Gene Edmonds for the rodeo and stock show. He'd fixed us up with dates and all. We was supposed to be at their house to pick em up at ten oclock in the mornin and it was after midnight fore we left out of El Paso. Gene had a brand new Olds Eighty-eight and he pitched me the keys and told me to drive. Quick as we hit highway eighty he looked over at me, told me to shower down on it. That thing would strictly motivate. I pushed it up to about eighty, eighty-five. Still had about a yard of pedal left. He looked over again. I said: How fast do you want to go? He said just whatever you feel comfortable with. Hell. I didnt do nothin but roll her on up to about a hundred and ten and here we went. Old long flat road. Had about six hundred miles of it in front of us.

Well there was all these jackrabbits in the road. They'd set there and freeze in the lights. Blap. Blap. I looked over at Gene and I said: What do you want to do about these rabbits? He looked at me and he said: Rabbits? I mean if you were lookin for somebody to give a shit I can tell you right now it sure as hell wasnt Gene. He didnt care if syrup went to thirty cents a sop.

We pulled into a filling station at Dimmitt Texas just about daybreak. Pulled up to the pumps and shut her down and set there and there was a car on the other side of the pumps and the old boy that worked there was fillin the tank and cleanin the windshield. Woman settin there in the car. The old boy drivin had gone in to take a leak or whatever. Anyway we pulled in facin this other car and I'm kindly layin there with my head back waitin on the old boy and I wasnt even thinkin about this woman but I could see her. Just settin there, sort of lookin around. Well directly she sat straight up and commenced to holler like she was bein murdered. I mean just a hollerin. I raised up, I didnt know what had happened. She was lookin over at us and I thought Gene had done somethin. Exposed hisself or somethin. You never knew what he was goin to do. I looked at Gene but he didnt know what the hell was goin on any more than I did. Well here come the old boy out of the men's room and I mean he was a big son of a bitch too. I got out and walked around the car. I thought I was goin crazy. The Oldsmobile had this big ovalshaped grille in the front of it was like a big scoop and when I got around to the front of the car it was just packed completely full of jackrabbit heads. I mean there was a hundred of em jammed in there and the front of the car the bumper and all just covered with blood and rabbit guts and them rabbits I reckon they'd sort of turned their heads away just at impact cause they was all lookin out, eyes all crazy lookin. Teeth sideways. Grinnin. I cant tell you what it looked like. I come damn near hollerin myself. I'd noticed the car was overheatin but I just put that down to the speed we was makin. This old boy wanted to fight us over it. I said: Damn, Sam. Rabbits. You know? Hell. Gene got out and started mouthin at him and I told him to get his ass back in the car and shut up. Old boy went over and told the woman to hush up and quit slobberin and all but I like to never got him pacified. I started to just go on and hit the big son of a bitch and be done with it.

Billy sat watching the night spool past. The roadside chaparral, the flat black scrim of the mountains cut into the starblown desert sky above them. Troy smoked. He reached for the whiskey and unscrewed the cap and sat holding the bottle.

I got discharged in San Diego. Took the first bus out. Me and another old boy got drunk on the bus and like to got throwed off. I got off in Tucson and went in a store and bought a new pair of Judson boots and a suit. I dont know what the hell I bought the suit for. I thought you was supposed to have one. I got on another bus and come on to El Paso and went up that evenin to Alamogordo and got my horses. I wandered all over this country. Worked in Colorado. Worked up in the panhandle. Got throwed in jail in this little old chickenshit town I wont even name it to you. State of Texas though. State of Texas. I hadnt done nothin. Just in the wrong place at the wrong time. I like to never got out of there. I'd got in a fight with a Mexican and like to killed him. I was in jail up there for nine months to the day. I wouldnt of wrote home for nothin. Time I got out and went to see about my horses they'd been sold for the feedbill. I didnt care about the one but I did the other cause I'd had him a long time. Nobody seemed to know nothin about it. I knew if I grabbed the old boy I'd be right back in the damn jail again. Asked all around. Finally somebody told me they'd sold my horse out of the state. They thought the buyer was from Alabama or some damn place. I'd had that horse since I was thirteen years old.

I lost a horse in Mexico I was awful partial to, Billy said. I'd had him since I was nine.

It's easy to do.

What, lose a horse?

Troy had tipped the bottle up and he drank and lowered it and screwed the cap back on and wiped his mouth with the back of his hand and laid the bottle on the seat. No, he said. Get partial to one.

Half an hour later they pulled off the highway and rumbled over the pipes of a cattleguard and drove up the mile-long dirt road to the ranch house. The porchlight was on and three heeler dogs came out and ran beside the truck barking. Elton came out and stood on the porch with his hands in his back pockets and his hat on.

They ate at a long table in the kitchen, passing bowls of hominy and okra and a great platter of fried steaks and biscuits.

This is awful good, mam, Billy said.

Elton's wife looked at him. You wouldnt mind not callin me mam would you?

No mam.

It makes me feel like a old woman.

Yes mam.

He cant help hisself, Troy said.

That's all right, the woman said.

You never let me off that easy.

Bein let off easy was never somethin you needed more of, the woman said.

I'll try not to say it, Billy said.

There was a seven year old girl at the table and she watched them with wide eyes. They ate. After a while she said: What's wrong with it?

What's wrong with what?

Sayin mam.

Elton looked up. There aint nothin wrong with it, honey. Your mama's just one of them modern kinds of women.

What's a modern kind of woman?

Eat your supper, the woman said. If your daddy had his way we wouldnt even have the wheel yet.

They sat in old canebottomed chairs on the porch and Elton set the three glass tumblers on the board floor between his feet and unscrewed the cap from the bottle and poured three measures and put the cap back and stood the bottle on the floor and passed the glasses round and leaned back in his rocker. Salud, he said.

He'd turned off the porchlight and they sat in the soft square of light from the window. He raised his glass to the light and looked through it like a chemist. You wont guess who's back at Bell's, he said.

Dont even say her name.

Well you did guess.

Who else would it be?

Elton leaned back in the chair and rocked. The dogs stood in the yard at the foot of the steps looking up at him.

What, said Troy. Did her old man finally run her off?

I dont know. She's supposed to be visitin. It's turned out to be kindly a long visit.

Yeah.

For whatever consolation there might be in that.

It aint no consolation.

Elton nodded. You're right, he said. It aint.

Billy sipped the whiskey and looked out at the shapes of the mountains. Stars were falling everywhere.

Rachel run smack into her in Alpine, said Elton. Little darlin just smiled and hidied like butter wouldnt melt in her mouth.

Troy sat leaning forward with his elbows on his knees, the glass in both hands before him. Elton rocked.

You remember we used to go down to Bloy's to try and pick up girls? That's where he met her at. Camp meetin. That'll make you ponder the ways of God. He asked her out and she told him she wouldnt go out with a man that drank. He looked her straight in the eye and told her he didnt drink. She like to fell over backwards. I guess it come as somethin of a shock to her to meet a even bigger liar than what she was. But he told the naked truth. Of course she called his hand on it. Said she knew for a fact he drank. Said everbody in Jeff Davis County knew he drank and drank plenty and was wild as a buck. He never batted a eye. Said he used to but he quit. She asked him when did he quit and he said I just now did. And she went out with him. And as far as I know he never took another drink. Till she quit him of course. By then he had a lot of catchin up to do. Tell me about the evils of liquor. Liquor aint nothin. But he was changed from that day.

Is she still as good lookin?

I dont know. I aint seen her. Rachel said she was. Satan hath power to assume a pleasing form. Them big blue eyes. Knew more ways to turn a man's head than the devil's grandmother. I dont know where they learn it at. Hell, she wasnt but seventeen.

They're born with it, Troy said. They dont have to learn it.

I hear you.

What they dont seem to learn is not to just run over the top of some poor son of a bitch for the pure enjoyment of it.

Billy sipped his whiskey.

Let me have your glass, Elton said.

He set it on the floor between his feet and poured the

whiskey and recapped the bottle and reached and passed the glass across.

Thanks, said Billy.

Were you in the war? Elton said.

No. I was four-F.

Elton nodded.

I tried to enlist three different times but they wouldnt take me.

I know you did. I tried to get overseas but I spent the whole war at Camp Pendleton. Johnny fought all over the Pacific theatre. He had whole companies shot out from under him. Never got a scratch. I think it bothered him.

Troy handed across his glass and Elton set it on the floor and poured it and passed it back. Then he poured his own. He sat back. What are you lookin at? he asked the dog. The dog looked away.

The thing that bothers me and then I'll shut up about it is that we had a hell of a row that mornin and I never had the chance to make it up. I told him to his face that he was a damn fool—which he was—and that the worst thing he could do to the old boy was to let him have her. Which it was. I knew all about her by then. We like to come to blows over it. I never told you that. It was bad. I never saw him alive again. I should of just kept out of it. Anybody in the state he was in you cant talk to em noway. No use to try even.

Troy watched him. You told me, he said.

Yeah. I guess I did. I dont dream about him anymore. I used to all the time. I'd have these conversations with him.

I thought you was goin to get off the subject.

All right. It still seems like about the only subject there is, though. Dont it?

He rose heavily from the chair with bottle and glass in hand. Let's walk out to the barn. I'll show you the foal that Jones mare throwed you never did think much of. Just bring your all's glasses. I got the bottle.

*   *   *

THEY RODE ALL MORNING through the open juniper country, keeping to the gravelly ridges. A storm was making up over the Sierra Viejas to the west and over the broad plain that ran south from the Guadalupes down around the Cuesta del Burro range and on to Presidio and the border. They crossed the upper reaches of the creek at noon and sat among the yellow leaves and watched leaves turn and drift in a pool while they ate the lunch that Rachel had packed for them.

Look at this, said Troy.

What is it?

A tablecloth.

Damn.

He poured coffee from a thermos into their cups. The turkey sandwiches they ate were wrapped in cloth.

What's in the other thermos?

Soup.

Soup?

Soup.

Damn.

They ate.

How long has he been manager down here?

About two years.

Billy nodded. Did he not offer to hire you on before now?

He did. I told him I didnt mind workin with him but I wasnt all that sure about workin for him.

What made you change your mind?

I aint changed it. I'm just thinkin about it.

They ate. Troy nodded downcountry. They say there's been a white man ambushed ever mile of this draw.

Billy studied the country. Looks like they'd of learned to stay out of it.

When they'd done eating Troy poured the rest of the coffee into their cups and screwed the cap back on the thermos and laid it by with the soup and the sandwich cloths and the still folded tablecloth to pack back in the saddlebags. They sat sipping the coffee. The horses standing downstream side by side looked up from their drinking in the creek. They had wet leaves stuck to their noses.

Elton's got his own notions about what happened, Troy said. Johnny if he hadnt of found that girl would of found somethin else. You couldnt head him. Elton says he changed. He never changed. He was four years older than me. Not a lot of years. But he walked ground I'll never see. Glad not to see. People always said he was bullheaded, but it wasnt just that. He fought Daddy one time he wasnt but fifteen. Fistfought him. Made the old man fight him. Told him to his face that he respected him and all but that he wasnt goin to take what he'd said. Somethin the old man had chewed him out over. I cried like a baby. He didnt cry. Kept gettin up. Nose all busted and all. The old man kept tellin him to stay down. Hell, the old man was cryin. I hope I never see nothin like it again. I can think about it now and it makes me sick. And there was nothin any mortal man could of done to of stopped it.

What happened?

The old man finally walked off. He was beat and he knew it. Johnny standin there. Couldnt hardly stand up. Callin to him to come back. The old man wouldnt even turn around. He just went on to the house.

Troy looked into the bottom of his cup. He slung the dregs out across the leaves.

It wasnt just her. There's a kind of man that when he cant have what he wants he wont take the next best thing but the worst he can find. Elton thinks he was that kind and maybe he was. But I think he loved that girl. I think he knew what she was and he didnt care. I think it was his own self he was blind to. I think he was just lost. This world was never made for him. He'd outlived it before he could walk. Get married. Hell. He couldnt even stand to wear lace-up shoes.

You liked him though.

Troy looked off down through the trees. Well, he said. I dont guess like really says it. I cant talk about it. I wanted to be like him. But I wasnt. I tried.

He was your dad's favorite I reckon.

Oh yeah. It wasnt a problem with anybody. It was just known. Accepted. Hell. It wasnt even a contest. You ready?

I'm ready.

He rose. He placed the flat of his hand in the small of his back and stretched. He looked at Billy. I loved him, he said. So did Elton. You couldnt not. That was all there was to it.

He folded the cloths under his arm together with the thermos bottles. They hadnt even looked to see what the soup was. He turned and looked back at Billy. So how do you like this country?

I like it.

I do too. Always have.

So you comin down here?

No.

It was dusk when they rode into Fort Davis. Nighthawks were circling over the old parade grounds when they passed and the sky over the mountains behind them was blood red. Elton was waiting with the truck and horsetrailer in front of the Limpia Hotel. They unsaddled the horses in the graveled parking lot and put the saddles in the bed of the truck and wiped the horses down and loaded them in the trailer and went into the hotel and through the lobby to the coffeeshop.

How did you like that little horse? said Elton.

I liked him fine, said Billy. We got along good.

They sat and studied the menus. What are you all havin? said Elton.

They left around ten oclock. Elton stood in the yard with his hands in his back pockets. He was still standing there, just the silhouette of him against the porchlight, when they rounded the curve at the end of the drive and went on toward the highway.

Billy drove. He looked over at Troy. You goin to stay awake aint you?

Yeah. I'm awake.

You've done decided?

Yeah, I think so.

We're goin to have to go somewheres.

Yeah. I know it.

You aint asked me what I thought.

Well. You aint comin down here unless I do and I aint. So what would be the use in me askin?

Billy didnt answer.

After a while Troy said: Hell, I knew I wasnt comin back down here.

Yeah.

You go back home and everthing you wished was different is still the same and everthing you wished was the same is different.

I know what you mean.

I think especially if you're the youngest. You wasnt the youngest in your family was you?

No. I was the oldest.

You dont want to be the youngest. I can tell you right now. There aint no percentage in it.

They drove on through the mountains. About a mile past the intersection with highway 166 there was a truckload of Mexicans pulled off onto the grass. They stood almost into the road waving their hats. Billy slowed.

The hell with that, said Troy.

Billy drove past. He looked in the rearview mirror but he could see nothing but the dark of the road and the deep of the desert night. He pulled the truck slowly to a halt.

Damn it, Parham, Troy said.

I know. I just cant do it.

You're fixin to get us in a jackpot here we wont get home till daylight.

I know it.

He put the truck into reverse and began to grind slowly back down the highway, using the white line running from under the front of the truck to steer by. When the other truck hove into view alongside them he could see that the right front tire was down.

They gathered around the cab. Punchada, they said. Tenemos una llanta punchada.

Puedo verlo, said Billy. He pulled off the road and climbed out. Troy lit a cigarette and shook his head.

They needed a jack. Did they have a spare? Sí. Por supuesto.

He got the jack out of the bed and they carried it back to the truck and commenced to jack the front end up. They had two spares and neither of them would hold air. They spelled each other at the antique tirepump. Finally they raised up and looked at Billy.

He got the tiretools out of the truckbed and came around and got the patchkit and a flashlight from under the seat. They carried one of the spares out into the road and laid it down and stood on it to break the bead and then the man who'd taken the tools from Billy stepped forward and began to pry the tire up off the rim while the others watched. The innertube that he snaked out of the tire's inner cavity was made of red rubber and there was a whole plague of patches upon it. He laid it out on the macadam and Billy trained the light over it. Hay parches sobre los parches, he said.

Es verdad, the man said.

La otra?

Está peor.

One of the younger men manned the tirepump and the tube bloated slowly up in the road and sat hissing. He knelt and put his ear to the various leaks. Billy flipped open the tin lid of the patchcan and thumbed the number of repairs it contained. Troy had climbed out of the truck and he walked back and stood smoking quietly and looking at the tire and the tube and the Mexicans.

The Mexicans wheeled the blown tire around the side of the truck and Billy put the light on it. There was a great ragged hole in the sidewall. It looked like it had been chewed by bulldogs. Troy spat quietly in the road. The Mexicans threw the tire up onto the bed of the truck.

Billy took the stub of chalk from the patchkit and circled the leaks in the tube and they unscrewed the valvestem from the valve and sat on the tube and then walked it down till it was dead flat. Then they sat in the road with the white line running past their elbows and the gaudy desert night overhead, the myriad constellations moving upon the blackness subtly as sealife, and they worked with the dull red shape of rubber in their laps, squatting like tailors or menders of nets. They scuffed the rubber with the little tin grater stamped into the lid of the kit and they laid on the patches and fired them with a match one by one till all were fused and all were done. When they had the tube pumped up again they sat in the road in the quiet desert dark and listened.

Oye algo? said Billy.

Nada.

They sat listening.

He unscrewed the valvestem again and when they had the tube deflated the man slid it down inside the tire and worked it around the rim and fitted the valve and the boy came forward with the pump and began to pump up the tire. He was a long time pumping. When the bead popped on the rim he stopped and they unscrewed the hose from the valve and the man took the valvestem from his mouth and screwed it into the hissing valve and then they stepped back and looked at Billy. He spat and turned and walked back to the truck to get the tiregauge.

Troy was asleep in the front seat. Billy got the gauge out of the glovebox and walked back and they gauged the tire and then rolled it over to the truck and slid it onto the hub and tightened down the lugnuts with a wrench made from a socket welded onto a length of heavy iron pipe. Then they let down the jack and pulled it from under the truck and handed it to Billy.

He took the jack and tiretools and put the patchkit and the

gauge in his shirtpocket and the flashlight in the back pocket of his jeans. Then they shook hands all the way around.

Adónde van? said Billy.

The man shrugged. He said that they were going to Sanderson Texas. He turned and looked off across the dark headlands to the east. The younger men stood about them.

Hay trabajo allá?

He shrugged again. Espero que sí, he said. He looked at Billy. Es vaquero?

Sí. Vaquero.

The man nodded. It was a vaquero's country and other men's troubles were alien to it and that was about all that could be said. They shook hands again and the Mexicans clambered aboard the truck and the truck cranked and coughed and started and lumbered slowly out onto the roadway. The men and boys in the bed of the truck stood and raised their hands. He could see them above the dark hump of the cab, against the deep burnt cobalt of the sky. The single taillight had a short in the wiring and it winked on and off like a signal until the truck had rounded the curve and vanished.

He put the jack and tools in the pickup and opened the door and nudged Troy awake.

Let's go, cowboy.

Troy sat and stared out at the empty road. He looked back behind them.

Where'd they go?

They're done gone.

What time is it do you reckon?

I dont know.

Are you done bein a Samaritan?

I'm done.

He leaned and opened the glovebox door and put the patchkit and the tiregauge and the flashlight in and shut the door and started the engine.

Where were they headed? Troy said.

Sanderson.

Sanderson?

Yeah.

Where were they comin from?

I dont know. They didnt say.

I bet they aint even goin to Sanderson, Troy said.

Where do you think they're goin?

Hell, who knows.

Why would anybody lie about goin to Sanderson Texas?

I dont know.

They drove on. Rounding a curve with a steep bank to the right of the road there was a sudden white flare and a solid whump of a sound. The truck veered, the tires squealing. When they got stopped they were halfway off the road into the bar ditch.

What in the hell, said Troy. What in the hell.

A large owl lay cruciform across the driver's windshield of the truck. The laminate of the glass was belled in softly to hold him and his wings were spread wide and he lay in the concentric rings and rays of the wrecked glass like an enormous moth in a web.

Billy shut off the engine. They sat looking at it. One of its feet shuddered and drew up into a claw and slowly relaxed again and it moved its head slightly as if to better see them and then it died.

Troy opened the door and got out. Billy sat looking at the owl. Then he turned off the headlights and got out too.

The owl was all soft and downy. Its head slumped and rolled. It was soft and warm to the touch and it felt loose inside its feathers. He lifted it free and carried it over to the fence and hung it from the wires and came back. He sat in the truck and turned the lights on to judge if he could drive with the windshield in that condition or whether he might have to kick it out completely. There was a clear place in the lower right corner and he thought he could see if he hunkered down and looked through the windshield there. Troy had walked up the road and was standing taking a leak.

He started the truck and pulled back onto the road. Troy had walked further up and was sitting in the roadside grass. He drove up and rolled down the window and looked at him.

What's wrong with you? he said.

Nothin, Troy said.

Are you ready to go?

Yeah.

He rose and walked around in front of the truck and got in. Billy looked over at him.

Are you all right?

Yeah. I'm all right.

It was just a owl.

I know. It aint that.

Well what is it?

Troy didnt answer.

He pulled the shiftlever in the floor down into first and let the clutch out. They moved down the highway. He could see pretty well. He could lean over and see through the glass on the other side of the division bar. Are you all right? he said. What is it?

Troy sat looking out the window at the passing darkness. Just everthing, he said. Just ever goddamned thing. Hell. Dont pay no attention to me. I ought not to drink whiskey in the first place.

They drove on to Van Horn and stopped for gas and coffee and by then the country that Troy'd grown up in and that he thought he might go back to and where his dead brother was buried was all behind them and it was two oclock in the morning.

Mac will have a few things to say when he sees the truck.

Billy nodded. I might be able to run into town and get it fixed in the mornin.

What do you reckon it'll cost?

I dont know.

You want to just split it?

That would suit me.

All right.

You sure you're okay?

Yeah. I'm all right. I just get to thinkin about things is all.

Yeah.

It dont help none though, does it?

Nope.

They sat drinking their coffee. Troy shook out a cigarette and lit it and put his cigarettes and his Zippo lighter on the table. How come you had to stop back there?

I just did.

You said you had to.

Yeah.

What is it? Some sort of religious thing?

No. It aint nothin like that. It's just that the worst day of my life was one time when I was seventeen years old and me and my bud—my brother—we was on the run and he was hurt and there was a truckload of Mexicans just about like them back yonder appeared out of nowhere and pulled our bacon out of the fire. I wasnt even sure their old truck could outrun a horse, but it did. They didnt have no reason to stop for us. But they did. I dont guess it would of even occurred to em not to. That's all.

Troy sat looking out the window. Well, he said. That's a pretty good reason.

Well. It was all the one I needed anyways. You ready?

Yeah. He drained his cup. I'm ready.

HE PAID HIS TWO PENNIES at the gate and pushed through the turnstile and went on across the bridge. On the banks of the river under the bridge small boys held up tin buckets nailed to the ends of poles and called out for money. He crossed the bridge into a sea of waiting vendors hustling cheap jewelry, leather goods, blankets. They followed him along for a distance and were spelled by others in a relay of huckstering down Juárez Avenue and up Ignacio Mejía to Santos Degollado where they fell away and watched him go.

He stood at the end of the bar and ordered a whiskey and propped his foot on the rail and looked across the room at the whores.

Dónde están sus compañeros? said the barman.

He raised the glass of whiskey and turned it in his hand. En el campo, he said. He drank.

He stood there for two hours. The whores came across the room one by one to solicit him and one by one returned. He didnt ask about her. When he left he'd had five whiskies and he paid for them with a dollar and put another dollar on top of it for the barman. He crossed Juárez Avenue and went limping up Mejía to the Napoleón and took a seat in front of the cafe and ordered a steak. He sat and drank coffee while he waited and he watched the life in the streets. A man came to the door and tried to sell him cigarettes. A man tried to sell him a Madonna made of painted celluloid. A man with a strange device with dials and levers asked him if he wished to electrocute himself. After a while the steak arrived.

He went again the following night. There were half a dozen soldiers from Fort Bliss there, young recruits, their heads all but shaved. They eyed him drunkenly, they looked at his boots. He stood at the bar and drank three whiskies slowly. She did not appear.

He walked up Juárez Avenue through the hucksters and pimps. He saw a boy selling stuffed armadillos. He saw a tourist drunk laboring up the sidewalk carrying a full suit of armor. He saw a beautiful young woman vomit in the street. Dogs turned at the sound and ran toward her.

He walked up Tlaxcala and up Mariscal and entered another such place and sat at the bar. The whores came to tug at his arm. He said that he was waiting for someone. After a while he left and walked back to the bridge.

HE'D PROMISED MAC he wouldnt ride the horse again until his ankle was better. Sunday after breakfast he worked the animal in the corral and in the afternoon he saddled Bird and rode up into the Jarillas. Atop a raw rock bluff he sat the horse and studied the country. The flooded saltflats shining in the evening sun seventy miles to the east. The peak of El Capitan beyond. All the high mountains of New Mexico paling away to the north beyond the red plains, the ancient creosote. In the steeply canted light the laddered shadows of the fences looked like railtracks running up the country and doves were crossing below him toward a watertank on the McNew spread. He could see no cattle anywhere in that cowtrodden scrubland. The doves called everywhere and there was no wind.

When he got back to the house it was dark and by the time he'd unsaddled the horse and put it up and gone to the kitchen Socorro had already cleared away and was washing the dishes. He got a cup of coffee and sat down and she brought him his supper and while he was eating Mac came and stood in the hallway door and lit a cigar.

You about ready? he said.

Yessir.

Take your time. Take your time.

He walked back up the hallway. Socorro brought the pot from the stove and spooned the last of the caldillo onto his plate. She brought him more coffee and poured a cup for Mac and left it steaming on the far side of the table. When he was done eating he rose and carried his plate and cup to the sink and he poured more coffee and then went to the old cherry-wood press hauled overland in a wagon from Kentucky eighty years ago and opened the door and took out the chess set from among the old cattleman's journals and the halfbound ledgers and leather daybooks and the old green Remington boxes of shotgun shells and rifle cartridges. On the upper shelf a dove-

tailed wooden box that held brass scaleweights. A leather folder
of drawing instruments. A glass horsecarriage that once held
candy for a Christmas in the long ago. He shut the door and
carried the board and the wooden box to the table and unfolded
the board and slid back the lid of the box and spilled out the
pieces, carved walnut, carved holly, and set them up. Then he
sat drinking his coffee.

Mac came out and pulled back the chair opposite and sat and
dragged the heavy glass ashtray forward from among the bottles of ketchup and hotsauce and laid his cigar in the ashtray
and took a sip of the coffee. He nodded toward John Grady's
left hand. John Grady opened his hand, he set the pawns on the
board.

I'm white again, said Mac.

Yessir.

He moved his pawn forward.

JC came in and got a cup of coffee from the stove and came
to the table and stood.

Set down, said Mac. You're makin the room untidy.

That's all right. I aint stayin.

Better set down, said John Grady. He needs all his powers of
concentration.

You got that right, said Mac.

JC sat down. Mac studied the board. JC glanced at the pile of
white chesspieces at John Grady's elbow.

Son, you better cut the old man some slack. You might could
be replaced with somebody that cowboys better and plays chess
worse.

Mac reached and moved his remaining bishop. John Grady
moved his knight. Mac took up his cigar and sat puffing quietly.

He moved his queen. John Grady moved his other knight
and sat back. Check, he said.

Mac sat studying the board. Damn, he said. After a while he
looked up. He turned to JC. You want to play him?

No sir. He's done made a believer out of me.

I know the feelin. He's beat me like a rented mule.

He looked at the wallclock and picked up his cigar again and put it in his teeth. I'll play you one more, he said.

Yessir, said John Grady.

Socorro took off her apron and hung it up and stood at the door.

Goodnight, she said.

Night Socorro.

JC rose from his chair. You all want some more coffee?

They played. When John Grady took the black queen JC pushed back his chair and got up.

I've tried to tell you, son. There's a cold winter comin.

He crossed the kitchen and set his cup in the sink and went to the door.

Night, he said.

Mac sat quietly studying the board. The cigar lay dead in the ashtray.

Night, said John Grady.

He pushed open the door and went out. The screendoor flapped shut. The clock ticked. Mac leaned back. He picked up the cigar stub and then he put it back in the ashtray. I believe I'll concede, he said.

You could still win.

Mac looked at him. Bullshit, he said.

John Grady shrugged. Mac looked at the clock. He looked at John Grady. Then he leaned and carefully turned the board around. John Grady moved Mac's remaining black knight.

Mac pursed his lips. He studied the board. He moved.

Five moves later John Grady mated the white king. Mac shook his head. Let's go to bed, he said.

Yessir.

He began to put away the pieces. Mac pushed back his chair and picked up the cups.

What time did Troy and Billy say they'd be back?

I dont reckon they said.

How come you not to go with em?

I just thought I'd stick around here.

Mac carried the cups to the sink. Did they ask you to go?

Yessir. I dont need to go everwhere they go.

He slid the cover shut on the box and folded the board and rose.

Is Troy fixin to go down there and go to work for his brother?

I dont know sir.

He crossed the room and put the chess set back in the press and closed the door and got his hat.

You dont know or you aint sayin?

I dont know. If I wasnt sayin I'd of said so.

I know you would.

Sir.

Yes.

I feel kind of bad about Delbert.

What do you feel bad about?

Well. I guess I feel like I took his job.

Well you didnt. He'd of been gone anyways.

Yessir.

You let me run the place. All right?

Yessir. Goodnight sir.

Switch on the barnlight yonder.

I can see all right.

You could see better with the light on.

Yessir. Well. It bothers the horses.

Bothers the horses?

Yessir.

He put on his hat and pushed open the door. Mac watched him cross the yard. Then he switched off the kitchen light and turned and crossed the room and went up the hallway. Bothers the horses, he said. Damn.

WHEN HE GOT UP in the morning and went down to Billy's room to wake him Billy wasnt there. The bed looked slept in and he limped out past the horse stalls and looked across the yard toward the kitchen. Then he went around to the side of the barn where the truck was parked. Billy was sitting in the seat leaning over the steering wheel taking the screws out of the metal sashframe that held the windshield and dropping the screws into the ashtray.

Mornin cowboy, he said.

Mornin. What happened to the windshield?

Owl.

Owl?

Owl.

He took the last screws out and pried up and lifted away the frame and began to pry the edges of the caved-in glass out of the rubber molding with the blade of the screwdriver.

Walk around and push in on this thing from the outside. Wait a minute. There's some gloves here.

John Grady pulled on the gloves and hobbled around and pushed on the edges of the glass while Billy pried with the screwdriver. They got the glass worked out of the molding along the bottom and one side and then Billy borrowed the gloves and pulled the whole thing out in one piece and lifted it over the steering wheel and laid it in the floor of the truck on the passenger side.

What did you do, drive with your head out the window?

No. I just sort of sat in the middle and looked out the good side.

He pushed at the windshield wiper lying inside across the dashboard.

I thought maybe you'd not got in yet.

We got in around five. What'd you do?

Nothin much.

You aint been rodeoin in the barn while I was gone have you?

Nope.

How's your foot?

It's all right.

Billy pushed the wiper up on its spring and pried the wiper

arm off the capstan with the screwdriver and laid it on the seat.

You goin to get a new glass for it?

I'll get Joaquín to bring one when he goes in. I dont want the old man to see it if I can help it.

Hell, anybody could run into a owl.

I know. But anybody didnt.

John Grady was leaning through the open window of the standing truck door. He turned and spat and leaned some more. Well, he said. I dont know what that means.

Billy laid the screwdriver in the seat. I dont either, he said. I dont know why I said it. Let's go in and see if she's got breakfast ready. I could eat the runnin gears of a bull moose.

When they sat down Oren looked up from his paper and studied John Grady over the tops of his glasses. How's your foot? he said.

It's all right.

I'll bet.

It's all right enough to ride a horse. That's what you wanted to know isnt it?

Can you get that in a stirrup?

I dont have to.

Oren went back to his paper. They ate. After a while he put the paper down and took off his glasses and laid them on the table.

There's a man sendin a two year old filly out here that he aims to give to his wife. I kept my own counsel on that. He dont know nothin about the horse other than its blood. Or any other horse I reckon probably you could say.

Is she broke?

The wife or the horse?

I'll lay eight to five they aint either one, said JC. Sight unseen.

I dont know, said Oren. Green broke or some kind of broke. He wants to leave her here two weeks. I said we'd give her all the trainin she was capable of absorbin in that length of time and he seemed satisfied with that.

All right.

Billy, are you all workin with us this week?

I reckon.

What time did the man say they'd be here? said John Grady.

He said after breakfast. JC. You all ready?

I was born that way.

Well the day advanceth, said Oren. He put his glasses in his shirtpocket and pushed back his chair.

THEY PULLED INTO the yard in a pickup truck towing a new single trailer at about eight-thirty. John Grady walked out to meet them. The trailer was painted black and had the name of a ranch somewhere up in New Mexico that he'd never heard of painted on the side in gold. The two men unlatching and taking down the gate on the trailer nodded at him and the taller of the two looked briefly around the yard and then they backed the horse down the ramp.

Where's Oren at? the tall man said.

John Grady watched the filly. She had a nervous look to her which was all right for a young mare offloaded onto strange terrain. He limped around to see her from the other side. Her eye followed him.

Walk her around.

What?

Walk her around.

Is Oren here?

No sir. He's not. I'm the trainer. Just walk her around a minute and let me watch her.

The man stood for a minute. Then he handed the halter rope to the other man. Walk her around some there, Louis. He looked at John Grady. John Grady was watching the filly.

What time you expect him back?

Not till this evenin.

They watched the little filly walk up and back.

Are you the trainer sure enough?

Yessir.

What is it you're lookin for?

John Grady studied the filly and he looked at the man. That horse is lame, he said.

Lame.

Yessir.

Shit, the man said.

The man walking the horse looked back over his shoulder.

Did you hear that, Louis? the man called to him.

Yeah. I heard it. You want to just go on and shoot her?

What makes you think that horse is lame? the man said.

Well sir. It's not really a matter of what I think. She's lame in the left foreleg. Let me look at her.

Bring her over here, Louis.

You reckon she can make it that far?

I dont know.

He brought the horse over and John Grady walked up to her and leaned against her with his shoulder and lifted her foreleg between his knees and examined the hoof. He ran his thumb around the frog and he examined the hoof wall. He leaned against the animal to feel her breathing and he talked to her and pulled his kerchief from his back pocket and wet it with spittle and began to clean the wall of the hoof.

Who put this on here? he said.

Put what?

This dressing. He held up the handkerchief to show them the stain from the hoof.

I dont know, the man said.

John Grady took out his pocketknife and opened it and ran the point of it down the side wall of the hoof. The man had come closer to watch him. He held up the knifeblade. See that? he said.

Yeah?

She's got a sandcrack in that hoof and somebody has filled it in with wax and then put that hoofdressing over it.

He rose and let the filly's foot down and stroked her shoulder and the three of them stood looking at the filly. The tall man put his hands in his back pockets. He turned and spat. Well, he said.

The man holding the horse toed the ground and looked away.

The old man will shit when he hears this.

Where did you all buy her at?

The man took one hand out of his back pocket and adjusted his hat. He looked at John Grady and he looked at the filly again.

Can I leave her with you? he said.

No sir.

Well let me leave her here till Oren gets back and me and him can talk about it.

I cant do that.

Why not?

I cant do it.

You're tellin me to load her and get her off the place.

John Grady didnt answer. He didnt take his eyes off the man either.

You can do better than that, the man said.

I dont believe I can.

He looked at the man holding the horse. He looked toward the house and he looked at John Grady again. Then he reached to his hip and took out his wallet and opened it and took out a tendollar bill and folded the bill and put the wallet back and tendered the bill toward the boy. Here, he said. Put that in your pocket and dont tell nobody where you got it.

I dont believe I can do that.

Go on.

No sir.

The man's face darkened. He stood holding out the bill. Then he stuck it in the pocket of his shirt.

It wouldnt be no skin off your ass.

John Grady didnt answer. The man turned and spat again.

I didnt have nothin to do with doctorin it thataway if that's what you're thinkin.

I never said you did.

You wouldnt help a man out though, would you?

Not that way I wouldnt.

The man stood looking at John Grady. He spat once more. He looked at the other man and he looked out across the spread.

Let's go, Carl, the other man said. Hell.

They walked the horse back across the lot toward the truck and trailer. John Grady stood watching them. They loaded the horse and raised the gate and shut the doors and latched them. The tall man walked around the side of the truck. Hey kid, he called.

Yessir.

You go to hell.

John Grady didnt answer.

You hear me?

Yessir. I hear you.

Then they got in the truck and turned and drove out across the lot and down the drive.

HE DROPPED THE REINS of his horse in the yard at the kitchen door and went in. Socorro was not in the kitchen and he called her and waited and then went back out. As he was mounting the horse she came to the door. She put her hands to her eyes against the sun. Bueno, she said.

A qué hora regresa el Señor Mac?

No sé.

He nodded. She watched him. She asked him what time he would be back and he said by dark.

Espérate, she said.

Está bien.

No. Espérate.

She went in. He sat the horse. The horse stamped at the bare ground and shook its head. All right, he said. We're goin.

When she came back out she had his lunch done up in a cloth and she handed it up to him at the stirrup. He thanked her and reached behind him and put it in the gamepocket of his ducking jacket and nodded and put the horse forward. She watched him ride to the gate and lean and undo the latch and push the gate open horseback and ride through and turn the horse and close the gate horseback and then set off down the road at a jog with the morning sun on his shoulders, his hat pushed back. Sitting very straight in the saddle. The wrapped and bootless foot at one side, the empty stirrup. The herefords and their calves following along the fence and calling after him.

He rode among the half wild cattle in the Bransford pasture all day and a cold wind blew down from the mountains of New Mexico. The cattle trotted off before him or ran with their tails up over the gravel plains among the creosote and he studied them for culls as they went. He was horsetraining as much as he was sorting cattle and the little blue horse he rode had the cuttinghorse's contempt for cows and would closeherd them along the crossfence and bite them. John Grady gave him his head and he cut out a big yearling calf and John Grady roped the calf and dallied but the calf didnt go down. The little horse stood spraddlelegged backed into the rope with the calf standing and twisting at the end of it.

What do you want to do now? he asked the horse.

The horse turned and backed. The calf went bucking.

I guess you think I'm goin to get down and flank that big son of a bitch and me on one leg.

He waited until the calf had bucked itself into a clear space among the creosote and then he put the horse forward at a gallop. He paid the slack rope over the horse's head and overtook the calf on its off side. The calf went trotting. The rope ran from its neck along the ground on the near side and trailed in a curve behind its legs and ran forward up the off side following the horse. John Grady checked his dally and then stood in one

stirrup and cleared his other leg of the trailing rope. When the
rope snapped taut it jerked the calf's head backward and
snatched its hind legs from under it. The calf turned endwise in
the air and slammed to the ground in a cloud of dust and lay
there.

John Grady was already off the horse and hobbling back
along the rope to where the calf lay and he knelt on its head
before it could recover and grabbed its hind leg and yanked the
pigginstring from his belt and tied it and waited till it quit
struggling. Then he leaned and pulled the leg up to take a
closer look at the swelling on the inside of its leg that had made
it run oddly and caused him to cut it out and rope it in the first
place.

The calf had a stob of wood embedded under the skin. He
tried to get hold of it with his fingers but it was broken off
almost flush. He felt along the length of it and pushed on the
end of it with his thumb and tried to feed it forward. He got a
bit more of it exposed and finally leaned forward and got hold
of it with his teeth and pulled it out. A watery serum ran. He
held the stick under his nose and sniffed it and then pitched it
away and went back to the horse to get his bottle of Peerless
and his swabs. When he turned the calf loose it was running
worse than before but he thought it would be all right.

He ate his lunch at noon in an outcropping of lava rock with
a view across the floodplain to the north and to the west. There
were ancient pictographs among the rocks, engravings of animals and moons and men and lost hieroglyphics whose meaning no man would ever know. The rocks were warm in the sun
and he sat sheltered from the wind and watched the silent
empty land. Nothing moved. After a while he folded away the
wrappings from his lunch and rose and went down and caught
the horse.

He was still currying the sweated animal by the light from
the barn stall when Billy walked down picking his teeth and
stood watching him.

Where'd you go?

Cedar Springs.

You up there all day?

Yep.

The man called that owned that filly.

I figured he would.

He wasnt pissed off or nothin.

He had no reason to be.

He asked Mac if he could get you to look at some horses for him.

Well.

He moved along the horse brushing. Billy watched him. She says she's fixin to throw it out if you dont come.

I'll be there in a minute.

All right.

What did you think about that country down there?

I thought it was some pretty nice country.

Yeah?

I aint goin nowheres. Troy aint either.

John Grady ran the brush down the horse's loins. The horse shuddered. We'll all be goin somewhere when the army takes this spread over.

Yeah, I know it.

Troy aint leavin?

Billy looked at the end of his toothpick and put it back in his mouth. The shadow of a bat come to hunt in the barnlight passed across the horse, across John Grady.

I think he just wanted to see his brother.

John Grady nodded. He leaned with both forearms across the horse and stripped the loose hairs from the brush and watched them drop.

When he entered the kitchen Oren was still at the table. He looked up from his paper and then went back to reading. John Grady went to the sink and washed and Socorro opened the warmer door over the oven and got down a plate.

He sat eating his supper and reading the news on the back side of Oren's paper across the table.

What's a plebiscite? said Oren.

You got me.

After a while Oren said: Dont be readin the back of the paper.

What?

I said dont be readin the back of the paper.

All right.

He folded the paper and slid it across the table and raised his coffee and sipped it.

How did you know I was readin the back of the paper?

I could feel it.

What's wrong with it?

Nothin. It just makes me nervous is all. It's a bad habit people got. If you want to read a man's paper you ought to ask him.

All right.

The man that owned that filly you wouldnt have on the property called out here tryin to hire you.

I already got a job.

I think he just wanted you to ride out to Fabens with him to look at a horse.

John Grady nodded. That aint what he wants.

Oren watched him. That's what Mac said.

Or it aint all he wants.

Oren lit a cigarette and laid the pack back on the table. John Grady ate.

What did Mac say?

Said he'd tell you.

Well. I been told.

Hell, call the man. You could do a little horsetradin on the weekend. Make yourself some money.

I guess I dont know how to work for but one man at a time.

Oren smoked. He watched the boy.

I went up to Cedar Springs. Worked them scrubs up there.

I wasnt askin.

I know it. I took that little blue horse of Watson's.

How did he do?

I thought he done awful good. Not braggin or nothin. He was a good horse fore I ever put a saddle on him.

You could of bought that horse.

I know it.

What didnt you like about him?

There wasnt nothin I didnt like about him.

You wont buy him now.

Nope.

He finished eating and wiped his plate with the last piece of tortilla and ate that and pushed the plate back and drank his coffee and set the cup down and looked at Oren.

He's just a good all around horse. He aint a finished horse but I think he'll make a cow horse.

I'm pleased to hear it. Of course your preference is for one that'll bow up like a bandsaw and run head first into the barn wall.

John Grady smiled. Horse of my dreams, he said. It aint exactly like that.

How is it then?

I dont know. I think it's just somethin you like. Or dont like. You can add up all of a horse's good points on a sheet of paper and it still wont tell you whether you'll like the horse or not.

What about if you add up all his bad ones?

I dont know. I'd say you'd probably done made up your mind at that point.

You think there's horses so spoiled you cant do nothin with em?

Yes I do. But probably not as many as you might think.

Maybe not. You think a horse can understand what a man says?

You mean like the words?

I dont know. Like can he understand what he says.

John Grady looked out the window. Water was beaded on the glass. Two bats were hunting in the barnlight. No, he said. I think he can understand what you mean.

He watched the bats. He looked at Oren.

I guess my feelin about a horse is that he mostly worries about what he dont know. He likes to be able to see you. Barring that, he likes to be able to hear you. Maybe he thinks that if you're talkin you wont be doin somethin else he dont know about.

You think horses think?

Sure. Dont you?

Yes I do. Some people claim they dont.

Well. Some people could be wrong.

You think you can tell what a horse is thinkin?

I think I can tell what he's fixin to do.

Generally.

John Grady smiled. Yeah, he said. Generally.

Mac always claimed a horse knows the difference between right and wrong.

Mac's right.

Oren smoked. Well, he said. That's always been a bit much for me to swallow.

I think if they didnt you couldnt even train one.

You dont think it's just gettin em to do what you want?

I think you can train a rooster to do what you want. But you wont have him. There's a way to train a horse where when you get done you've got the horse. On his own ground. A good horse will figure things out on his own. You can see what's in his heart. He wont do one thing while you're watchin him and another when you aint. He's all of a piece. When you've got a horse to that place you cant hardly get him to do somethin he knows is wrong. He'll fight you over it. And if you mistreat him it just about kills him. A good horse has justice in his heart. I've seen it.

You got a lot higher opinion of horses than I got, Oren said.

I really dont have all that much in the way of opinions where horses are concerned. When I was a kid I thought I knew all there was to know about a horse. Where horses are concerned I've just got dumber and dumber.

Oren smiled.

If a man really understood horses, John Grady said. If a man really understood horses he could just about train one by lookin at it. There wouldnt be nothin to it. My way is a long way from workin one over with a tracechain. But it's a long way from what's possible too.

He stretched his legs out. He crossed the sprained foot over his boot.

You're right about one thing, he said. They're mostly ruint before they ever bring em out here. They're ruined at the first saddle. Before that, even. The best horses are the ones been around kids. Or maybe even just a wild horse in off the range that's never even seen a man. He's got nothin to unlearn.

You might have a hard time gettin anyone to agree with you on that last one.

I know it.

You ever break a wild horse?

Yeah. You hardly ever train one though.

Why not?

People dont want em trained. They just want em broke. You got to train the owner.

Oren leaned and stubbed out his cigarette. I hear you, he said.

John Grady sat studying the smoke rising into the lampshade over the table. That probably aint true what I said about the one that aint never seen a man. They need to see people. They need to just see em around. Maybe what they need is to just think people are trees until the trainer comes along.

IT WAS STILL LIGHT OUT, a gray light with the rain falling in the streets again and the vendors huddled in the doorways looking out at the rain without expression. He stomped the water from his boots and entered and crossed to the bar and took off his hat and laid it on the barstool. There were no other customers. Two whores lounging on a sofa watched him without much interest. The barman poured his whiskey.

He described the girl to the barman but the barman only shrugged and shook his head.

Eres muy joven.

He shrugged again. He wiped the bar and leaned back and took a cigarette from his shirtpocket and lit it. John Grady motioned for another whiskey and doled his coins onto the counter. He took his hat and his glass over to the sofa and queried the whores but they only tugged at his clothing and asked him to buy them a drink. He looked into their faces. Who they might be behind the caked sizing and the rouge, the black greasepaint lining their dark indian eyes. They seemed alien and sad. Like madwomen dressed for an outing. He looked at the neon deer hanging on the wall behind them and the garish tapestries of plush, of foil and braid. He could hear the rain on the roof to the rear and the steady small drip of water falling from the ceiling into puddles in the bloodred carpeting. He drained his whiskey and set the glass on the low table and put on his hat. He nodded to them and touched the brim of his hat to go.

Joven, said the oldest.

Sí.

She looked furtively about but there was no one there to hear.

Ya no está, she said.

He asked where she had gone but they did not know. He asked if she would return but they did not think so.

He touched his hat again. Gracias, he said.

Ándale, said the whores.

At the corner a sturdy cabdriver in a blue suit of polished serge hailed him. He held an antique umbrella, rare to see in that country. One of the panels between the ribs had been replaced by a sheet of blue cellophane and under it the driver's face was blue. He asked John Grady if he wanted to go see the girls and he said that he did.

They drove through the flooded and potholed streets. The driver was slightly drunk and commented freely on pedestrians that crossed before them or that stood in the doorways. He commented on aspects of their character deducible from their appearance. He commented on crossing dogs. He talked about what the dogs thought and where they might be going and why.

They sat at a whorehouse bar on the outskirts of the city and the driver pointed out the virtues of the various whores that were in the room. He said that men out for an evening were often likely to accept the first proposal but that the prudent man would be more selective. That he would not be misled by appearances. He said that it was best to move freely where whores were concerned. He said that in a healthy society choice should always be the prerogative of the buyer. He turned to regard the boy with dreamy eyes.

De acuerdo? he said.

Claro que sí, said John Grady.

They drank up and moved on. Outside it was dark and in the streets the colored lights lay slurred and faintly peened in the fine rain. They sat at the bar of an establishment called the Red Cock. The driver saluted with his glass aloft and drank. They studied the whores.

I can take you some other places, the driver said. Maybe she is go home.

Maybe.

Maybe she is get married. Sometimes these girls is get married.

I seen her down here two weeks ago.

The driver reflected. He sat smoking. John Grady finished his drink and rose. Vamos a regresar a La Venada, he said.

In the Calle de Santos Degollado he sat at the bar and waited. After a while the driver returned and leaned and whispered to him and then looked about with studied caution.

You must talk to Manolo. Manolo only can give us this information.

Where is he?

I take you to him. I take you. It is arrange. You have to pay.

John Grady reached for his wallet. The driver stayed his arm.

He looked toward the barman. Afuera, he said. No podemos hacerlo aquí.

Outside he again reached for his billfold but the driver said for him to wait. He looked about theatrically. Es peligroso, he hissed.

They got into the cab.

Where is he? said John Grady.

We go to him now. I take you.

He started the engine and they pulled away down the street and turned right. They drove half way up the block and turned again and pulled into an alley and parked. The driver cut the engine and switched off the lights. They sat in the darkness. They could hear a radio in the distance. They could hear rain-water from the canales dripping in the puddles in the alley. After a while a man appeared and opened the rear door of the cab and got in.

The domelight was out in the cab and John Grady could not see the man's face. He was smoking a cigarette and he cupped his hand over it when he smoked in the manner of country people. John Grady could smell the cologne he wore.

Bueno, the man said.

You pay him now, said the cabdriver. He will tell you where the girl is.

How much do I pay him?

You pay me fifty dollars, the man said.

Fifty dollars?

No one answered.

I dont have fifty dollars.

The man sat for a moment. Then he opened the door again and got out.

Wait a minute, said John Grady.

The man stood in the alley, one hand on the door. John Grady could see him. He was wearing a black suit and a black tie. His face was small and wedgeshaped.

Do you know this girl? said John Grady.

Of course I know this girl. You waste my time.

What does she look like?

She is sixteen years old. She is the epiléptica. There is only one. She is gone two weeks now. You waste my time. You have no money and you waste my time.

I'll get the money. I'll bring it tomorrow night.

The man looked at the driver.

I'll come to the Venada. I'll bring it to the Venada.

The man turned his head slightly and spat and turned back. You cant come to the Venada. On this business. What is the matter with you? How much do you have?

John Grady took out his billfold. Thirty somethin, he said. He thumbed through the bills. Thirty-six dollars.

The man held out his hand. Give it to me.

John Grady handed him the money. He wadded it into his shirtpocket without even looking at it. The White Lake, he said. Then he shut the door and was gone. They couldnt even hear his footsteps going back up the alley. The driver turned in his seat.

You want to go to the White Lake?

I dont have any more money.

The driver drummed his fingers on the back of the seat. You dont have no monies?

No.

The driver shook his head. No monies, he said. Okay. You want to go back to the Avenida?

I cant pay you.

Is okay.

He started the engine and backed down the alley toward the street. You pay me next time. Okay?

Okay.

Okay.

WHEN HE PASSED Billy's room the light was on and he stopped and pushed open the canvas and looked in. Billy was lying in bed. He lowered the book he was reading and looked over the top of it and then laid it down.

What are you readin?

Destry. Where you been?

You ever been to a place called the White Lake?

Yes I have. One time.

Is it real expensive?

It's real expensive. Why?

I was just wonderin about it. See you in the mornin.

He let the canvas fall and turned and went on down the bay to his room.

You better stay out of the White Lake, son, Billy called.

John Grady pushed open the curtain and felt for the lightchain.

It aint no place for a cowboy.

He found the chain and pulled the light on.

You hear me?

HE LIMPED DOWN the hallway after breakfast with his hat in his hand. Mr Mac? he called.

McGovern came to the door of his office. He had some papers in his hand and some more wedged under his elbow. Come on in, son, he said.

John Grady stood in the door. Mac was at his desk. Come on in, he said. What do you need that I aint got?

He looked up from his papers. John Grady was still standing in the doorway.

I wonder if I could draw some on next month's pay.

Mac reached for his billfold. How much did you need.

Well. I'd like to get a hundred if I could.

Mac looked at him. You can have it if you want, he said. What did you aim to do next month?

I'll make out.

He opened the billfold and counted out five twenties. Well,

he said. I guess you're big enough to handle your own affairs. It aint none of my business, is it?

I just needed it for somethin.

All right.

He shuffled the bills together and leaned and laid them on the desk. John Grady came in and picked them up and folded them and stuck them in his shirtpocket.

Thank you, he said.

That's all right. How's your foot?

It's doin good.

You're still favorin it I see.

It's all right.

You still intend to trade for that horse?

Yessir. I do.

How did you know Wolfenbarger's filly had a bad hoof?

I could see it.

She didnt walk lame.

No sir. It was her ear.

Her ear?

Yessir. Ever time that foot hit the ground one ear would move a little. I just kept watchin her.

Sort of like a poker tell.

Yessir. Sort of.

You didnt want to go off horsetradin with the old man though.

No sir. Is he a friend of yours?

I know him. Why?

Nothin.

What were you goin to say?

That's all right.

You can say it. Go ahead.

Well. I guess I was goin to say that I didnt think I could keep him out of trouble on no part time basis.

Like it would be a full time job?

I didnt say that.

Mac shook his head. Get your butt out of here, he said.

Yessir.

You didnt tell him that did you?

No sir. I aint talked to him.

Well. That's a shame.

Yessir.

He put on his hat and turned but stopped again at the door.

Thank you sir.

Go on. It's your money.

When he came in that evening Socorro had already left the kitchen and there was no one at the table except the old man. He was smoking a homerolled cigarette and listening to the news on the radio. John Grady got his plate and his coffee and set them on the table and pulled back the chair and sat.

Evenin Mr Johnson, he said.

Evenin son.

What's the news?

The old man shook his head. He leaned across the table to the windowsill where the radio sat and turned it off. It aint news no more, he said. Wars and rumors of wars. I dont know why I listen to it. It's a ugly habit and I wish I could get broke of it but I think I just get worse.

John Grady spooned pico de gallo over his rice and his flautas and rolled up a tortilla and commenced to eat. The old man watched him. He nodded at the boy's boots.

You look like you been in some pretty mirey country today.

Yessir. I was. Some.

That old greasy clay is hard to clean off of anything. Oliver Lee always said he come out here because the country was so sorry nobody else would have it and he'd be left alone. Of course he was wrong. At least about bein left alone.

Yessir. I guess he was.

How's your foot doin.

It's all right.

The old man smiled. He drew on his cigarette and tapped the ash into the ashtray on the table.

Dont be fooled by the good rains we've had. This country is fixin to dry up and blow away.

How do you know?

It just is.

You want some more coffee?

No thanks.

The boy got up and went to the stove and filled his cup and came back.

Country's overdue, the old man said. Folks have got short memories. They might be glad to let the army have it fore they're done.

The boy ate. How much do you think the army will take?

The old man drew on his cigarette and stubbed it out thoughtfully. I think they'll take the whole Tularosa basin. That's my guess.

Can they just take it?

Yeah. They can take it. Folks will piss and moan about it. But they dont have a choice. They ought to be glad to get shut of it.

What do you think Mr Prather will do?

John Prather will do whatever he says he'll do.

Mr Mac said he told em the only way he'd leave was in a box.

Then that's how he'll leave. You can take that to the bank.

John Grady wiped his plate and sat back with his cup of coffee. I ought not to ask you this, he said.

Ask it.

You dont have to answer.

I know it.

Who do you think killed Colonel Fountain?

The old man shook his head. He sat for a long time.

I ought not to of asked you.

No. It's all right. You know his daughter's name was Maggie too. She was the one told Fountain to take the boy with him. Said they wouldnt bother a eight year old boy. But she was wrong, wasnt she?

Yessir.

A lot of people think Oliver Lee killed him. I knew Oliver

pretty well. We was the same age. He had four sons himself. I just dont believe it.

You dont think he could of done it?

I'll say it stronger than that. I'll say he didnt.

Or cause it to be done?

Well. That's another matter. I'll say he never shed no tears over it. Over the colonel, leastways.

You didnt want some more coffee?

No thank you son. I'd be up all night.

Do you think they're still buried out there somewheres?

No. I dont.

What do you think happened?

I always thought the bodies were taken to Mexico. They had a choice to bury em out there somewhere south of the pass where they might be discovered or to go another thirty miles to where they could drop em off the edge of the world and I think that's what they done.

John Grady nodded. He sipped his coffee. Were you ever in a shooting scrape?

I was. One time. I was old enough to know better too.

Where was it?

Down on the river east of Clint. It was in nineteen and seventeen just before my brother died and we were on the wrong side of the river waitin for dark to cross some stolen horses we'd recovered and we got word they was layin for us. We waited and waited and after a while the moon come up—just a piece of a moon, not even a quarter. It come up behind us and we could see it reflected in the windshield of their car over in the trees along the river breaks. Wendell Williams looked at me and he said: We got two moons in the sky. I dont believe I ever seen that before. And I said: Yes, and one of em is backwards. And we opened fire on em with our rifles.

Did they shoot back?

Sure they did. We laid there and shot up about a box of shells apiece and then they left out.

Was anybody hit?

Not that I ever heard of. We hit the car a time or two. Knocked the windshield out.

Did you get the horses across?

We did.

How many head was it?

It was a few. About seventy head.

That's a lot of horses.

It was a lot of horses. We was paid good money, too. But it wasnt worth gettin shot over.

No sir. I guess not.

It does funny things to a man's head.

What's that, sir?

Bein shot at. Havin dirt thowed on you. Leaves cut. It changes a man's perspective. Maybe some might have a appetite for it. I never did.

You didnt fight in the revolution?

No.

You were down there though.

Yes. Tryin to get the hell out. I'd been down there too long. I was just as glad when it did start. You'd wake up in some little town on a Sunday mornin and they'd be out in the street shootin at one another. You couldnt make any sense out of it. We like to never got out of there. I saw terrible things in that country. I dreamt about em for years.

He leaned and put his elbows on the table and took his makings from his shirtpocket and rolled another smoke and lit it. He sat looking at the table. He talked for a long time. He named the towns and villages. The mud pueblos. The executions against the mud walls sprayed with new blood over the dried black of the old and the fine powdered clay sifting down from the bulletholes in the wall after the men had fallen and the slow drift of riflesmoke and the corpses stacked in the streets or piled into the woodenwheeled carretas trundling over the cobbles or over the dirt roads to the nameless graves. There were thousands who went to war in the only suit they owned. Suits in which they'd been married and in which they would be buried. Standing in the streets in their coats and ties and hats behind the upturned carts and bales and firing their rifles like irate accountants. And the small artillery pieces on wheels that scooted backwards in the street at every round and had to be retrieved and the endless riding of horses to their deaths bearing flags or banners or the tentlike tapestries painted with portraits of the Virgin carried on poles into battle as if the mother of God herself were authoress of all that calamity and mayhem and madness.

The tallcase clock in the hallway chimed ten.

I reckon I'd better get on to bed, the old man said.

Yessir.

He rose. I dont much like to, he said. But there aint no help for it.

Goodnight sir.

Goodnight.

THE CABDRIVER would see him through the wroughtiron gate in the high brick wall and up the walk to the doorway. As if the surrounding dark that formed the outskirts of the city were a danger. Or the desert plains beyond. He pulled a velvet bellpull in an alcove in the archway and stood back humming. He looked at John Grady.

You like for me to wait I can wait.

No. It's all right.

The door opened. A hostess in evening attire smiled at them and stood back and held the door. John Grady entered and took off his hat and the woman spoke with the driver and then shut the door and turned. She held out her hand and John Grady reached for his hip pocket. She smiled.

Your hat, she said.

He handed her his hat and she gestured toward the room and he turned and went in, brushing down his hair with the flat of his hand.

There was a bar to the right up the two stairs and he stepped up and passed along behind the stools where men were drinking and talking. The bar was mahogany and softly lit and the barmen wore little burgundy jackets and bowties. Out in the salon the whores lounged on sofas of red damask and gold brocade. They wore negligees and floorlength formal gowns and sheath dresses of white satin or purple velvet that were split up the thigh and they wore shoes of glass or gold and sat in studied poses with their red mouths pouting in the gloom. A cutglass chandelier hung overhead and on a dais to the right a string trio was playing.

He walked to the far end of the bar. When he put his hand on the rail the barman was already there placing a napkin.

Good evening sir, he said.

Evenin. I'll have a Old Grandad and water back.

Yessir.

The barman moved away. John Grady put his boot on the polished brass footrail and he watched the whores in the glass of the backbar. The men at the bar were mostly welldressed Mexicans with a few Americans dressed in flowered shirts of an intemperately thin cloth. A tall woman in a diaphanous gown passed through the salon like the ghost of a whore. A cockroach that had been moving along the counter behind the bottles ascended to the glass where it encountered itself and froze.

He ordered another drink. The barman poured. When he looked into the glass again she was sitting by herself on a dark velvet couch with her gown arranged about her and her hands composed in her lap. He reached for his hat, not taking his eyes from her. He called for the barman.

La cuenta por favor.

He looked down. He remembered that he'd left his hat with the hostess at the door. He took out his wallet and pushed a fivedollar bill across the mahogany and folded the rest of the bills and put them in his shirtpocket. The barman brought the change and he pushed a dollar back toward him and turned and looked across the room to where she sat. She looked small and lost. She sat with her eyes closed and he realized that she was listening to the music. He poured the shot of whiskey into the glass of water and set the shotglass on the bar and took his drink and set out across the room.

His faint shadow under the lights of the great glass tiara above them may have brought her from her reveries. She looked up at him and smiled thinly with her painted child's mouth. He almost reached for his hatbrim.

Hello, he said. Do you care if I set down?

She recomposed herself and smoothed her skirt to make room on the couch beside her. A waiter moved out from the shadows along the walls and laid down two napkins on the low glass table before them and stood.

Bring me a Old Grandad and water back. And whatever she's drinkin.

He nodded and moved away. John Grady looked at the girl. She leaned forward and smoothed her skirt again.

Lo siento, she said. Pero no hablo inglés.

Está bien. Podemos hablar español.

Oh, she said. Qué bueno.

Qué es su nombre?

Magdalena. Y usted?

He didnt answer. Magdalena, he said.

She looked down. As if the sound of her name were troubling to her.

Es su nombre de pila? he said.

Sí. Por supuesto.

No es su nombre . . . su nombre profesional.

She put her hand to her mouth. Oh, she said. No. Es mi nombre propio.

He watched her. He told her that he had seen her at La Venada but she only nodded and did not seem surprised. The waiter arrived with the drinks and he paid for them and tipped the man a dollar. She did not pick up her drink then or later. She spoke so softly he had to lean to catch her words. She said that the other women were watching but that it was nothing. It was only that she was new to this place. He nodded. No importa, he said.

She asked why he had not spoken to her at La Venada. He said that it was because he was with friends. She asked him if he had a sweetheart at La Venada but he said that he did not.

No me recuerda? he said.

She shook her head. She looked up. They sat in silence.

Cuántos años tiene? he said.

Bastantes.

He said it was all right if she did not wish to say but she didnt answer. She smiled wistfully. She touched his sleeve. Fue mentira, she said. Lo que decía.

Cómo?

She said that it was a lie that she did not remember him. She said that he was standing at the bar and she thought that he would come to talk to her but that he had not and when she looked again he was gone.

Verdad?

Sí.

He said that she had not really lied. He said she'd only shook her head, but she shook her head again and said that these were the worst lies of all. She asked him why he had come to the White Lake alone and he looked at the drinks untouched on the table before them and he thought about that and about lies and he turned and looked at her.

Porque la andaba buscando, he said. Ya tengo tiempo buscándola.

She didnt answer.

Y cómo es que me recuerda?

She half turned away, she almost whispered. También yo, she said.

Mande?

She turned and looked at him. También yo.

In the room she turned and closed the door behind them. He

couldnt even remember how they got there. He remembered her hand in his, small and cold, so strange to feel. The prism-broken light from the chandelier that ran in a river over her naked shoulders when they passed beneath. Half stumbling after her like a child.

She went to the bedside and lit two candles and then turned off the lamp. He stood in the room with his hands at his sides. She reached to the back of her neck and undid the clasp of her gown and reached behind and pulled down the zipper. He began to unbutton his shirt. The room was small and the bed all but filled it. It was a fourpost bed with a canopy and curtains of winecolored organza and the candles shone through onto the pillows with a winey light.

There was a light knock at the door.

Tenemos que pagar, she said.

He took the folded bills from his pocket. Para la noche, he said.

Es muy caro.

Cuánto? He was counting out the bills. He had eighty-two dollars. He held it out to her. She looked at the money and she looked at him. The knock came again.

Dame cincuenta, she said.

Es bastante?

Sí, sí. She took the money and opened the door and held it out and whispered to the man on the other side. He was tall and thin and he smoked a cigarette in a silver holder and he wore a black silk shirt. He looked at the client for just a moment through the partly opened door and he counted the money and nodded and turned away and she shut the door. Her bare back was pale in the candlelight where the dress was open. Her black hair glistened. She turned and withdrew her arms from the sleeves of the dress and caught the front of it before her. She stepped from the pooled cloth and laid the dress across a chair and stepped behind the gauzy curtains and turned back the covers and then she pulled the straps of her chemise from her shoulders and let it fall and stepped naked into the bed and pulled the satin quilt to her chin and turned on her side and put her arm beneath her head and lay watching him.

He took off his shirt and stood looking for some place to put it.

Sobre la silla, she whispered.

He draped the shirt over the chair and sat and pulled off his boots and put his socks in the tops of them and stood them to one side and stood and unbuckled his belt. He crossed the room naked and she reached and turned back the covers for him and he slid beneath the tinted sheets and lay back on the pillow and looked up at the softly draped canopy. He turned and looked at her. She'd not taken her eyes from him. He raised his arm and she slid against him the whole length of her soft and naked and cool. He gathered her black hair in his hand and spread it across his chest like a blessing.

Es casado? she said.

No.

He asked her why she wished to know. She was silent a moment. Then she said that it would be a worse sin if he were married. He thought about that. He asked her if that was really why she wished to know but she said he wished to know too much. Then she leaned and kissed him. In the dawn he held her while she slept and he had no need to ask her anything at all.

She woke while he was dressing. He pulled on his boots and crossed to the bedside and sat and put his hand against her cheek and smoothed her hair. She turned sleepily and looked up at him. The candles in their holders had burned out and the bits of wick lay blackened in the scalloped shapes of wax.

Tienes que irte?

Sí.

Vas a regresar?

Sí.

She studied his eyes to see if he spoke the truth. He leaned and kissed her.

Vete con Dios, she whispered.

Y tú.

She put her arms around him and held him against her breast and then she let him go and he rose and walked to the door. He turned and stood looking back at her.

Say my name, he said.

She reached and parted the canopy curtain. Mande? she said.

Di mi nombre.

She lay there holding the curtain. Tu nombre es Juan, she said.

Yes, he said. Then he pulled the door closed and went down the hall.

The salon was empty. It smelled of stale smoke and sweet ferment and the fading lilac rose and spice of the vanished whores. There was no one at the bar. In the gray light there were stains on the carpet, worn places on the arms of the furniture, cigarette burns. In the foyer he unlatched the painted half door and entered the little cloakroom and retrieved his hat. Then he opened the front door and walked out into the morning cold.

A landscape of low shacks of tin and cratewood here on the outskirts of the city. Barren dirt and gravel lots and beyond them the plains of sage and creosote. Roosters were calling and the air smelled of burning charcoal. He took his bearings by the gray light to the east and set out toward the city. In the cold dawn the lights were still burning out there under the dark cape of the mountains with that precious insularity common to cities of the desert. A man was coming down the road driving a donkey piled high with firewood. In the distance the churchbells had begun. The man smiled at him a sly smile. As if they knew a secret between them, these two. Something of age and youth and their claims and the justice of those claims. And of the claims upon them. The world past, the world to come. Their common transiencies. Above all a knowing deep in the bone that beauty and loss are one.

THE OLD ONE-EYED CRIADA was the first to reach her, trotting stoically down the hallway in her broken slippers and pushing open the door to find her bowed in the bed and raging as if some incubus were upon her. The old woman carried her keys tied by a thong to a short length of broomstick and she wrapped the stick with a quick turn of the bedclothes and forced it between the girl's teeth. The girl arched herself stiffly and the criada climbed up onto the bed and pinned her down and held her. A second woman had come to the doorway bearing a glass of water but she waved her away with a toss of her head.

Es como una mujer diabólica, the woman said.

Vete, called the criada. No es diabólica. Vete.

But the housewhores were gathering in the doorway and they began to push through into the room all of them in facecream and hairpapers and dressed in their varied nightwear and they gathered clamoring about the bed and one pushed forward with a statue of the Virgin and raised it above the bed and another took one of the girl's hands and commenced to tie it to the bedpost with the sash from her robe. The girl's mouth was bloody and some of the whores came forward and dipped their handkerchiefs in the blood as if to wipe it away but they hid the handkerchiefs on their persons to take away with them and the girl's mouth continued to bleed. They pulled her other arm free and tied it as well and some of them were chanting and some were blessing themselves and the girl bowed and thrashed and then went rigid and her eyes white. They'd brought little figures from their rooms and votive shrines of gilt and painted plaster and some were at lighting candles when the owner of the establishment appeared in the doorway in his shirtsleeves.

Eduardo! Eduardo! they cried. He strode into the room backhanding them away. He swept icons and candles to the floor and seized the old criada by one arm and flung her back.

Basta! he cried. Basta!

The whores huddled whimpering, clutching their robes about their rolling breasts. They retreated to the door. The criada alone stood her ground.

Por qué estás esperando? he hissed.

Her solitary eye blinked. She would not move.

He'd brought from somewhere in his clothes an italian switchblade knife with black onyx handles and silver bolsters and he leaned and cut the sashes from the girl's wrists and seized the covers and pulled them up over her nakedness and folded the knife away as silently as it had appeared.

No la moleste, hissed the criada. No la moleste.

Cállate.

Golpéame si tienes que golpear a alguien.

He turned and seized the old woman by the hair and forced her to the door and shoved her into the hallway with the whores and shut the door behind her. He'd have latched it but those doors latched only from without. The old woman nevertheless did not enter again but stood outside calling that she needed her keys. He stood looking at the girl. The piece of broomstick had fallen from her mouth and lay on the blood-stained sheets. He picked it up and went to the door and opened it. The old woman shrank back and raised one arm but he only threw the keys rattling and clattering down the corridor and then slammed the door shut again.

She lay breathing quietly. There was a cloth lying on the bed and he picked it up and held it for a moment almost as if he might bend to wipe the blood from her mouth but then he flung it away also and turned and looked once more at the wreckage of the room and swore softly to himself and went out and shut the door behind him.

WARD BROUGHT THE STALLION out of the stall and started down the bay with it. The stallion stopped in the middle of the bay and stood trembling and took small steps as if the ground had got unsteady under its feet. Ward stood close to the stallion and talked to it and the stallion jerked its head up and down in a sort of frenzied agreement. They'd been through it all before but the stallion was no less crazy for that and Ward no less patient. He led the horse prancing past the stalls where the other horses circled and rolled their eyes.

John Grady was holding the mare by a twitch and when the stallion entered the paddock she tried to stand upright. She turned at the end of the rope and shot out one hindfoot and then she tried to stand again.

That is a pretty decent lookin mare, Ward said.

Yessir.

What happened to her eye?

Man that owned her knocked it out with a stick.

Ward led the walleyed stallion around the perimeter of the paddock. Knocked it out with a stick, he said.

Yessir.

He couldnt put it back though, could he?

No sir.

Easy, said Ward. Easy now. That's a sweet mare.

Yessir, said John Grady. She is.

He walked the stallion forward by fits and starts. The little mare rolled her good eye till it was white as the blind one. JC and another man had entered the paddock and closed the gate behind them. Ward turned and looked past them toward the paddock walls.

I aint tellin you all again, he called. You go on to the house like I told you.

Two teen-age girls came out and started across the yard toward the house.

Where's Oren at? said Ward.

John Grady turned with the skittering mare. He was leaning all over her and trying to keep her from stepping on his feet.

He had to go to Alamogordo.

Hold her now, Ward said. Hold her.

The stallion stood, his great phallus swinging.

Hold her, said Ward.

I got her.

He knows where it's at.

The mare bucked and kicked one leg. On the third try the stallion mounted her, clambering, stamping his hindlegs, the great thighs quivering and the veins standing. John Grady stood holding all of this before him on a twisted tether like a child holding by a string some struggling and gasping chimera invoked by sorcery out of the void into the astonished day-world. He held the twitchrope in one hand and laid his face against the sweating neck. He could hear the slow bellows of her lungs and feel the blood pumping. He could hear the slow dull beating of the heart within her like an engine deep in a ship.

He and JC loaded the mare in the trailer. She look knocked up to you? JC said.

I dont know.

He bowed her back, didnt he?

They raised the tailgate on the trailer and latched it at either side. John Grady turned and leaned against the trailer and wiped his face with his kerchief and pulled his hat back down.

Mac's done got the colt sold.

I hope he aint spent the money.

Yeah?

She's been bred twice before and it didnt take.

Ward's stud?

No.

I got my money on Ward's studhorse.

So does Mac.

Are we done?

We're done. You want to swing by the cantina?

Are you buyin?

Hell, said JC. I thought I'd get you to back me on the shuffleboard. Give us a chance to improve our financial position.

Last time I done that the position we wound up in wasnt financial.

They climbed into the truck.

Are you broke sure enough? said JC.

I aint got a weepin dime.

They started slowly down the drive. The horsetrailer clanked behind. Troy was counting change in his hand.

I got enough for a couple of beers apiece, he said.

That's all right.

I'm ready to blow in the whole dollar and thirty-five cents.

We better get on back.

HE WATCHED BILLY RIDE down along the fenceline from where it crested against the red dunes. He rode past and then sat the horse and looked out across the windscoured terrain and he turned and looked at John Grady. He leaned and spat.

Hard country, he said.

Hard country.

This used to be grama grass to a horse's stirrups.

I've heard that. Did you see any more of that bunch?

No. They're scattered all to hell and gone. Wild as deer. A man needs three horses to put in a day up here.

Why dont we ride up Bell Springs Draw.

Were you up there last week?

No.

All right.

They crossed the red creosote plain and picked their way up along the dry arroyo over the red rock scree.

John Grady Cole was a rugged old soul, Billy sang.

The trail crossed through the rock and led out along a wash. The dirt was like red talc.

With a buckskin belly and a rubber asshole.

An hour later they sat their horses at the spring. The cattle had been and gone. There were wet tracks at the south end of the ciénega and wet tracks in the trail leading out south down the side of the ridge.

There's at least two new calves with this bunch, Billy said.

John Grady didnt answer. The horses raised their dripping mouths from the water one and then the other and blew and leaned and drank again. The dead leaves clinging to the pale and twisted cottonwoods rattled in the wind. Set in a flat above the springs was a small adobe house in ruins these many years. Billy took his cigarettes from his shirtpocket and shook one out and hunched his shoulders forward and lit it.

I used to think I'd like to have a little spread up in the hills somewhere like this. Run a few head on it. Kill your own meat. Stuff like that.

You might one day.

I doubt it.

You never know.

I wintered one time in a linecamp up in New Mexico. You get a pretty good ration of yourself after a while. I wouldnt do it again if I could help it. I like to froze in that damn shack. The wind would blow your hat off inside.

He smoked. The horses raised their heads and looked out. John Grady pulled the latigo on his catchrope and retied it. You think you'd of liked to of lived back in the old days? he said.

No. I did when I was a kid. I used to think rawhidin a bunch of bony cattle in some outland country would be just as close to heaven as a man was likely to get. I wouldnt give you much for it now.

You think they were a tougher breed back then?

Tougher or dumber?

The dry leaves rattled. Evening was coming on and Billy buttoned his jacket against the cold.

I could live here, John Grady said.

Young and ignorant as you are you probably could.

I think I'd like it.

I'll tell you what I like.

What's that?

When you throw a switch and the lights come on.

Yeah.

If I think about what I wanted as a kid and what I want now they aint the same thing. I guess what I wanted wasnt what I wanted. You ready?

Yeah. I'm ready. What do you want now?

Billy spoke to the horse and reined it around. He sat and looked back at the little adobe house and at the blue and cooling country below them. Hell, he said. I dont know what I want. Never did.

They rode back in the dusk. The dark shapes of cattle moved off sullenly before them.

This is the tag end of that bunch, Billy said.

Yep.

They rode on.

When you're a kid you have these notions about how things are goin to be, Billy said. You get a little older and you pull back some on that. I think you wind up just tryin to minimize the pain. Anyway this country aint the same. Nor anything in it. The war changed everthing. I dont think people even know it yet.

The sky to the west darkened. A cold wind blew. They could see the aura of the lights from the city come up forty miles away.

You need to wear more clothes than that, Billy said.

I'm all right. How did the war change it?

It just did. It aint the same no more. It never will be.

EDUARDO STOOD at the rear door smoking one of his thin cigars and looking out at the rain. There was a sheetiron warehouse behind the building and there was nothing much there to see except the rain and black pools of water standing in the alley where the rain fell and the soft light from the yellow bulb screwed into the fixture over the back door. The air was cool. The smoke drifted in the light. A young girl who limped on a withered leg passed carrying a great armload of soiled linen down the hall. After a while he closed the door and walked back up the hallway to his office.

When Tiburcio knocked he did not even turn around. Adelante, he said. Tiburcio entered. He stood at the desk and counted out money. The desk was of polished glass and fruitwood and there was a white leather sofa against one wall and a low coffeetable of glass and chrome and there was a small bar against the other wall with four white leather stools. The carpeting on the floor was a rich cream color. The alcahuete counted out the money and stood waiting. Eduardo turned and looked at him. The alcahuete smiled thinly under his thin moustache. His black greased hair shone in the soft light. His black shirt bore a glossy sheen from the pressings of an iron too hot.

Eduardo put the cigar between his teeth and came to the desk. He stood looking down. He fanned with one slender jeweled hand the bills on the glass and he took the cigar from his teeth and looked up.

El mismo muchacho?

El mismo.

He pursed his lips, he nodded. Bueno, he said. Ándale.

When Tiburcio had gone he unlocked his desk drawer and took from it a long leather wallet with a chain hanging from it and put the bills in the wallet and put the wallet back in the drawer and locked it again. He opened his ledgerbook and made an entry in it and closed it. Then he went to the door and stood smoking quietly and looking out up the hallway. His hands clasped behind him at the small of his back in a stance he had perhaps admired or read of but a stance native to some other country, not his.

THE MONTH OF NOVEMBER passed and he saw her but once more. The alcahuete came to the door and tapped and went away and she said that he must leave. He held her hands in his, both of them sitting tailorwise and fully dressed in the center of the canopy bed. Leaning and talking to her very quickly and with great earnestness but she would only say it was too dangerous and then the alcahuete rapped at the door again and did not go away.

Prométeme, he said. Prométeme.

The alcahuete rapped with the heel of his fist. She clutched his hand, her eyes wide.

Debes salir, she whispered.

Prométeme.

Sí. Sí. Lo prometo.

When he passed through the salon it was all but empty. The blind pianist who sat in for the string trio at these late hours was at the bench but he was not playing. His young daughter stood beside him. On the piano lay the book which she had been reading to him as he played. John Grady crossed the room and took his last dollar but one and dropped it into the barglass atop the piano. The maestro smiled and bowed slightly. Gracias, he said.

Cómo estás, said John Grady.

The old man smiled again. My young friend, he said. How are you? You are well?

Yes, thank you. And you?

He shrugged. His thin shoulders rose in the dull black stuff of his suit and fell again. I am well, he said. I am well.

Are you done for the night?

No. We go for our supper.

It is very late.

Oh yes. It is late.

The blind man spoke an old-world english, a language from another place and time. He steadied himself and rose and turned woodenly.

Will you join us?

No thank you sir. I need to get on.

And how is your suit advancing?

He wasnt sure what that meant. He turned the words over in his mind. The girl, he said.

The old man bowed his head in affirmation.

I dont know, John Grady said. All right, I think. I hope so.

It is an uncertain business, the old man said. You must persevere. To persevere is everything.

Yessir.

The girl had taken her father's hat from the piano and stood holding it. She took his hand but he made no motion to leave. He faced the room, empty save for two whores and a drunk at the bar. We are friends, he said.

Yessir, John Grady said. He wasnt sure of whom the old man spoke.

May I speak in confidence?

Yes.

I believe she is favorable. He placed one delicate and yellowed finger to his lips.

Thank you sir. I appreciate that.

Of course. He held out one hand palm up and the girl placed the brim of his hat in his grip and he took it in both hands and turned and placed it on his head and looked up.

Do you think she's a good person? John Grady said.

Oh my, said the blind man. Oh my.

I think she is.

Oh my, said the blind man.

John Grady smiled. I'll let you get on to your supper. He nodded to the girl and turned to go.

Her condition, the blind man said. You know her condition?

He turned back. Sir? he said.

Little is known. There is a great deal of superstition. Here they are divided in two camps. Some take a benign view and others do not. You see. But this is my belief. My belief is that she is at best a visitor. At best. She does not belong here. Among us.

Yessir. I know she dont belong here.

No, said the blind man. I do not mean in this house. I mean here. Among us.

He walked back through the streets. Carrying the blind man's words concerning his prospects as if they were a contract with the world to come. Cold as it was the Juárenses stood in the open doorways and smoked or called to one another. Along the sandy unpaved streets nightvendors trundled their carts or drove their small burros before them. They called out leeen-ya. They called out quero-seeen-a. Plying the darkened streets and calling out like old suitors in search themselves of maids long lost to them.

II

H E WAITED but she didnt come. He stood at the window with the hangings of old lace gathered back in his hand and watched the life in the streets. Anyone who would have looked up to see him there behind the untrue panes of dusty glass could have told his story. The afternoon grew quiet. Across the street a merchant closed and locked the iron shutters of his hardware shop. A taxi stopped in front of the hotel and he leaned with his face against the cold pane but he could not see if anyone got out. He turned and went to the door and opened it and walked out to the head of the stairwell where he could look down into the lobby. No one came. When he went back and stood at the window again the taxi was gone. He sat on the bed. The shadows grew long. After a while it was dark in the room and the green neon of the hotel sign came on outside the window and after a while he rose and took his hat from the top of the bureau and went out. He turned at the door and looked back into the room and then pulled the door shut behind him. If he'd stood longer he'd have passed the criada La Tuerta in the shabby stairwell instead of the lobby as he did, he any lodger, she any old woman with one clouded eye struggling in from the street. He stepped out into the cool evening and she labored up the stairs and knocked at the door and waited and knocked again. A door down the hallway opened and a man looked out. He told her that he had no towels.

H E WAS LYING on his bunk staring up at the roughsawed boards of the ceiling of the bunkroom when Billy came and stood in the doorway. He was slightly drunk. His hat was pushed back on his head. What say, cowboy, he said.

Hey Billy.

How you doin?

I'm doin all right. Where'd you all go?

We went to a dance at Mesilla.

Who all went?

Everbody but you.

He sat in the doorway and jacked one boot against the jamb and took off his hat and put it on his knee and leaned his head back. John Grady watched him.

Did you dance?

Danced my ass off.

I didnt know you were a big dancer.

I aint.

I guess you give it your best.

It's a thing that's got to be seen. Oren tells me that squirrel-headed horse you think so much of is eatin out of your hand.

That might be a bit of an exaggeration.

What do you tell em?

Who?

Horses.

I dont know. The truth.

I guess it's a trade secret.

No.

How can you lie to a horse?

He turned and looked at John Grady. I dont know, the boy said. Do you mean how do you go about it or how can you bring yourself to do it?

Go about it.

I dont know. I think it's just what's in your heart.

You think a horse knows what's in your heart?

Yeah. Dont you?

Billy didnt answer. After a while he said: Yeah. I do.

I aint a very good liar.

You just aint had enough practice at it.

Down the barn bay in the stalls they could hear the wheeze and stir of the animals.

Have you got a girl you're seein?

John Grady crossed his boots one over the other. Yeah, he said. Tryin to.

JC said you did.

How did JC know?

He just said you manifested all the symptoms.

Manifested?

Yeah.

What are they?

He didnt say. You intend to bring her around some time where we can get a look at her?

Yeah. I'll bring her around.

Well.

He took his hat from his knee and put it on his head and rose.

Billy?

Yeah.

I'll tell you about it. It's kind of a mess. Right now I'm just a bit wore out.

I dont doubt it for a minute, cowboy. I'll see you in the mornin.

HE WENT the following week with no more money in his pocket than would buy a drink at the bar. He watched her in the mirror. She sat upright alone on the dark velvet couch with her hands composed in her lap like a debutante. He drank the whiskey slowly. When he looked in the mirror again he thought she had been watching him. He finished the whiskey and paid for it and turned to go. He had not meant to look directly at her but he did. He could not even imagine her life.

He got his hat and gave the woman the last of his change and she smiled and thanked him and he put his hat on and turned. He had his hand on the ornate onyx handle of the door when one of the waiters stepped in front of him.

Un momento, he said.

He stopped. He looked at the hatcheck girl and he looked at the waiter.

The waiter stood between him and the door. The girl, he said. She say you no forget her.

He looked toward the salon but he could not see her from the door.

Dígame? he said.

She say you no . . .

En español, por favor. Dígame en español lo que dice ella.

The man would not. He repeated the words again in english and then he turned and was gone.

He sat the next night in the Moderno and waited for the maestro and his daughter. He waited for a long time and he thought perhaps they had already been or perhaps they were not coming. When the little girl pushed open the door she saw him and looked up at her father but she said nothing. They took a table near the door and the waiter came and poured a glass of wine.

He rose and crossed the room and stood at their table. Maestro, he said.

The blind man turned his face up and smiled at the space alongside John Grady. As if some unseen double stood there.

Buenas noches, he said.

Cómo está?

Ah, said the blind man. My young friend.

Yes.

Please. You must join us. Sit down.

Thank you.

He sat. He looked at the girl. The blind man hissed at the waiter and the waiter came over.

Qué toma? said the maestro.

Nothing. Thank you.

Please. I insist.

I cant stay.

Traiga un vino para mi amigo.

The waiter nodded and moved away. John Grady thumbed back his hat and leaned forward with his elbows on the table. What is this place? he said.

The Moderno? It is a place where the musicians come. It is a very old place. It has always been here. You must come on Saturday. Many old people come. You will see them. They come to dance. Very old people dancing. Here. In this place. The Moderno.

Are they going to play again?

Yes, yes. Of course. It is early. They are my friends.

Do they play every night?

Yes. Every night. They will play soon now. You will see.

Good as the maestro's word the violinists began to tune their instruments in the inner room. The cellist leaned listening with his head inclined and drew his bow across the strings. A couple who had been sitting at a table against the far wall rose and stood in the archway holding hands and then sallied forth onto the concrete floor as the musicians struck up an antique waltz. The maestro leaned forward to hear. Are they dancing? he said. Are any dancing now?

The little girl looked at John Grady. Yes, John Grady said. They're dancing.

The old man leaned back, he nodded. Good, he said. That is good.

THEY SAT AGAINST a rock bluff high in the Franklins with a fire before them that heeled in the wind and their figures cast up upon the rocks behind them enshadowed the petroglyphs carved there by other hunters a thousand years before. They could hear the dogs running far below them. Their cries trailed off down the side of the mountain and sounded again more faintly and then faded away where they coursed out along some rocky draw in the dark. To the south the distant lights of the city lay strewn across the desert floor like a tiara laid out upon a jeweler's blackcloth. Archer had stood and turned toward the running dogs the better to listen and after a while he squatted again and spat into the fire.

She aint goin to tree, he said.

I dont believe she will either, said Travis.

How do you know it's the same lion? said JC.

Travis had taken his tobacco from his pocket and he smoothed and cupped a paper with his fingers. She's done us thisaway before, he said. She'll run plumb out of the country.

They sat listening. The cries grew faint and after a while there were no more. Billy had gone off up the side of the mountain to look for wood and he came back dragging a dead cedar stump. He picked it up and dropped it on top of the fire. A shower of sparks rose and drifted down the night. The stump sat all black and twisted over the small flames. Like some amorphous thing come in out of the night to warm itself among them.

Couldnt you find a bigger chunk of wood, Parham?

It'll take here in a minute.

Parham's put the fire plumb out, said JC.

The darkest hour is just before the storm, said Billy. It'll take here in a minute.

I hear em, Travis said.

I do too.

She's crossed at the head of that big draw where the road cuts back.

We wont get that Lucy dog back tonight.

What dog is that?

Bitch out of that Aldridge line. Them dogs was bred by the Lee Brothers. They just forgot to build in the quit.

Best dog we ever had was her grandaddy, said Archer. You remember that Roscoe dog, Travis?

Of course I do. People thought he was part bluetick but he was a full leopard cur with a glass eye and he did love to fight. We lost him down in Nyarit. Jaguar caught him and bit him damn near in two.

You all dont hunt down there no more.

No.

We aint been back since before the war. It got to be a long ways to go them last few trips. Lee Brothers had about quit goin. They brought a lot of jaguars out of that country, too.

JC leaned and spat into the fire. The flames were snaking up along the sides of the stump.

You all didnt care bein way off down there in old Mexico thataway?

We always got along with them people.

You dont need to go far to get in trouble, said Archer. You want trouble you can find all you can say grace over right across that river yonder.

That's an amen on that.

You cross that river you in another country. You talk to some of these old waddies along this border. Ask em about the revolution.

Do you remember the revolution, Travis?

Archer here can tell you moren what I can.

You was in swaddlin clothes wasnt you, Travis?

Just about it. I do remember bein woke up one time and goin to the window and we looked out and you could see the guns goin off over there like it was the fourth of July.

We lived on Wyoming Street, said Archer. After Daddy died. Mama's Uncle Pless worked in a machine shop on Alameda and they brought in the firingpins out of two artillery pieces and asked him could he turn new ones and he turned em and wouldnt take a dime for it. They was all on the side of the rebels. He brought the old pins home and give em to us boys. There was one shop turned some cannon barrels out of railroad axles and they dragged em back across the river behind a team of mules. The trunnions was made out of Ford truck axle housings and they set em in wood sashes and used the wheels off of fieldwagons to mount em in. That was in November of nineteen and thirteen. Villa come into Juárez at two oclock in the mornin on a train he'd highjacked. It was just a flat-out war. Lots of folks in El Paso had their windowlights shot out. Some people killed, for that matter. They'd go down and stand along the river there and watch it like it was a ballgame.

Villa come back in nineteen and nineteen. Travis can tell ye. We'd slip over there and hunt for souvenirs. Empty shellcases and what not. There was dead horses and mules in the street. Storewindows shot out. We seen bodies laid out in the alameda with blankets over em or wagonsheets. That sobered us up, I can tell you. They made us take showers with the Mexicans fore they'd let us back in. Disinfected our clothes and all. There was typhus down there and people had died of it.

They sat smoking quietly and looking out at the distant lights in the valley floor below them. Two of the dogs came in out of the night and passed behind the hunters. Their shadows trotted across the stone bluff and they crossed to a place in the dry dust under the rocks where they curled up and were soon asleep.

None of it done anybody any good, Travis said. Or if it did I never heard of it.

I been all over that country down there. I was a cattlebuyer for Spurlocks. Supposed to be one. I was just a kid. I rode all over northern Mexico. Hell, there wasnt no cattle. Not to speak of. Mostly I just visited. I liked it. I liked the country and I liked the people in it. I rode all over Chihuahua and a good part of Coahuila and some of Sonora. I'd be gone weeks at a time and not have hardly so much as a peso in my pocket but it didnt make no difference. Those people would take you in and put you up and feed you and feed your horse and cry when you left. You could of stayed forever. They didnt have nothin. Never had and never would. But you could stop at some little estancia in the absolute dead center of nowhere and they'd take you in like you was kin. You could see that the revolution hadnt done them no good. A lot of em had lost boys out of the family. Fathers or sons or both. Nearly all of em, I expect. They didnt have no reason to be hospitable to anybody. Least of all a gringo kid. That plateful of beans they set in front of you was hard come by. But I was never turned away. Not a time.

Three more dogs passed by the fire and sought out beds under the bluff. The stars swung west. The hunters talked of other things and after a while another dog came in. He was favoring a forefoot and Archer got up and walked up under the bluff to see about him. They heard the dog whine and when he came back he said they'd been in a fight.

Two more dogs came in and then all were in save one.

I'll wait a while if you all want to head back, Archer said.

We'll wait with ye.

I dont mind.

We'll wait a while. Wake up young Cole yonder.

Let him sleep, said Billy. He's been fightin that bear.

The fire burned down and it grew colder and they sat close to the flames and hand fed them with sticks and with old brittle limbs they broke from the windtwisted wrecks of trees along the rimrock. They told stories of the old west that once was. The older men talked and the younger men listened and light began to show in the gap of the mountain above them and then faintly along the desert floor below.

The dog they were waiting for came in limping badly and circled the fire. Travis called to her. She halted with her red eyes and looked at them. He rose and called her again and she came up and he took hold of her collar and turned her to the light. There were four bloody furrows along her flank. There was a flap of skin ripped loose at her shoulder exposing the muscle underneath and blood was dripping slowly from one ripped ear onto the sandy dirt where she stood.

We need to get that sewed up, Travis said.

Archer pulled a leash from among those he'd strung through his belt and he clipped it onto the D-ring of her collar. She carried the only news they would have of the hunt, bearing witness to things they could only imagine or suppose out there in the night. She winced when Archer touched her ear and when he let go of her she stepped back and stood with her forefeet braced and shook her head. Blood sprayed the hunters and hissed in the fire. They rose to go.

Let's go, cowboy, Billy said.

John Grady sat up and reached about on the ground for his hat.

Hell of a lionhunter you turned out to be.

Is the peeler awake? said JC.

The peeler's awake.

A man that's been huntin that bear I dont believe these old mountain lions hold much interest.

I think you got that right.

Chips all down and where was he? And us at the mercy of the old folks here. Could of used some help, son. We been outlied till it's pitiful. I mean sent to the showers. Wasnt even a contest, was it Billy?

Not even a contest.

John Grady squared his hat and walked out along the edge of the bluff. The desert plain lay cold and blue below them in the graying light and the shape of the river running down from the north through the break of gray winter trees lay in a pale serpentine of mist. To the south the cold gray grid of the distant city and the shape of the older city across the river like stampings in the desert soil. Beyond them the mountains of Mexico. The injured hound had come from the fire where the men were sorting and chaining the dogs and it walked out and stood beside John Grady and studied with him the plain below. John Grady sat and let his boots dangle over the edge of the rock and the dog lay down and rested its bloody head alongside his leg and after a while he put his arm around it.

BILLY SAT LEANING with his elbows on the table and his arms crossed. He watched John Grady. John Grady pursed his lips. He moved the remaining white knight. Billy looked at Mac. Mac studied the move and he looked at John Grady. He sat back in his chair and studied the board. No one spoke.

Mac picked up the black queen and held it a moment and

then set it back. Then he picked up the queen again and moved. Billy leaned back in his chair. Mac reached and took the cold cigar from the ashtray and put it in his mouth.

Six moves later the white king was mated. Mac sat back and lit the cigar. Billy blew a long breath across the table.

John Grady sat looking at the board. Good game, he said.

It's a long road, said Mac, that has no turning.

They walked out across the yard toward the barn.

Tell me somethin, Billy said.

All right.

And I know you'll tell me the truth.

I already know what the question is.

What's the answer.

The answer is no.

You didnt slack up on him just the littlest bit?

No. I dont believe in it.

The horses stirred and snuffled in their stalls as they passed down the bay. John Grady looked at Billy.

You dont reckon he thinks that do you?

I hope not. He damn sure wouldnt like it a bit.

He damn sure wouldnt.

HE WALKED into the pawnshop with the gun in the holster and the holster and belt slung over his shoulder. The pawn-broker was an old man with white hair and he was reading the paper spread out on the glass top of a display case at the rear of the shop. There were guns in racks along one wall and guitars hanging from overhead and knives and pistols and jewelry and tools in the cases. John Grady laid the gunbelt on the counter and the old man looked at it and looked at John Grady. He drew the pistol from the holster and cocked it and let the hammer down on the halfcock notch and spun the cylinder and opened the gate and looked at the chambers and closed the gate and cocked the hammer and let it back down with his thumb.

He turned it over and looked at the serial numbers on the frame and triggerguard and on the bottom of the backstrap and then slid it back into the holster and looked up.

How much do you want? he said.

I need about forty dollars.

The old man sucked his teeth and shook his head gravely.

I been offered fifty for it. I just need to pawn it.

I could let you have maybe twenty-five.

John Grady looked at the gun. Let me have thirty, he said.

The pawnbroker shook his head doubtfully.

I dont want to sell it, John Grady said. I just need to borrow on it.

The belt and holster too, yes?

Yes. It all goes together.

All right.

He brought out his pad of forms and slowly copied out the serial number and he wrote down John Grady's name and address and turned the paper on the glass for the boy to read and sign. Then he separated the sheets and handed a copy to John Grady and took the gun to his cage at the rear of the shop. When he returned he had the money and he laid it on the counter.

I'll be back for it, John Grady said.

The old man nodded.

It belonged to my grandfather.

The old man opened his hands and closed them again. A gesture of accommodation. Not quite a blessing. He nodded toward the glass case where half a dozen old Colt revolvers lay displayed, some nickelplated, some with grips of staghorn. One with old worn grips of guttapercha, one with the front sight filed away.

All of them belonged to somebody's grandfather, he said.

As he was going up Juárez Avenue a shineboy spoke to him. Hey cowboy, he said.

Hey.

Better let me shine those boots for you.

All right.

He sat on a little folding campstool and put his boot on the shineboy's homemade wooden box. The shineboy turned up the leg of his trousers and began to take out his rags and brushes and tins of polish and lay them to hand.

You goin to see your girl?

Yeah.

I hope you werent goin up there with these boots.

I guess it's a good thing you hollered at me. She might of run me off.

The boy dusted off the boot with his rag and lathered it. When are you gettin married? he said.

What makes you think I'm gettin married?

I dont know. You kind of got the look. Are you?

I dont know. Maybe.

Are you a cowboy sure enough?

Yep.

You work on a ranch?

Yeah. Small ranch. Estancia, you might say.

You like it?

Yeah. I like it.

He wiped off the boot and opened his can and began to slap polish onto the leather with the stained fingers of his left hand.

It's hard work, aint it?

Yeah. Sometimes.

What if you could be somethin else?

I wouldnt be nothin else.

What if you could be anything in the world?

John Grady smiled. He shook his head.

Were you in the war?

No. I was too young.

My brother was too young but he lied about his age.

Was he American?

No.

How old was he?

Sixteen.

I guess he was big for his age.

He was a big bullshitter for his age.

John Grady smiled.

The boy put the lid back on the tin and took out his brush.

They asked him if he was a pachuco. He said all the pachucos he knew of lived in El Paso. He told em he didnt know any Mexican pachucos.

He brushed the boot. John Grady watched him.

Was he a pachuco?

Sure. Of course he was.

He brushed the boot and then chucked the brush back into the box and took out his cloth and popped it and bent and began to rifle the cloth back and forth over the toe of the boot.

He joined the marines. He got two purple hearts.

What about you?

What about me what.

What did you join.

He glanced up at John Grady. He whipped the cloth around the counter of the boot. I sure didnt join no marines, he said.

What about the pachucos.

Nah.

You're not a pachuco?

Nah.

Are you a bullshitter?

Sure.

A big one?

Pretty big. Let me have the other foot.

What about the black around the edges?

I do that last. Dont worry about everything.

John Grady put his other foot on the box and turned up his trouserleg.

Appearance is important with women, the boy said. Dont think they dont look at your boots.

You got a girl?

Shit no.

You sound like you've had some bad experiences.

Who aint? You fool with em and that's the kind you'll have.

There'll be some sweet young thing nail you down one of these days.

I hope not.

How old are you?

Fourteen.

You lie about your age?

Yeah. Sure.

I guess if you admit it then it aint a lie.

The boy ceased rubbing in the polish for a moment and sat looking at the boot. Then he began again.

If there's somethin I want to be a different way from what it is then that's how I say it is. What's wrong with that?

I dont know.

Who else is goin to?

Nobody, I guess.

Nobody is right.

Is your brother married?

Which brother? I got three.

The one that was in the marines.

Yeah. He's married. They're all married.

If they're all married why did you ask which one?

The shineboy shook his head. Man, he said.

I guess you're the youngest.

No. I got a brother ten years old is married with three kids. Of course I'm the youngest. What do you think?

Well maybe marriage runs in the family.

Marriage dont run in families. Anyway I'm an outlaw. Oveja negra. You speak spanish?

Yeah. I speak spanish.

Oveja negra. That's me.

Black sheep.

I know what it is.

I am too.

The boy looked up at him. He reached and got his brush from the box. Yeah? he said.

Yeah.

You dont look like no outlaw to me.

What does one look like?

Not like you.

He brushed the boot and put away the brush and got his cloth out and popped it. John Grady watched him. What about you? What if you could be anything you wanted?

I'd be a cowboy.

Really?

The boy looked up at him with disgust. Shit no, he said. What's wrong with you? I'd be a rico and lay around on my ass all day. What do you think?

What if you had to do something?

I dont know. Maybe be a airplane pilot.

Yeah?

Sure. I'd fly everywhere.

What would you do when you got there?

Fly somewhere else.

He finished polishing the boot and got out his bottle of blacking and began to paint the heel and the edges of the sole with the swab.

Other boot, he said.

John Grady put his other foot up and the boy painted the edges. Then he put the swab back in the bottle and screwed the cap shut and pitched the bottle into the box. You're done, he said.

John Grady turned his cuffs back down and stood and reached into his pocket and took out a coin and handed it to the boy.

Thanks.

He looked down at his boots. What do you think.

She might let you in the door. Where's your flowers at?

Flowers?

Sure. You're goin to need all the help you can get.

You're probably right.

I shouldnt even be tellin you this stuff.

Why not?

You'd be better off just to be put out of your misery.

John Grady smiled. Where are you from? he said.

Right here.

No you're not.

I grew up in California.

What are you doin over here?

I like it over here.

Yeah?

Yeah.

You like shinin shoes?

I like it all right.

You like the street.

Yeah. I dont like goin to school.

John Grady adjusted his hat and looked off up the street. He looked down at the boy. Well, he said. I never much liked it myself.

Outlaws, the boy said.

Outlaws. I think maybe you're a bigger outlaw than me.

I think you're right.

I'm just kind of gettin the hang of it.

You need any pointers come see me. I'll be happy to show you the ropes.

John Grady smiled. Okay, he said. I'll see you around.

Adiós, vaquero.

Adiós, bolero.

The boy smiled and waved him on.

THE CRIADA STOOD behind her in the full-length mirror, her mouth bristling with hairpins. She looked at the girl in the mirror, so pale and so slender in her shift with her hair piled atop her head. She looked at Josefina. Josefina stood to the side with one arm crossed and her other elbow propped upon it, her fist to her chin. No, she said. No.

She shook her head and waved her hand as if to dismiss some

outrage and the criada began to withdraw the pins and combs from the girl's hair until the long black fall descended again over her shoulders and her back. She took her brush and began again to brush the girl's hair, following with the flat of her hand beneath, holding up the silky blackness with each stroke and letting it fall again. Josefina came forward and took a silver haircomb from the table and swept back the girl's hair along the side and held it there. She studied the girl and she studied the girl in the mirror. The criada had stepped back and stood holding the brush in both hands. She and Josefina studied the girl in the mirror, the three of them in the yellow light of the table-lamp standing there within the gilded plaster scrollwork of the mirror's frame like figures in an antique flemish painting.

Cómo es, pues, said Josefina.

She was speaking to the girl but the girl did not answer.

Es más joven. Más . . .

Inocente, said the girl.

The woman shrugged. Inocente pues, she said.

She studied the girl's face in the glass. No le gusta?

Está bien, the girl whispered. Me gusta.

Bueno, said the woman. She let go her hair and placed the comb in the criada's hand. Bueno.

When she was gone the old woman put the comb back on the table and came forward with her brush again. Bueno, she said. She shook her head and clucked her tongue.

No te preocupes, the girl said.

The old woman brushed her hair more fiercely. Bellísima, she hissed. Bellísima.

She assisted her with care. With solicitude. One by one the hooks and stays. Passing her hands across the lilac velvet, cupping her breasts each in turn and adjusting the border of the decolletage, pinning gown to undergarment. She brushed away bits of lint. She held the girl by her waist and turned her like a toy and she knelt at her feet and fastened the straps of her shoes. She rose and stood back.

Puedes caminar? she said.

No, said the girl.

No? Es mentira. Es una broma. No?

No, said the girl.

The criada made a shooing motion. The girl stepped archly about the room on the tall gold spikes of the slippers.

Te mortifican? said the criada.

Claro.

She stood again before the mirror. The old woman stood behind her. When she blinked only the one eye closed. So that she appeared to be winking in some suggestive complicity. She brushed the gathered hair with her hand, she plucked the shoulders of the sleeves erect.

Como una princesa, she whispered.

Como una puta, said the girl.

The criada seized her by the arm. She hissed at her, her eye glaring in the lamplight. She told her that she would marry a great rich man and live in a fine house and have beautiful children. She told her that she had known many such cases.

Quién? said the girl.

Muchas, hissed the criada. Muchas. Girls, she told her, with no such beauty as hers. Girls with no such dignity or grace. The girl did not answer. She looked across the old woman's shoulder into the eyes in the glass as if it were some sister there who weathered stoically this beleaguerment of her hopes. Standing in the gaudy boudoir that was itself a tawdry emulation of other rooms, other worlds. Regarding her own false arrogance in the pierglass as if it were proof against the old woman's entreaties, the old woman's promises. Standing like some maid in a fable spurning the offerings of the hag which do conceal within them unspoken covenants of corruption. Claims that can never be quit, estates forever entailed. She spoke to that girl standing in the glass and she said that one could not know where it was that one had taken the path one was upon but only that one was upon it.

Mande? said the criada. Cuál senda?

Cualquier senda. Esta senda. La senda que escoja.

But the old woman said that some have no choice. She said that for the poor any choice was a gift with two faces.

She was kneeling in the floor repinning the hem of the dress. She'd taken the pins from her mouth and now she laid them on the carpet and took them up one by one. The girl watched her image in the glass. The old woman's gray head bowed at her feet. After a while she said that there was always a choice, even if that choice were death.

Cielos, said the old woman. She blessed herself quickly and went on pinning.

When she entered the salon he was standing at the bar. The musicians were assembling their pieces on the dais and tuning them and the few notes or chords sounded in the quiet of the room as if some ceremony were at hand. Within the shadows of the niche beyond the dais Tiburcio stood smoking, his fingers laced about the thin niellate ebony holder of his cigarette. He looked at the girl and he looked toward the bar. He watched the boy turn and pay and take up his glass and come down the broad stairs where the velvetcovered rope railings led into the salon. He blew smoke slowly from his thin nostrils and then he opened the door behind him. The brief light framed him in silhouette and his long thin shadow fell briefly across the floor of the salon and then the door closed again as if he had not been there at all.

Está peligroso, she whispered.

Cómo?

Peligroso. She looked around the salon.

Tenía que verte, he said.

He took her hands in his but she only looked in anguish toward the door where Tiburcio had been standing. She took hold of his wrists and begged him to leave. A waiter glided forth from the shadows.

Estás loco, she whispered. Loco.

Tienes razón.

She took his hand and rose. She turned and whispered to the

waiter. John Grady rose and put money in the waiter's hand and turned toward her.

Debemos irnos, she said. Estamos perdidos.

He said that he would not. He said that he would not do that again and that she must meet him but she said that it was too dangerous. That now it was too dangerous. The music had begun. A long low chord from the cello.

Me matará, she whispered.

Quién?

She only shook her head.

Quién, he said. Quién te matará?

Eduardo.

Eduardo.

She nodded. Sí, she said. Eduardo.

HE DREAMT THAT NIGHT of things he'd heard and that were so although she'd never spoke of them. In a room so cold his breath smoked and where the corrugated steel walls were hung with bunting and a scaffolding covered with cheap red carpet rose in tiers for the folding slatwood chairs of the spectators. A raw wooden stage trimmed like a fairground float and BX cable running to a boom overhead made from galvanized iron pipe that held floodlights covered each in cellophanes of red and green and blue. Curtains of calendered velour in loops as red as blood.

The tourists sat in chairs with operaglasses hanging from their necks while waiters took their orders for drinks. When the lights dimmed the master of ceremonies strode onto the boards and doffed his hat and bowed and smiled and held up his whitegloved hands. In the wings the alcahuete stood smoking and behind him milled a great confusion of obscene carnival folk, painted whores with their breasts exposed, a fat woman in black leather with a whip, a pair of youths in ecclesiastical robes. A priest, a procuress, a goat with gilded horns and hooves who wore a ruff of purple crepe. Pale young debauchees with rouged cheeks and blackened eyes who carried candles. A trio of women holding hands, gaunt and thin as the inmates of a spitalhouse and attired the three alike in the same cheap finery, their faces daubed in fard and pale as death. At the center of all a young girl in a white gauze dress who lay upon a palletboard like a sacrificial virgin. Arranged about her are artificial flowers that appear in their varied pale and pastel colors to be faded from the sun. As if perhaps replevined from some desert grave. Music has begun. Some ancient rondel, faintly martial. There is a periodic click in the piece from a scratch in the black bakelite plate turning under a stylus somewhere behind the curtains. The houselights dim till just the stage is lit. Chairs shuffle. A few coughs. The music fades until only the whisper of the stylus remains, the periodic click like a misset metronome, a clock, a portent. A measure of something periodic and otherwise silent and vastly patient which only darkness could accommodate.

When he woke it was not from this dream but from another and the pathway from dream to dream was lost to him. He was alone in some bleak landscape where the wind blew without abatement and where the presence of those who had gone before still lingered on in the darkness about. Their voices carried back to him, or perhaps the echo of those voices. He lay listening. It was the old man wandering the yard in his nightclothes and John Grady swung his legs over the side of the bunk and reached and got his trousers and pulled them on and stood and buckled his belt and reached and got his boots. When he went out Billy was standing in the doorway in his shorts.

I'll get him, said John Grady.

That's pitiful, Billy said.

He caught him going past the corner of the barn and on to God knows where. He had on his hat and his boots and dressed in these and his long white unionsuit he looked like the ghost of some ancient waddy wandering there.

John Grady took him by the arm and they started for the house. Come on, Mr Johnson, he said. You dont need to be out here.

The light had come on in the kitchen and Socorro was standing in the door in her robe. The old man stopped again in the yard and turned and looked again toward the darkness. John Grady stood holding his elbow. Then they went on to the house.

Socorro swung the screendoor wide. She looked at John Grady. The old man steadied himself with one hand against the doorjamb and entered the kitchen. He asked Socorro if she had any coffee. As if that was what he'd been in search of.

Yes, she said. I fix some coffee.

He's all right, said John Grady.

Quieres un cafecito?

No gracias.

Pásale, she said. Pásale. Puedes encontrar sus pantalones?

Sí. Sí.

He helped the old man to a chair at the table and went on down the hallway. Mac's light was on and he was standing in the door.

Is he all right?

Yessir. He's all right.

He went on to the end of the hall and entered the room on the left and got the old man's britches off the bedpost where he'd hung them. The pockets were weighted with change, with a pocketknife, a billfold. With a ring of keys to doors long since forgotten. He came back down the hallway holding them by the belt. Mac was still standing in the doorway. He was smoking a cigarette.

He aint got any clothes on?

Just his longjohns.

He'll take off out of here one of these nights naked as a jaybird. Socorro'll quit us for sure.

She wont quit.

I know it.

What time is it, sir?

It's after five. Damn near time to get up anyways.

Yessir.

Would you mind settin with him a bit?

No sir.

Make him feel better about it. Like he was gettin up any-ways.

Yessir. I will.

You didnt know you'd hired on at a loonyfarm, did you?

He aint loony. He's just old.

I know it. Go on. Fore he catches cold. Them old dropseats he wears are probably drafty to set around in.

Yessir.

He sat with the old man and drank coffee until Oren came in. Oren looked at them but he didnt say anything. Socorro fixed breakfast and brought the eggs and biscuits and chorizo sausage and they ate. When John Grady took his plate to the sideboard and went out it was just breaking day. The old man was still sitting at the table in his hat. He'd been born in east Texas in eighteen sixty-seven and come out to this country as a young man. In his time the country had gone from the oil lamp and the horse and buggy to jet planes and the atomic bomb but that wasnt what confused him. It was the fact that his daughter was dead that he couldnt get the hang of.

THEY SAT IN THE FRONT ROW of the bleachers near the auctioneer's table and Oren leaned forward from time to time to spit carefully over the top boards into the dust of the arena. Mac had a small notebook in his shirtpocket and he took it out and consulted his notes and put it back again and then he took it out and sat holding it in his hand.

Did we look at this little horse? he said.

Yessir, said John Grady.

He studied his notebook again.

He said it was Davis but it aint.

No sir.

Bean, said Oren. It's a Bean horse.

I know what horse it is, said Mac.

The auctioneer blew into the microphone. The speakers were hung from the lightstandards at the far end of the arena and his voice quavered and echoed high in the auction barn.

Ladies and gentlemen a correction on that. This horse is entered by Mr Ryle Bean.

The bidding was started at five hundred. Someone at the far side of the arena touched the brim of his hat and the spotter raised one hand and turned and the auctioneer said now six now six I have six who'll give me seven seven seven. Seven now.

Oren leaned and spat thoughtfully into the dust. Over yonder's your buddy, he said.

I see him, said John Grady.

Who's that? said Mac.

Wolfenbarger.

Does he see us?

Yeah, said Oren. He sees us.

Did you know who that was, John Grady?

Yessir. He come out one afternoon.

I thought you wouldnt talk to him.

I didnt.

Just pretend like he aint even here.

Yessir.

When was he out?

Last week. I dont know. Wednesday maybe.

Just dont pay no attention to him.

Yessir. I aint.

I got more to do than worry about him.

Yessir.

Eighty, seven-eighty, called the auctioneer. Will you do it. The man wont take less.

The rider rode the horse around the arena. He crossed diagonally and stopped and backed.

That's a good usin horse and a good ropin horse, the auctioneer said. The horse is worth a thousand dollars. All right now. I've got eight got eight got eight. Eight and a half now. Eight-fifty eight-fifty eight-fifty.

The horse sold for eight and a quarter and they brought in an Arabian mare that sold for seventeen. Mac watched them lead her back out again.

I wouldnt have that crazy bitch on the place, he said.

They auctioned off a flashy palomino gelding that brought thirteen hundred dollars. Mac looked up from his notes. Where the hell do people get that kind of money? he said.

Oren shook his head.

Did Wolfenbarger bid on him?

You said not to look over there.

I know it. Did he?

Yep.

He didnt buy him though, did he.

No.

I thought you wasnt goin to look over there.

I didnt have to. He was wavin his hand like the place had caught fire.

Mac shook his head and sat looking at his notes.

They're fixin to run that rough string in here in a minute, Oren said.

What kind of money you think we're talkin about?

I would expect a man could buy them horses for a hundred dollars a head.

What would you do with the other three, run em back through?

Run em back through. Or you might do better to sell em off out at the place.

Mac nodded. Might, he said. He glanced across the stands. I hate that sumbuck goin to school on me.

I know it.

He lit a cigarette. They watched the stableboy bring in the next horse.

I'd say he's come to buy, said Oren.

I'd say he has too.

He'll bid on ever one of them horses of Red's. See if he dont.

I know it. We ought to shill him just a little bit.

Oren didnt answer.

A fool and his money, said Mac. John Grady what's wrong with that horse?

Not a thing that I know of.

I thought you said it was some kind of a mongrel outcross. A Martian horse or somethin.

Horse might be a little coldblooded.

Oren spat over the boards and grinned.

Coldblooded? said Mac.

Yessir.

The horse was bid in at three hundred dollars.

How old was that thing. You remember?

It was eleven.

Yeah, said Oren. About six years ago it was.

The bidding went to four and a half. Mac tugged at his ear. I'm just a horsetradin fool, he said. The spotter pointed to the auctioneer.

I got five got five got five got five now, called the auctioneer.

I thought you didnt like to do that, said Oren.

Do what? said Mac.

The bidding went to six and then six and a half.

He's not opened that mouth or shook his head or done nothin, the auctioneer said. Horse worth a little more money than that, folks.

The horse was sold at seven hundred. Wolfenbarger never bid. Oren glanced at Mac.

Cute sumbuck, aint he? Mac said.

You care if I say somethin.

Say it.

Why dont we do what we said and just trade like he wasnt here.

Damn if you aint awful hard on a man. Callin on him to follow his own advice.

It's hell, aint it.

You're probably right. Be the best strategy anyway for a ned like him.

The stableboy brought out the roan four year old from McKinney and they bid the horse in at six hundred.

Where's that string at? said Mac.

I dont know.

Well, we're fixin to get down to the nutcuttin.

He put one finger to his ear. The spotter raised his hand. The auctioneer's voice clapped back from the high speakers. I got six got six got six. Do we hear seven. Who'll give me seven. Seven now. Seven seven seven.

Yonder he goes with that hand.

I see him.

The horse went to seven and seven and a half and eight. The horse went to eight and a half.

Bidders all over the barn, aint they? said Oren.

All over the barn.

Well there aint nothin you can do about it. What's this horse worth?

I dont know. Whatever it sells for. John Grady?

I liked the horse.

I wish they'd of run that string through first.

I know you got a figure in mind.

I did have.

It's the same horse out here that it was in the paddock.

Spoke like a gentleman.

The bidding was stalled at eight and a half. The auctioneer took a drink of water. This is a nice horse, boys, he said. You're way off on this one.

The rider rode the horse down and turned it and came back. He rode it with no bridle but only a rope looped around its neck and he turned and sat the horse. I'll tell you what now, he called. I dont own a hair on him but this is a gaited horse.

It'll cost you a thousand dollars to breed to his mama, said the auctioneer. What do you say boys?

The spotter raised his hand.

I got nine got nine got nine. Now half half half. Nine and a half. Now half. Niner and now half.

Can I say somethin, said John Grady.

I wish you would.

You aint buyin him to sell, are you?

No, I aint.

Well then I think you ought to get the horse you want.

You think a lot of him.

Yessir.

Oren shook his head and leaned and spat. Mac sat looking in his book.

He's goin to cost me no matter what I do, one way of lookin at it.

The horse?

No, not the damn horse.

The bidding went to nine and a half and then a thousand.

John Grady looked at Mac and then looked out at the arena.

I know that old boy up yonder in the checked shirt, said Mac.

I do too, said Oren.

I'd like to see em buy back their own horse.

I would too.

Mac bought the horse for eleven hundred dollars. Put me in the damn poorhouse, he said.

That's a good horse, said John Grady.

I know how good a horse it is. Dont go tryin to make me feel better.

Dont pay no attention to him, son, said Oren. He wants you to brag on his horse only he's just a little backwards about it is all.

What do you think old highpockets cost me on that trade?

Probably didnt cost you nothin on that one, Oren said. He might be fixin to cost you on the next one though.

The groom was wetting down the dust in the barn with a waterhose. They brought in the four-horse string and Mac bought them too.

Like a thief in the dark, called the auctioneer. Number one o four. Sold at five and a quarter.

That could of been more painful than what it was I reckon, Mac said.

Skippin through the raindrops.

Yep.

He watched the groom lead the next horse out.

You remember this horse, John Grady.

Yessir. I remember all of em.

Mac thumbed his notes. You get in the habit of writin everthing down and after a while you cant remember nothin.

The reason you started writin stuff down in the first place was cause you couldnt remember nothin, Oren said.

I know this little horse, said Mac. I'd sure like to sell him to Wolfenbarger.

I thought you was goin to leave him be.

He could start a circus.

This is a smoothmouthed horse about eight year old, called the auctioneer. A good usin horse and a good ropin horse and he's worth quite a bit more than what you got him started at.

He needs to buy that horse. It'll do about anything except travel in a straight line. Ought to suit him right down to the ground.

The rider rode the horse hard up and back before the stands, closereining the horse and doubling back.

Five five five, called the auctioneer. This is a good horse, boys. Guaranteed to be sound. Work close like that. Like a cat in a stovepipe, folks. Now half now half now half.

Mac tugged at his ear. Five and a half now six now six now six, called the auctioneer.

Oren looked disgusted.

Hell, said Mac. We can have a little fun with the old boy cant we?

The bidding went to seven. The owner stood up in the stands. I'll tell you what, he said. If you can make him go through the bridle I'll give him to you.

The bidding went to seven and a half, it went to eight.

John Grady did you hear about the preacher that sold the old boy the blind horse?

No sir.

He was always justifyin everthing with scripture. They come around wantin to know how he could do the old boy thataway and he told em, said: Well, he was a stranger and I took him in.

I think you told me that.

Mac nodded. He thumbed his notes.

He didnt know how to bid on that string. I think it just confused him.

Yessir.

He's ready to buy a horse.

He might be.

You a poker player, son?

I've sat in a time or two, yessir.

You think this horse will sell for under a thousand?

No sir. I kindly doubt it.

If it does bust a thousand what will it go to?

I dont know.

I dont know either.

Mac bid the horse to eight and a half and then to nine and a half. There it stopped. Oren leaned and spat.

What Oren dont understand is that the more money that nedhead is got in his pockets the more that Welburn horse is goin to cost me.

Oren understands that, said Oren. He just thinks you ought to go on and buy the horse for what the bid is and not risk not havin the money to do it with. Anyway, that sumbuck's got more money than Carter has liver pills.

The spotter raised his hand.

I got ten got ten got ten, called the auctioneer. Now eleven now eleven.

The horse went to eleven and Wolfenbarger bid it to twelve and Mac bid it to thirteen.

I aint responsible, said Oren.

The man's a horsebuyer.

You remember what the horse was bid in at?

Yeah. I remember.

Just go on then.

Old Oren, Mac said.

Wolfenbarger bought the horse for seventeen hundred dollars.

Fine piece of horseflesh, said Mac. Ought to suit him just about right.

He reached in his pocket and took out a dollar.

Why dont you run get us some Cokes, John Grady.

Yessir.

Oren watched him climb down through the stands.

You think he'd tout you off of a horse as well as he would on?

Yes. I do.

I think he would too.

I wish I had about six more just like him.

You know there's things about a horse he can only say in spanish?

I dont care if he only knows em in greek. Why?

I just thought it was curious. You think he's from San Angelo?

I think he's from wherever he says he's from.

I guess he is.

He learned it out of a book.

Out of a book?

Joaquín says he knows the name of ever bone a horse has got.

Oren nodded. Well, he said. He might at that. I know some things that he didnt learn out of no book.

I do too, said Mac.

The next horse they brought out the auctioneer read from the horse's papers at some length.

I believe this here is a biblical horse, Mac said.

Aint that the truth.

The horse was bid in at a thousand dollars and went to eighteen five and was a no sale. Oren leaned and spat. Man thinks a lot of his horse, he said.

The man does, said Mac.

They trotted in the Welburn horse and Mac bought him for fourteen hundred dollars.

Boys, he said. Let's go home.

You dont want to stick around and spend some more of Wolfenbarger's money?

Wolfenbarger who?

SOCORRO FOLDED and hung her towel, she untied and hung her apron. She turned at the door.

Buenas noches, she said.

Buenas noches, said Mac.

She shut the door. He could hear her winding her old tin clock. A little later he heard the faint ratcheting sound of his father-in-law winding the tallcase clock in the hallway. The glass doorcase closed softly. Then it was quiet. It was quiet in the house and it was quiet in the country about. He sat smoking. The cooling stove ticked. Far away in the hills behind the house a coyote called. When they had used to spend winters at the old house on the southeasternmost section of the ranch the last thing he would hear before he fell asleep at night was the bawl of the train eastbound out of El Paso. Sierra Blanca, Van Horn, Marfa, Alpine, Marathon. Rolling across the blue prairie through the night and on toward Langtry and Del Rio. The white bore of the headlamp lighting up the desert scrub and the eyes of trackside cattle floating in the dark like coals. The herders in the hills standing with their serapes about their shoulders watching the train pass below and the little desert foxes stepping into the darkened roadbed to sniff after it where the warm steel rails lay humming in the night.

That part of the ranch was long gone and the rest would soon follow. He drank the last of his coffee cold in the cup and lit his last cigarette before bed and then he rose from his chair and turned off the light and came back and sat smoking in the dark. A storm front had moved down from the north in the afternoon and it had turned off cold. No rain. Maybe in the eastern sections. Up in the Sacramentos. People imagined that if you got through a drought you could expect a few good years to try and get caught up but it was just like the seven on a pair of dice. The drought didnt know when the last one was and nobody knew when the next one was coming. He was about out of the cattle business anyway. He drew slowly on the cigarette. It flared and faded. His wife would be dead three years in February. Socorro's Candlemas Day. Candelaria. Something to do with the Virgin. As what didnt. In Mexico there is no God. Just her. He stubbed out the cigarette and rose and stood looking out at the softly lit barnlot. Oh Margaret, he said.

JC PULLED UP in front of Maud's and got out and slammed the truck door and he and John Grady went in.

Yonder come two good'ns, said Troy.

They stood at the bar. What'll you boys have, said Travis.

Give us two Blue Ribbons.

He got the bottles out of the cooler and opened them and set them on the bar.

I got it, said John Grady.

I got it, said JC.

He put forty cents on the bar and took the bottle by the neck and swigged down a long drink and wiped his mouth with the back of his hand and leaned against the bar.

You put in a hard day in the saddle? said Troy.

I'm mostly a nightrider, said JC.

Billy stood bent over the shuffleboard sliding the puck up and back. He looked at Troy and he looked at JC and then he slid the puck down the hardwood alleyway. The pins at the end swung up and the strike light lit up on the scoreboard and the small bells counted up the score. Troy grinned and put the

cigar he was smoking in the corner of his mouth and stepped
forward and took the puck and bent over the board.

You want to play?

JC'll play.

You want to play, JC?

Yeah, I'll play. What are we playin for?

Troy scored a strike on the bowling machine and stepped
back and popped his fingers.

Me and JC'll play you and Askins.

Askins stood by the machine with one hand in his back
pocket and the other holding a beer. Me and Jessie'll play you
and Troy, he said.

Billy lit a cigarette. He looked at Askins. He looked at JC.

You and Troy play them, he said.

Go on and play.

You and Troy play. Go on.

What are we playin for? said JC.

I dont care.

Make it light on yourself.

What are we playin for, Troy?

Whatever they want to play for.

We'll play for a dollar.

High rollers. Get your quarters up. Jessie, you in?

I'm in, said Jessie.

Billy sat on the stool at the bar next to John Grady. They
watched while the players put their quarters in the machine.
The numbers rolled back and the bells chinged. Troy poured
powdered wax from a can onto the alley and slid the puck
back and forth and bent to shoot. Bowlin school is now open,
he said.

Show us somethin.

You'd be surprised what all you can learn from a experienced
player.

He slid the puck down the boards. The bells rang. He
stepped back and popped his fingers. Things, he said, that will
stand you in good stead all your life.

I need to talk to you, said John Grady.

Billy blew smoke across the room. All right, he said.

Let's go back in the back.

All right.

They took their beers and walked to the rear of the place where there were tables and chairs and a bandstand and a polished concrete dancefloor. They kicked back two chairs and sat at one of the tables and set their bottles down. The place was dim and musty.

I'll bet I know what this is about, said Billy.

Yeah. I know.

He sat peeling the label from his beerbottle with his thumbnail while he listened. He didnt even look up at John Grady. John Grady told him about the girl and about the White Lake and about Eduardo and he told him what the blind maestro had said. When he'd finished Billy still hadnt looked up but he'd stopped peeling the beerlabel. He didnt say anything. After a while he took his cigarettes from his pocket and lit one and laid the pack and his lighter on the table.

You are shittin me aint you? he said.

No. I guess I aint.

What the hell's wrong with you? Have you been drinkin paint thinner or somethin?

John Grady pushed his hat back. He looked out across the floor. No, he said.

Let me see if I got this straight. You want me to go to a whorehouse in Juárez Mexico and buy this whore cash money and bring her back across the river to the ranch. Is that about the size of it?

John Grady nodded.

Shit, said Billy. Smile or somethin, will you? Goddamn. Tell me you aint gone completely crazy.

I aint gone completely crazy.

The hell you aint.

I'm in love with her, Billy.

Billy slumped back in his chair. His arms hung uselessly by his side. Aw goddamn, he said. Goddamn.

I cant help what it sounds like.

My own damn fault. I never should of took you down there. Never in this world. It's my fault. Hell, I dont even know what I'm complainin about.

He leaned and took his lighted cigarette from the tin ashtray where he'd put it and took a pull on it and blew the smoke across the table. He shook his head. Tell me this, he said.

All right.

What in the goddamn hell would you do with her if you did get her away from down there? Which you aint.

Marry her.

Billy paused with the cigarette half way to his mouth. He put it down again.

Well that's it, he said. That's it. I'm havin your ass committed.

I mean it, Billy.

Billy leaned back in the chair. After a while he threw up one hand. I cant believe my goddamn ears. I think I'm the one that's gone crazy. I'm a son of a bitch if I dont. Have you lost your rabbit-assed mind? I'm an absolute son of a bitch, bud. I never in my goddamn life heard the equal of this.

I know. I cant help it.

The hell you cant.

Will you help me?

No and hell no. Do you know what they're goin to do with you? They're goin to hook your head up to one of them machines and throw a big switch and fry your brains to where you wont be a menace to yourself no more.

I mean it, Billy.

You think I dont mean it? I'm goin to help em hook up the wires.

I cant go down there. He knows who I am.

Look at me, son. You're not makin no sense. What the hell

kind of people do you think it is you're talkin about? Do you really think you can go down there and dicker with some greaser pimp that buys and sells people outright like you was goin down to the courthouse lawn to trade knives?

I cant help it.

Will you quit sayin that, goddamn it? What the hell do you mean you cant help it?

Just let it go. It's all right.

It's all right? Shit.

He slumped in the chair.

You want another beer?

No, I dont. I want a goddamn quart of whiskey.

I dont blame you for not wantin no part of it.

Well I'm glad as all hell to hear that.

He shook a cigarette out of the pack.

You got one lit, John Grady said.

Billy paid him no mind. You got no money, he said. So I dont know how in the hell you propose to go shoppin for whores.

I'll get it.

Get it where?

I'll get it.

How much were you plannin to offer him?

Two thousand dollars.

Two thousand dollars.

Yeah.

Well. If there was any doubt at all there sure aint now. You've gone completely crazy and that's all there is to be said about it. Aint it?

I dont know.

Well I do. Where in the hell, where in the goddamn hell, do you think you're goin to get two thousand dollars at?

I dont know. I'll get it.

You dont make that in a year.

I know it.

You're in a dangerous frame of mind, son. Did you know that?

Maybe.

I've seen it before. You know you been actin peculiar since you had that wreck? Have you thought about that? Look at me. I'm serious.

I aint crazy, Billy.

Well one of us is. Shit. I blame myself. That's all. Blame myself.

It dont have nothin to do with you.

The hell it dont.

It's all right. Just let it go.

Billy leaned back in his chair. He stared at the two cigarettes burning in the ashtray. After a while he pushed his hat back and passed his hand across his eyes and across his mouth and pulled the hat down again and looked across the room. Out at the bar the shuffleboard bells rang. He looked at John Grady.

How did you ever get in such a mess?

I dont know.

How did you let it get this far?

I dont know. I feel some way like I didnt have nothin to do with it. Like it's just the way it is. Like it always was this way.

Billy shook his head sadly. More craziness, he said. It aint too late, you know.

Yes it is.

It's never too late. You just need to make up your mind.

It's done made up.

Well unmake it. Start again.

Two months ago I'd of agreed with you. Now I know better. There's some things you dont decide. Decidin had nothin to do with it.

They sat for a long time. He looked at John Grady and he looked out across the room. The dusty dancefloor, the empty bandstand. The shapes of a covered drumset. He pushed back his chair and stood and set the chair back carefully at its place at the table and then he turned and walked out across the room and through the bar and out the door.

* * *

LATE THAT NIGHT lying in his bunk in the dark he heard the kitchen door close and heard the screendoor close after it. He lay there. Then he sat and swung his feet to the floor and got his boots and his jeans and pulled them on and put on his hat and walked out. The moon was almost full and it was cold and late and no smoke rose from the kitchen chimney. Mr Johnson was sitting on the back stoop in his duckingcoat smoking a cigarette. He looked up at John Grady and nodded. John Grady sat on the stoop beside him. What are you doin out here without your hat? he said.

I dont know.

You all right?

Yeah. I'm all right. Sometimes you miss bein outside at night. You want a cigarette?

No thanks.

Could you not sleep either?

No sir. I guess not.

How's them new horses?

I think he done all right.

Them was some boogerish colts I seen penned up in the corral.

I think he's goin to sell off some of them.

Horsetradin, the old man said. He shook his head. He smoked.

Did you used to break horses, Mr Johnson?

Some. Mostly just what was required. I was never a twister in any sense of the word. I got hurt once pretty bad. You can get spooked and not know it. Just little things. You dont hardly even know it.

But you like to ride.

I do. Margaret could outride me two to one though. As good a woman with a horse as I ever saw. Way bettern me. Hard thing for a man to admit but it's the truth.

You worked for the Matadors didnt you?

Yep. I did.

How was that?

Hard work. That's how it was.

I guess that aint changed.

Oh it probably has. Some. I was never in love with the cattle business. It's just the only one I ever knew.

He smoked.

Can I ask you somethin? said John Grady.

Ask it.

How old were you when you got married?

I was never married. Never found anybody that'd have me.

He looked at John Grady.

Margaret was my brother's girl. Him and his wife both was carried off in the influenza epidemic in nineteen and eighteen.

I didnt know that.

She never really knowed her parents. She was just a baby. Well, five. Where's your coat at?

I'm all right.

I was in Fort Collins Colorado at the time. They sent for me. I shipped my horses and come back on the train with em. Dont catch cold out here now.

No sir. I wont. I aint cold.

I had ever motivation in the world but I never could find one I thought would suit Margaret.

One what?

Wife. One wife. We finally just give it up. Probably a mistake. I dont know. Socorro pretty much raised her. She spoke better spanish than Socorro did. It's just awful hard. It liked to of killed Socorro. She still aint right. I dont expect she ever will be.

Yessir.

We tried ever way in the world to spoil her rotten but it didnt take. I dont know why she turned out the way she did. It's just a miracle I guess you could say. I dont take no credit for it, I'll tell you that.

Yessir.

Look yonder. The old man nodded toward the moon.

What?

You cant see em now. Wait a minute. No. They're gone.

What was it?

Birds flyin across the moon. Geese maybe. I dont know.

I didnt see em. Which way were they headed?

Upcountry. Probably headed for that marsh country on the river up around Belen.

Yessir.

I used to love to ride of a night.

I did too.

You'll see things on the desert at night that you cant understand. Your horse will see things. He'll see things that will spook him of course but then he'll see things that dont spook him but still you know he seen somethin.

What sort of things?

I dont know.

You mean like ghosts or somethin?

No. I dont know what. You just knows he sees em. They're out there.

Not just some class of varmint?

No.

Not somethin that will booger him?

No. It's more like somethin he knows about.

But you dont.

But you dont. Yes.

The old man smoked. He watched the moon. No further birds flew. After a while he said: I aint talkin about spooks. It's more like just the way things are. If you only knew it.

Yessir.

We was up on the Platte River out of Ogallala one night and I was bedded down in my soogan out away from the camp. It was a moonlit night just about like tonight. Cold. Spring of the year. I woke up and I guess I'd heard em in my sleep and it was just this big whisperin sound all over and it was geese just by the thousands headed up the river. They passed for the better part of a hour. They blacked out the moon. I thought the herd would get up off the grounds but they didnt. I got up and walked out and stood watchin em and some of the other young waddies in the outfit they had got up too and we was all standin out there in our longjohns watchin. It was just this whisperin sound. They was up high and it wasnt loud or nothin and I wouldnt of thought about somethin like that a wakin us wore out as we was. I had a nighthorse in my string named Boozer and old Boozer he come to me. I reckon he thought the herd'd get up too but they didnt. And they was a snuffy bunch, too.

Did you ever have a stampede?

Yes. We was drivin to Abilene in eighteen and eighty-five. I wasnt much more than a button. And we had got into it with a rep from one of the outfits and he followed us to where we crossed the Red River at Doane's store into Indian Territory. He knew we'd have a harder time gettin our stock back there and we did but we caught the old boy and it was him for you could still smell the coaloil on him. He come by in the night and set a cat on fire and thowed it onto the herd. I mean slung it. Walter Devereaux was comin in off the middle watch and he heard it and looked back. Said it looked like a comet goin out through there and just a squallin. Lord didnt they come up from there. It took us three days to shape that herd back and whenever we left out of there we was still missin forty some odd head lost or crippled or stole and two horses.

What happened to the boy?

The boy?

That threw the cat.

Oh. Best I remember he didnt make out too well.

I guess not.

People will do anything.

Yessir. They will.

You live long enough you'll see it.

Yessir. I have.

Mr Johnson didnt answer. He flipped the butt of his cigarette out across the yard in a slow red arc.

Aint nothin to burn out there. I remember when you could have grassfires in this country.

I didnt mean I'd seen everthing, John Grady said.

I know you didnt.

I just meant I'd seen things I'd as soon not of.

I know it. There's hard lessons in this world.

What's the hardest?

I dont know. Maybe it's just that when things are gone they're gone. They aint comin back.

Yessir.

They sat. After a while the old man said: The day after my fiftieth birthday in March of nineteen and seventeen I rode into the old headquarters at the Wilde well and there was six dead wolves hangin on the fence. I rode along the fence and ran my hand along em. I looked at their eyes. A government trapper had brought em in the night before. They'd been killed with poison baits. Strychnine. Whatever. Up in the Sacramentos. A week later he brought in four more. I aint heard a wolf in this country since. I suppose that's a good thing. They can be hell on stock. But I guess I was always what you might call superstitious. I know I damn sure wasnt religious. And it had always seemed to me that somethin can live and die but that the kind of thing that they were was always there. I didnt know you could poison that. I aint heard a wolf howl in thirty odd years. I dont know where you'd go to hear one. There may not be any such a place.

When he walked back through the barn Billy was standing in the doorway.

Has he gone back to bed?

Yeah.

What was he doin up?

He said he couldnt sleep. What were you?

Same thing. You?

Same thing.

Somethin in the air I reckon.

I dont know.

What was he talkin about?

Just stuff.

What did he say?

I guess he said cattle could tell the difference between a flight of geese and a cat on fire.

Maybe you dont need to be hangin around him so much.

You might be right.

You all seem to have a lot in common.

He aint crazy, Billy.

Maybe. But I dont know as you'd be the first one I'd come to for an opinion about it.

I'm goin to bed.

Night.

Night.

HE TOLD THE WOMAN in spanish that he intended to keep his hat and he carried it with him up the two steps to the bar and then he put it on again. There were some Mexican businessmen standing at the bar and he nodded to them as he passed. They nodded back curtly. The barman placed a napkin down. Señor? he said.

Old Grandad and water back.

The barman moved away. Billy took out his cigarettes and lighter and laid them on the bar. He looked in the backbar mirror. Several whores were draped about on the couches in the lounge. They looked like refugees from a costume ball. The barman returned with the shot of whiskey and set it and the glass of water on the bar and Billy picked up the whiskey and rocked it once in a slow circular motion and then raised it and drank. He reached for his cigarettes, he nodded to the barman.

Otra vez, he said.

The barman came with the bottle. He poured.

Dónde está Eduardo, said Billy.

Quién?

Eduardo.

The barman poured reflectively. He shook his head.

El patrón, said Billy.

El patrón no está.

Cuándo regresa?

No sé. He stood holding the bottle. Hay un problema? he said.

Billy shook a cigarette from the pack and put it in his mouth and reached for the lighter. No, he said. No hay un problema. I need to see him on a business deal.

What is your business?

He lit the cigarette and laid the lighter on top of the pack and blew smoke across the bar and looked up.

I dont feel like we're makin much progress here, he said.

The barman shrugged.

Billy took his money from his shirtpocket and laid a ten-dollar bill on the bar.

That aint for the drinks.

The barman looked down the bar to where the businessmen were standing. He looked at Billy.

Do you know what this job is worth? he said.

What?

I said do you know what this job is worth?

You mean you make pretty good on tips.

No. I mean do you know what it costs to buy a job like this?

I never heard of nobody buyin a job.

You do lots of business in Mexico?

No.

The barman stood with the bottle. Billy took out his money again and put down two fives on top of the ten. The barman palmed the money off the bar and put it in his pocket. Un momento, he said. Espérate.

Billy took up the whiskey and swirled it and drank. He set the glass down and passed the back of his wrist across his mouth. When he looked in the backbar glass the alcahuete was standing at his left elbow like Lucifer.

Sí señor, he said.

Billy turned and looked at him.

Are you Eduardo?

No. How may I help you?

I wanted to see Eduardo.

What do you want to see him about?

I wanted to talk to him.

Yes. Talk to me.

Billy turned to look at the barman but the barman had moved away to serve the other patrons.

It's just somethin personal, Billy said. Hell, I aint goin to hurt him.

The alcahuete's eyebrows moved slightly upward. That is good to know, he said. You find something you dont like?

I got a deal he might be interested in.

Who is the dealer.

What?

Who is the dealer.

Me. I'm the dealer.

Tiburcio studied him for a long time. I know who you are, he said.

You know who I am?

Yes.

Who am I?

You are the trujamán.

What's that?

You dont speak spanish?

I speak spanish.

You come with the mordida.

Billy took out his money and laid it on the bar. I got eighteen dollars. That's all I got. And I aint paid for the drinks yet.

Pay for the drinks.

What?

Pay for the drinks.

Billy left a five on the bar and put the thirteen dollars in his shirtpocket along with his cigarettes and lighter and stood.

Follow me.

He followed him out through the lounge past the whores in their whore's finery. Through the kaleidoscope of pieced light from the overhead chandelier and past the empty bandstand to a door at the rear.

The door was covered in winecolored baize and there was no doorknob to it. The alcahuete opened it anyway and they entered a corridor with blue walls and a single blue bulb screwed into the ceiling above the door. The alcahuete held the door and he stepped through and the alcahuete closed it behind them and turned and went down the corridor. The musky spice of his cologne hung in the air. At the farthest end of the corridor he stopped and tapped twice with his knuckles upon a door embossed with silver foil. He turned, waiting, his hands crossed before him at the wrist.

A buzzer buzzed and the alcahuete opened the door. Wait here, he said.

Billy waited. An old woman with one eye came down the corridor and tapped at one of the doors. When she saw him there she blessed herself with the sign of the cross. The door opened and she disappeared inside and the door closed and the corridor stood empty once again in the soft blue light.

When the silver door opened the alcahuete motioned him inside with a cupping motion of his thin ringed fingers. He stepped in and stood. Then he took off his hat.

Eduardo was sitting at his desk smoking one of his slender black cigars. He was sitting sideways with his feet crossed before him propped in the open lower drawer of his desk and he appeared to be examining his polished lizardskin boots. How may I help you? he said.

Billy looked back at Tiburcio. He looked again at Eduardo. Eduardo lifted his feet from the drawer and swiveled slowly in his chair. He was dressed in a black suit with a pale green shirt open at the neck. He rested his arm on the polished glass top of the desk, he held the cigar. He looked like he had nothing much on his mind.

I got a business proposition for you, Billy said.

Eduardo held up the little cigar and studied it. He looked at Billy again.

Somethin you might be interested in, Billy said.

Eduardo smiled thinly. He looked past Billy at the alcahuete and he looked at Billy again. My fortunes are to change for the better, he said. How very good.

He took a long slow pull on the cigar. He made a strange and graceful gesture with the hand that held it, turning it in an arc and holding it palm up. As if it cupped something unseen. Or were accustomed to holding something now absent.

Do you care if we talk alone? Billy said.

He nodded and the alcahuete withdrew and closed the door. When he was gone Eduardo leaned back in his chair and turned again and recrossed his boots in the drawer. He looked up and waited.

What I wanted, said Billy, was to buy one of these girls.

Buy, said Eduardo.

Yessir.

How do you mean, buy.

I give you the money and take her out of here.

You believe these girls are here against their will.

I dont know what they are.

But that's what you think.

I dont think anything.

Of course you do. Otherwise what would there be to buy?

I dont know.

Eduardo pursed his lips. He studied the end of the cigar. He doesnt know, he said.

You're tellin me that these girls are free to just walk out of here.

That is a good question.

Well what would be a good answer.

I would say that they are free in their persons.

In their what?

In their persons. They are free in their persons. Whether they are free here? He placed his forefinger alongside his temple. Well, who can say?

If one of em wanted to leave she could leave.

They are whores. Where would they go?

Suppose one of em wanted to get married.

Eduardo shrugged. He looked up at Billy.

Tell me this, he said.

All right.

Are you principal or agent?

Am I what?

Is it you who wishes to buy this girl?

Yes.

Do you come often to the White Lake?

I was here one time.

Where did you meet this girl?

At La Venada.

And now you wish to marry her.

Billy didnt answer.

The pimp pulled slowly on the cigar and blew the smoke slowly toward his boots. I think you are the agent, he said.

I aint no agent. I work for Mac McGovern at the Cross Fours out of Orogrande New Mexico and you can ask anybody.

I think you are not here on your own behalf.

I'm here to make you a offer.

Eduardo smoked.

Cash money, Billy said.

This girl has an illness. Does your friend know that?

I didnt say I had a friend.

She has not told him that, has she?

How do you know what girl it is.

Her name is Magdalena.

Billy studied him. You knew that because of what I said about La Venada.

This girl will not leave here. Perhaps your friend thinks that she will but she will not. Perhaps even she thinks it. She is very young. Let me ask you this.

Ask it.

What is wrong with your friend that he falls in love with whores?

I dont know.

Does he think she is not really a whore?

I couldnt tell you.

You cannot talk to him?

No.

Because she is whore to the bone. I know her.

I expect you do.

Your friend is very rich?

No.

What can he offer this girl? Why would she leave?

I dont know. I reckon he thinks she's in love with him.

Heavens, said Eduardo. Do you believe such a thing?

I dont know.

Do you believe such a thing?

No.

What are you going to do?

I dont know. What do you want me to tell him?

There is nothing to tell him. He drinks a great deal, your friend?

No. Not especially.

I am trying to help you.

Billy tapped his hat against the side of his leg. He looked at Eduardo and he looked around the room that was his office. In the corner against the far wall there was a small bar. A sofa upholstered in white leather. A glasstopped coffeetable.

You dont believe me, said Eduardo.

I dont believe you dont have some money invested in this girl.

Did I say that?

I thought you did.

She owes me a certain amount. Money that was advanced to her for her costumes. Her jewelry.

How much money.

Would I ask you such a question?

I dont know. I guess I wouldnt be in a position to be asked.

You think I am a whiteslaver.

I didnt say that.

That is what you think.

What do you want me to tell him.

What difference does it make?

I guess it might make a difference to him.

Your friend is in the grip of an irrational passion. Nothing you say to him will matter. He has in his head a certain story. Of how things will be. In this story he will be happy. What is wrong with this story?

You tell me.

What is wrong with this story is that it is not a true story. Men have in their minds a picture of how the world will be. How they will be in that world. The world may be many different ways for them but there is one world that will never be and that is the world they dream of. Do you believe that?

Billy put his hat on. I thank you for your time, he said.

You are welcome.

He turned to go.

You didnt answer my question, said Eduardo.

He turned back. He looked at the pimp. His cigar in his gracefully cupped fingers, his expensive boots. The windowless room. The furniture in it that looked as if it had been brought in and set in place solely for the purpose of this scene. I dont know, he said. I guess probably I do. I just dont like to say it.

Why is that?

It seems like a betrayal of some kind.

Can the truth be a betrayal?

Maybe. Anyway, some men get what they want.

No man. Or perhaps only briefly so as to lose it. Or perhaps only to prove to the dreamer that the world of his longing made real is no longer that world at all.

Yeah.

Do you believe that?

I'll tell you what.

Tell me.

Let me sleep on it.

The pimp nodded. Ándale pues, he said. The door opened by no visible means or signal. Tiburcio stood waiting. Billy turned again and looked back. You didnt answer mine, he said.

No?

No.

Ask it again.

Let me ask you this instead.

All right.

He's in trouble, aint he?

Eduardo smiled. He blew cigar smoke across the glass top of his desk. That is not a question, he said.

IT WAS LATE when he got back but the light was still on in the kitchen. He sat in the truck for a minute, then he shut off the engine. He left the key in the ignition and got out and walked across the yard to the house. Socorro had gone to bed but there was cornbread in the warmer over the oven and a plate of beans and potatoes with two pieces of fried chicken. He carried the plates to the table and went back and got silver out of the dishdrainer and got down a cup and poured his coffee and set the pot back over the eye of the stove where there was still a dull red glow of coals and he took his coffee to the table and sat and ate. He ate slowly and methodically. When he'd finished he carried the dishes to the sink and opened the refrigerator and bent to scout the interior for anything in the way of dessert. He found a bowl of pudding and took it to the sideboard and got down a small dish and filled it and put the pudding back in the refrigerator and got more coffee and sat eating the pudding and reading Oren's newspaper. The clock ticked in the hallway. The cooling stove creaked. When John Grady came in he went on to the stove and got a cup of coffee and came to the table and sat down and pushed back his hat.

You up for the day? said Billy.

I hope not.

What time is it?

I dont know.

Billy sipped his coffee. He reached in his pocket for his cigarettes.

Did you just get in? John Grady said.

Yep.

I reckon the answer was no.

You reckon right, little hoss.

Well.

It's about what you expected aint it?

Yeah. Did you offer him the money?

Oh we had a pretty good visit, take it all around.

What did he say.

Billy lit his cigarette and laid the lighter on top of the pack. He said she didnt want to leave there.

Well that's a lie.

Well that may be. But he says she aint leavin.

Well she is.

Billy blew smoke slowly across the table. John Grady watched him.

You just think I'm crazy, dont you?

You know what I think.

Well.

Why dont you take a good look at yourself. Look at what it's brung you to. Talkin about sellin your horse. It's just the old story all over again. Losin your head over a piece of tail. Cept in your case there aint nothin about it makes any sense. Nothin.

In your eyes.

In mine or any man's.

He leaned forward and began to count off on the fingers of the hand that held the cigarette: She aint American. She aint a citizen. She dont speak english. She works in a whorehouse. No, hear me out. And last but not least—he sat holding his thumb—there's a son of a bitch owns her outright that I guarangoddamntee you will kill you graveyard dead if you mess with him. Son, aint there no girls on this side of the damn river?

Not like her.

Well I'll bet that's the truth if you ever told it.

He stubbed out the cigarette. Well. I've gone as far as I can go with you. I'm goin to bed.

All right.

He pushed back his chair and rose and stood. Do I think you're crazy? he said. No. I dont. You've rewrote the book for crazy. If all you are is crazy then all them poor bastards in the loonybin that they're feedin under the door need to be set loose in the street.

He put the cigarettes and lighter in his shirtpocket and carried the cup and bowl to the sink. At the door he stopped again and looked back. I'll see you in the mornin, he said.

Billy?

Yeah.

Thanks. I appreciate it.

I'd say you're welcome but I'd be a liar.

I know it. Thanks anyway.

You aim to sell that stallion?

I dont know. Yeah.

Maybe Wolfenbarger will buy him.

I thought about that.

I expect you did. I'll see you in the mornin.

John Grady watched him walk across the yard toward the barn. He leaned and wiped the beaded water from the window glass with his sleeve. Billy's shadow shortened across the yard until he passed under the yellow light over the barn door and

then he stepped through into the dark of the barn and was lost
to view. John Grady let the curtains fall back across the glass
and turned and sat staring into the empty cup before him.
There were grounds in the bottom of the cup and he swirled
the cup and looked at them. Then he swirled them the other
way as if he'd put them back the way they'd been.

HE STOOD IN THE GROVE of willows with his back to the
river and watched the road and the vehicles that moved along
the road. There was little traffic. The dust of the few cars hung
in the dry air long after the cars were gone. He walked on down
to the river and squatted and watched the passing water murky
with clay. He threw in a rock. Then another. He turned and
looked back toward the road.

The cab when it came stopped at the turnoff and then backed
and turned and came rocking and bumping down the rutted
mud road and pulled up in the clearing. She got out on the far
side and paid the driver and spoke briefly with him and the
driver nodded and she stepped away. The driver put the cab in
gear and put his arm across the seat and backed the cab and
turned. He looked toward the river. Then he pulled away out
to the road and went back toward town.

He took her hand. Tenía miedo que no vendrías, he said.

She didnt answer. She leaned against him. Her black hair
falling about her shoulders. The smell of soap. The flesh and
bone living under the cloth of her dress.

Me amas? he said.

Sí. Te amo.

He sat on a cottonwood log and watched her while she
waded in the gravel shallows. She turned and smiled at him.
Her dress gathered about her brown thighs. He tried to smile
back but his throat caught and he looked away.

She sat on the log beside him and he took her feet in his
hands each in turn and dried them with his kerchief and fastened with his own fingers the small buckles of her shoes. She

leaned and put her head on his shoulder and he kissed her and
he touched her hair and her breasts and her face as a blind man
might.

Y mi respuesta? he said.

She took his hand and kissed it and held it against her heart
and she said that she was his and that she would do whatever he
asked her if it take her life.

She was from the State of Chiapas and she had been sold at
the age of thirteen to settle a gambling debt. She had no family. In Puebla she'd run away and gone to a convent for protec-
tion. The procurer himself appeared on the convent steps the
following morning and in the pure light of day paid money into
the hand of the mother superior and took the girl away again.

This man stripped her naked and beat her with a whip made
from the innertube of a truck tire. Then he held her in his arms
and told her that he loved her. She ran away again and went to
the police. Three officers took her to a room in the basement
where there was a dirty mattress on the floor. When they were
through with her they sold her to the other policemen. Then
they sold her to the prisoners for what few pesos they could
muster or traded her for cigarettes. Finally they sent for the
procurer and sold her back to him.

He beat her with his fists and slammed her against the wall
and knocked her down and kicked her. He said that if she ran
away again he would kill her. She closed her eyes and offered
him her throat. In his rage he seized her up by the arm but the
arm broke in his hand. A muted snap, like a dry stick. She
gasped and cried out with the pain.

Mira, he shouted. Mira, puta, que has hecho.

The arm was set by a curandera and now would not
straighten. She showed him. Mires, she said. The house was
called La Esperanza del Mundo. Where a painted child in a
stained kimono with her arm in a sling wept in silence or went
wordlessly with men to a room at the rear for a price of less
than two dollars.

He had bent forward weeping with his arms around her. He

put his hand over her mouth. She took it away. Hay más, she said.

No.

She would tell him more but again he placed his fingers against her mouth. He said that there was only one thing he wished to know.

Lo que quieras, she said.

Te casas conmigo.

Sí, querido, she said. La respuesta es sí. I marry you.

WHEN HE ENTERED the kitchen Oren and Troy and JC were sitting there and he nodded to them and went on to the stove and got his breakfast and his coffee and came to the table. Troy scooted his chair slightly to make room. You aint about give out under this heavy courtin schedule are you son?

Shit, said JC. Dont even think about tryin to keep up with the cowboy.

I talked to Crawford about your horse, said Oren.

What did he say.

He said he thought he had a buyer if you could come to his figures.

Same figures?

Same figures.

I dont believe I can do it.

He might do a little better. But not much.

John Grady nodded. He ate.

You might do better to run him through the auction.

The auction aint for three more weeks.

Two and a half.

Tell him I'll take three and a quarter.

JC got up and carried his dishes to the sink. Oren lit a cigarette.

When will you see him? said John Grady.

I'll talk to him today if you want.

All right.

He ate. Troy got up and took his dishes to the sink and he and JC went out. John Grady wiped his plate with the last bite of biscuit and ate it and pushed back his chair.

These four-minute breakfasts are goin to get you in trouble with the union, Oren said.

I got to see the old man a minute.

He carried his plate and cup to the sink and wiped his hands on the sides of his trousers and crossed the room and went down the hall.

He knocked on the jamb of the office doorway and looked in but the room was empty. He went on down the hall to Mac's bedroom and tapped at the open door. Mac came out of the bathroom with a towel around his neck and his hat on.

Mornin son, he said.

Mornin sir. I wondered if I could talk to you for a minute.

Come on in.

He hung the towel over a chairback and went to the oldfashioned chifforobe and took out a shirt and shook it unfolded and stood undoing the buttons. John Grady stood in the doorway.

Come on in, Mac said. Put your damn hat back on.

Yessir. He took a couple of steps into the room and put his hat on and stood there. On the wall opposite were framed photographs of horses. On the dresser in an ornate silver frame a photograph of Margaret Johnson McGovern.

Mac pulled on his shirt and stood buttoning it. Set down, son, he said.

That's all right.

Go on. You look like you got a lot on your mind.

There was a heavy oak chair covered with dark leather at the far side of the bed and he crossed the floor and sat in it. Some of Mac's clothes were thrown across one arm of the chair. He put his elbow on the other arm. Mac swept up and tucked in his shirt front and back and buttoned his trousers and buckled his belt and got his keys and his change and his billfold from the dresser. He came over to the bed carrying his socks and sat and unrolled them and began to pull them on. Well, he said. You wont never have no better of a chance.

John Grady started to take off his hat again but then he put his hands back in his lap. Then he leaned forward with his elbows on his knees.

Just pretend it's a cold stockpond on a hot day and jump on in, said Mac.

Yessir. Well. I want to get married.

Mac stopped midsock. Then he pulled the sock on and reached down for his boot. Married, he said.

Yessir.

All right.

I want to get married and I thought for one thing if you didnt care I'd just go on and sell that horse.

Mac pulled on the boot and picked up the other boot and sat with it in his hand. Son, he said. I can understand a man wantin to get married. I lacked about a month bein twenty when I did. We kind of finished raisin one another. But I might of been fixed a little better than you. You think you can afford it?

I dont know. I thought maybe if I sold the horse.

How long have you been thinkin about this?

Well. A while.

This aint a have-to kind of thing is it?

No sir. It aint nothin like that.

Well why dont you hold off for a while. See if it wont keep.

I cant really do that.

Well, I dont know what that means.

There's some problems.

Well I got time to listen if you want to tell me about it.

Yessir. Well. For one thing she's Mexican.

Mac nodded. I've known that to work, he said. He pulled on the boot.

So I got the problem of gettin her over here.

Mac put his foot down on the floor and put his hands on his knees. He looked up at the boy. Over here? he said.

Yessir.

You mean across the river?

Yessir.

You mean she's a Mexican Mexican?

Yessir.

Damn, son.

He looked off across the room. The sun was just up over the barn. He looked at the white lace curtains on the window. He looked at the boy sitting stiffly there in his father's chair. Well, he said. That's somethin of a problem, I reckon. Aint the worst one I ever heard of. How old is she?

Sixteen.

Mac sat with his lower lip between his teeth. It keeps gettin worse, dont it? Does she speak english?

No sir.

Not word one.

No sir.

Mac shook his head. Outside they could hear the cattle calling along the fence by the road. He looked at John Grady. Son, he said, have you give this some thought?

Yessir. I sure have.

I take it you've pretty much made up your mind.

Yessir.

You wouldnt be here if you hadnt, would you?

No sir.

Where do you plan on livin at?

Well sir, I wanted to talk to you about that. I thought if you didnt care I'd see if I could fix up the old place at Bell Springs.

Damn. It dont even have a roof anymore does it?

Not much of a one. I looked it over. It could be fixed up.

It would take some fixin.

I could fix it up.

You probably could. Probably could. You aint said nothin about money. I cant raise you. You know that.

I aint asked for a raise.

I'd have to raise Billy and JC both. Hell. I might have to raise Oren.

Yessir.

Mac sat leaning forward with his fingers laced together. Son, he said, I think you ought to wait. But if you got it in your head to go on, then go ahead. I'll do whatever I can for you.

Thank you sir.

He put his hands on his knees and rose. John Grady rose. Mac shook his head, half smiling. He looked at the boy.

Is she pretty?

Yessir. She sure is.

I'll bet she is, too. You bring her in here. I want to see her.

Yessir.

You say she dont speak no english?

No sir.

Damn. He shook his head again. Well, he said. Go on. Get your butt out of here.

Yessir.

He crossed the room to the door and stopped and turned.

Thank you sir.

Go on.

HE AND BILLY rode to Cedar Springs. They rode to the top of the draw and rode back down again throwing all the cattle out downcountry before them and roping everything that looked suspicious, heading and heeling them and stretching the screaming animals on the ground and dismounting and dropping the reins while the horses backed and held the catchropes taut. There were new calves on the ground and some of them had worms in their navels and they doused them with Peerless and swabbed them out and doused them again and turned them loose. In the evening they rode up to Bell Springs and John Grady dismounted and left Billy with the horses while they drank and crossed through the swales of sacaton grass to the old adobe and pushed open the door and went in.

He stood very quietly. Sunlight fell the length of the room from the small sash set in the western wall. The floor was of packed clay beaten and oiled and it was strewn with debris, old clothes and foodtins and curious small cones of mud that had formed from water percolating down through the mud roof and dripping through the latillas to stand about like the work of old-world termites. In the corner stood an iron bedstead with random empty beercans screwed into the bare springs. On the back wall a 1928 Clay Robinson and Co. calendar showing a cowboy on nightherd under a rising moon. He passed on through the long core of light where he set the motes to dancing and went through the doorless framework into the other room. There was a small two-eyed woodburning stove against the far wall with the rusted pipes fallen into a pile behind it and there were a couple of old Arbuckle coffeeboxes nailed to the wall and a third one lying in the floor. A few jars of home-canned beans and tomatoes and salsa. Broken glass in the floor. Old newspapers from before the war. An old rotted Fish brand slicker hanging from a peg in the wall by the kitchen door and some pieces of old tackleather. When he turned around Billy was standing in the doorway watching him.

This the honeymoon suite? he said.

You're lookin at it.

He leaned in the doorframe and took his cigarettes from his shirtpocket and shucked one out and lit it.

The only thing you aint got here is a dead mule in the floor.

John Grady had crossed to the back door and stood looking out.

You think you're goin to be able to get the truck up here?

I think we might could comin up the other side.

What's this we shit? You got a rat in your pocket?

John Grady smiled. From the kitchen door you could see the late sun high on the bare ridgerock of the Jarillas. He shut the door and looked back at Billy and walked over to the stove and lifted one of the castiron eyeplates and looked in and lowered it again.

I may be wrong about this, said Billy, but it's my feelin that once they get used to lights and runnin water it's kindly hard to wean em back off again.

Got to start somewhere.

Is she goin to cook on that?

John Grady smiled. He went past Billy into the other room. Billy straightened up in the doorway to let him by and then stood looking after him. I hope she's a country girl, he said.

What do you say we ride back down on the back side and see what the old road looks like.

Whatever you want to do. We'll be late gettin in.

John Grady stood in the doorway looking out. Yeah, he said. All right. I can ride up on Sunday.

Billy watched him. He unlimbered himself out of the doorframe and crossed the room. Let's do it, he said. We're goin to be ridin back in the dark either way.

Billy?

Yeah.

It dont make any difference, you know. What anybody thinks.

Yeah. I know it too well.

That's a pretty picture, aint it.

He looked at the horses across the creek where they stood footed to their darkening shapes in the ford with their heads raised looking toward the house and the cottonwoods and the mountains and the red sweep of the evening sky beyond.

You think I'll outgrow whatever it is I got.

No. I dont. I used to but I dont no more.

I'm too far gone, is that it?

It aint just that. It's you. Most people get smacked around enough after a while they start to pay attention. More and more you remind me of Boyd. Only way I could ever get him to do anything was to tell him not to.

There used to be a pipe from the spring to the house.

You could run it again I would reckon.

Yeah.

I'd say the water's still good. There aint nothin above here.

Billy walked out in the yard and took a long drag on his cigarette and stood looking at the horses. John Grady pulled the door shut. Billy looked at him.

You never did tell me what Mac said.

He didnt say much. If he thought I was crazy he was too much of a gentleman to mention it.

What do you think he'd say if he knew she worked at the White Lake?

I dont know.

The hell you dont.

He wont know it unless you tell him.

I've thought about it.

Yeah?

He'd shit green apples.

Billy flipped the butt of the cigarette out across the yard. It was already dark enough that it made an arc in the fading light. Arcs within the arc. We better get on, he said.

HE DIDNT SELL the horse to Wolfenbarger. On Saturday two friends of McGovern's came out and they leaned on the fender of their truck and smoked and talked while he saddled the horse and led it out. They straightened up when they saw the horse. He nodded to them and took the animal out to the corral.

Mac came from the kitchen and nodded to the men.

Mornin.

He crossed the yard. Crawford introduced him to the other man and the three of them walked out to the corral.

That looks like the horse old man Chávez used to ride, the man said.

As far as I know there's no connection.

That was a funny story about that horse.

Yes it was.

You think a horse can grieve for a man?

No. Do you?

No. Still it was a funny kind of story.

It was.

The man walked around the horse while John Grady held it. He put his hand behind the horse's front leg and he looked into its eye. He backed up against the horse and picked up one hindleg and put it down again but he didnt look at the hoof and he didnt look into the horse's mouth.

You say this is a three year old?

Yessir.

Ride him around some.

They stood watching while John Grady rode the horse up and back and turned the horse and backed him and then cantered him around the corral.

How come the boy wants to sell him?

Mac didnt answer. They watched the horse. After a while he said: He just needs the money. The horse is sound.

What do you think, Junior?

You aint goin to pay no attention to me. Get me on Mac's wrong side.

It aint my horse, said Mac.

What do you think?

Crawford spat. Pretty good lookin horse I think.

What will he take for him?

What he's askin.

They stood.

I might go two and a half.

Mac shook his head.

It's his horse to sell aint it? the man said.

Mac nodded. Yes, he said. It is. But if he was to let that horse go for two hundred and fifty dollars I'd pay him off. I wouldnt want anybody that ignorant on the place. Liable to do themselves a injury.

The man toed the dirt. He looked at Crawford and he studied the horse again and he looked at Mac.

Will he take three?

Will you give three?

Yessir.

John Grady, called Mac.

Yessir?

Bring that man's horse over here and get your saddle off of him.

Yessir, said John Grady.

WHEN HE CAME IN that night Oren and Troy were still at the table drinking coffee and he got his plate from the warmer and filled his cup and joined them.

They tell me you're damn near afoot, said Oren.

Just about it.

I guess you decided that varmint was just too crazy to make a horse out of.

I just needed the money.

Mac said the man never even rode him.

He didnt.

I suppose the critter's reputation had done preceded him.

Could be.

You may not of heard the last from him.

Could be.

They watched him eat.

The cowboy thinks horses are sane and people are crazy, Troy said.

He might have a point.

You all have been around different horses from what I have.

More likely we been around different people.

I dont know, said Troy. I been acquainted with some lulus.

How did you all get along?

John Grady looked up. He smiled. Oren was shucking a cigarette out of the pack. All horses are crazy, he said. To a degree. Only thing to be said in their favor is that they dont try to hide it from you.

He reached down and popped a wooden match on the underside of his chair and lit his cigarette and shook the match out and laid it in the ashtray.

Why do you think they're crazy? said John Grady.

Why do I think it or why are they?

Why are they.

They're just made that way. A horse has got two brains. He dont see the same thing out of both eyes at once. He's got a eye for each side.

So does a fish, said Troy.

Well. That's true.

So does a fish have two brains?

I dont know. I dont know that a fish has got any brains at all to speak of.

Maybe a fish just aint smart enough to be crazy.

I think you got a point. A horse aint really all that dumb.

They're too dumb to shade up and a dumb-assed cow will do that.

So will a fish. Or a rattlesnake for that matter.

You think a snake is dumber than a fish?

Hell, Troy. I dont know. Who in the hell would know such a thing? They're both dumbern hell in my opinion.

Well I didnt mean to get you stirred up.

I aint stirred up.

Well go on with the story.

It aint a story. It was just a observation about horses.

Well what was it.

I dont know. I forgot.

No you aint.

You were talkin about a horse havin two brains, said John Grady.

Oren pulled on the cigarette. He looked at John Grady. He leaned and tapped the ash into the ashtray.

All I was sayin is that a horse is a different proposition from what a lot of people think. A lot of what people take for igno-rance on the part of the horse is just confusion between the righthand horse and the lefthand horse. Like if you was to saddle a horse and all and then walk around to his off side and start to mount up. You know what's goin to happen.

Sure. All hell's goin to bust loose.

That's right. That particular horse aint even seen you yet.

Oren jerked up his elbows and drew back in alarm from his own off side. Shit, he said. Who's that?

Troy grinned. John Grady drank from his cup and set it back on the table. Why couldnt it be that he's just not used to bein mounted from that side? he said.

It is. But the point is he cant ask the other half of the horse if he's ever seen this man before or get his advice about what to do.

Well it seems to me that if the two sides of the horse aint even speakin to one another you'd have some real problems. The whole horse wouldnt even start off together in the same direction. What about that?

Oren smoked. He looked at Troy. I aint a authority on horses' brains. I'm just tellin you what one cowboy's experience has been. There's two sides to a horse and it's been my experience that what you got to do is work the one side and let the other side go.

I've known some people the same way. Several, in fact.

Yes. I have too. But I think it's somethin they've worked at. A horse comes by it natural.

You dont think you could train both sides of the horse the same?

You're wearin me out.

Hell, that's a fair question.

I suppose you could. Maybe. It'd be hard to do. There would just about have to be two of you.

Well suppose you had a twin brother.

I suppose in principle maybe you could work with a horse thataway. I dont know. But what would you have when you got done?

You'd have a two-sided balanced horse.

No you wouldnt. You'd just have a horse that thought there was two of you. Suppose one day he sees you both on the same side. What then?

I reckon he'd think you was quadruplets.

Oren stubbed out the cigarette. No, he said. He'd think the same thing as everbody else.

What's that?

That you're as crazy as a shithouse rat.

He pushed back his chair and rose. I'll see you all in the mornin.

The kitchen door closed. Troy shook his head. Old Oren is losin his sense of humor.

John Grady smiled. He thumbed his plate back from the edge of the table and leaned back in his chair. Through the window he could see Oren adjust his hat as he set out down the drive toward the small house he shared with his cat. As if the dead world past might take pains to notice. He'd not always been a cowboy. He'd been a miner in northern Mexico and he'd fought in wars and revolutions and he'd been an oilfield roustabout in the Permian Basin and a mariner under three different flags. He'd even been married once.

John Grady drained the last dark dregs from the bottom of the cup and set the cup on the table. Oren's all right, he said.

III

WHEN HE CROSSED at the top of the draw he smelled what the horse had been smelling. A reek of carrion wafted up on some vector of the cooling evening air. He sat the horse and turned in the saddle and tested the air with his nose but the smell had passed and vanished. He turned the horse and sat facing back down the draw and then he put the horse forward again down the narrow cattletrail. The horse watched the cattle moving out before them through the scrub and pricked his ears about.

I'll let you know what it is you need to do, John Grady told him.

A hundred yards down the far side of the draw he smelled it again and he halted the horse. The horse stood waiting.

You wouldnt scout out a dead cow for me, would you? he said.

The horse stood. He put him forward again and they rode down another quarter mile or so and the horse settled into his gait such as it was and paid no more mind to the distant cattle. A little further on and he halted the horse and tested the air. He sat the horse. Then he turned and started back up the way they'd come.

He cut for sign and finally picked up the scent ripe and strong and in the dusk he dismounted and stood looking down at the flyblown carcass of a new calf that had been dragged into the center of a ring of creosote bush in broad open country. There'd been no rain in two weeks and the dragmarks were visible across the gravel and he walked out a ways on the backtrack looking for sand or dirt where there might be a foot track but he didnt find one. He came back and picked up the reins and mounted up and looked out at the surrounding countryside to mark the spot and then rode out and back down the draw.

HE AND BILLY STOOD over the dead calf and Billy walked back out following the dragmarks and stood looking over the country.

How far out did you go? he said.

Not far.

It's been a stout somethin to drag that big calf.

You think it's been a lion?

No. A lion'd of covered it up. Or tried to.

They mounted up and rode out on the backtrack. They lost the track on the hard ground and picked it up again. Billy followed the track over the gravels by raising or lowering his head and catching a certain angle of the light. He said that the disturbed ground had a different look and after a while John Grady could see it too. The day was cool. The horses were fresh with the morning and the weather and seemed unworried.

Range riders, said Billy.

Range riders.

Detectives.

Pinkertons.

The calf had been cut out and run down and killed in open country. Billy dismounted and walked over the ground. There was blood on the rocks, black from the sun.

You dont think it's just been coyotes? said John Grady.

I dont think so.

What do you think it's been?

I know what it's been.

What?

Dogs.

Dogs?

Yep.

I aint never seen any dogs out here.

I aint either. But they're here.

In the days that followed they found two more dead calves. They rode the Cedar Springs pasture and they crossed the floodplain below it and they rode the surrounding traprock bluffs and the mesa that ran east toward the old mine. They found tracks of the dogs but they did not see them. Before the week was out they'd found another freshkilled calf not dead a day.

There were some old Oneida number three doublespring traps on a shelf in the saddleroom and Billy boiled and waxed them and they carried them out the next day and buried three of them around the carcass. They rode out before daybreak to check the sets and when they got to the kill the traps were all dug out and lying on the ground. One of them was not even sprung. The carcass itself was little more than skin and bones.

I didnt know dogs were that smart, said John Grady.

I didnt either. They probably didnt know we were that dumb.

You ever trap dogs before?

No.

What do you want to do?

Billy picked up the unsprung trap and reached under the jaw and sprang it with his thumb. It chopped shut with a dead metal sound in the quiet morning air. He cut the wires and wired the rings together and hung the traps over the horn of his saddle and mounted up. He looked at John Grady.

We just aint found where they're usin is all. They might walk in a blind set.

You think Travis's dogs would run em?

Billy sat looking out at the long morning light on the rocks of the mesa. I dont know, he said. That's a pretty good question.

They took a packhorse and carried a kitchen box and their soogans out to the mesa and made camp. They sat drinking coffee from tin cups and watching the coals flare and lapse in the wind's fanning of them. Far out on the plain below the lights of the cities lay shimmering in their grids with the dark serpentine of the river dividing them.

I thought you had other business to attend to, Billy said.

I do.

You think it can wait.

I hope it can wait. I aint sure this can.

Well I'm glad you aint forgot all of your raising.

I aint forgot anything.

You're tired of me gettin on your ass though.

You're entitled.

They sipped their coffee. The wind blew. They pulled their blankets about their shoulders.

I aint jealous you know.

I never said you were.

I know. You might of thought it. Truth is, I wouldnt pull your boots on at gunpoint.

I know.

Billy lit a cigarette with a brand from the fire and laid the brand back. He smoked. It looks a lot better from up here than it does down there, dont it?

Yes. It does.

There's a lot of things look better at a distance.

Yeah?

I think so.

I guess there are. The life you've lived, for one.

Yeah. Maybe what of it you aint lived yet, too.

They stayed out Saturday and they rode the country under the rim Sunday morning and midday they found a freshkilled calf lying in a gravel wash out on the floodplain. The mother was standing looking at it and they hazed her away and she walked off bawling and stood and looked back.

Them old-time brocklefaces wouldnt of give up a calf that-away, Billy said. I'll bet they aint a mark on her.

I'll bet there aint either, said John Grady.

You aint good for nothin but to eat and shit, are you? Billy told the cow. The cow stared dully.

You know they're holed up in them rocks somewhere under the rim.

Yeah. I know it. But you'd have a hell of a time tryin to ride it and I sure aint goin to walk it.

John Grady looked down at the dead calf. He leaned and spat. What do you want to do?

Why dont we just pack up and ride back and call Travis and see what he says.

All right. If he'd come out this evenin we could lay for em.

Well he wont be comin out this evenin, I can tell you that.

Why is that?

Shit, said Billy. That old man wont hunt on a Sunday.

John Grady smiled. What if our ox was in the ditch?

He wouldnt give a damn if the whole outfit was in the ditch and you and me and Mac with it.

Maybe he'd just let us borrow the dogs.

He wouldnt do that. Anyways the dogs wont hunt on Sunday either. They're Christian dogs.

Christian dogs.

Yep. Raised that way.

As they rode out along the upper end of the floodplain they heard another cow bawl and they halted and sat their horses and scanned the country below them.

Do you see her? said Billy.

Yeah. Yonder she is.

Is it that same one?

No.

Billy leaned and spat. Well, he said. You know what that means. You want to ride down there?

I dont see what would be the use in it.

THEY SET OUT across the broad creosote flats of the valley in the darkness before dawn on Tuesday. Archer had a set of six dogboxes that fitted atop the bed of the Reo truck they drove and the truck groaned along in low gear and the headlights swung up and down in pale yellow fulcrums picking up the riders that went before them in the dark and the shapes of the creosote bushes and the red eyes of the horses where they turned their heads or crossed ahead of the truck. The dogs jostling in their boxes rode in silence and the riders smoked or talked quietly among themselves. Their hats low, the corduroy collars of their duckingjackets turned up. Riding slowly up the broad flat valley ahead of the truck.

The truck pulled up in a gravel fan at the head of the valley and the riders dismounted and dropped the reins on their horses and helped Travis and Archer unload the dogs and snap them onto the big harnessleather gangleads. The dogs backed and danced and whined and some raised their mouths and howled and the howls echoed off of the rimrock and back again and Travis halfhitched the first cast of dogs to the front bumper of the truck where their collective breath clouded whitely in the headlamps and the horses standing along the edge of the dark stamped and snorted and leaned to test the yellow lightbeams with their noses. They handed down the dogs by their collars from the boxes on the other side of the truck and leashed them up as well and the stars in the east began to dim out one by one.

They walked the dogs baying out along the gravel and Billy and John Grady rode below them and cut back and forth until they located the dead calf in the wash. It had been eaten to the bones and the bones had been dragged about over the ground. The ribcage lay with its curved tines upturned on the gravel plain like some great carnivorous plant brooding in the barren dawn.

They called out to the doghandlers and Travis called back to the others and they came down the wash with the big bluetick and treeing walker hounds lunging at their leads and slobbering and sucking at the air with their noses. When they fetched up at the remains of the calf they drew back and shied and sniffed the ground and looked at Travis.

Keep the horses back, called Travis. Let's give em a chance.

He set about unleashing the dogs and urging them on. They padded about snuffing at the ground and the dogs that Archer was bringing down began to howl and moan and Archer turned them loose and they came barreling down the draw.

Travis walked over to where Billy sat his horse. He stood with the leads braided up together and slung across his shoulder and listened.

What do you think? said Billy.

I dont know.

I'll bet them calfkillin sons of bitches aint been gone from here long.

I bet they aint either.

What do you think?

I dont know. If Smoke wont run em they aint goin to be run.

Is that your best dog?

No. But he's the dog for the job.

Why is that?

Cause he's run dogs before.

What did he think about it?

He never said.

The dogs were casting about in the dark, returning and setting out again.

It looks to me like they've left out of here in ever direction. How many are they up here do you reckon?

I dont know. Three or four.

I'll bet they's moren that.

You may be right.

Yonder he goes now.

One of the dogs had sorted out the track and set off baying. The others came tearing out of the creosote and within seconds all eight hounds were in full cry.

That sounds pretty hot on that dry ground, said Travis. Where's my horse at?

JC did have him but I think he's gone on.

You know where they're headed dont you?

Up towards them rocks under the mesa yonder I'd say.

Archer came leading Travis's horse by the bridlereins. Travis stepped up into the saddle and looked toward the east. It's about to get light enough to see.

There's goin to be one godawful dogfight up in them rocks.

I hear you. Let's go boys.

John Grady and JC were sitting their horses at the upper end of the wash when Archer and Travis and Billy rode up.

Where's Troy and Joaquín?

Done gone on.

Let's go.

You hear that?

What?

Listen.

From the rimrock of the far western edge of the floodplain beyond the cries of the trailing hounds they could hear short chopping barks, a balesome howling.

Them ignorant sons of bitches is answerin back, said Billy.

I guess they want to be in on the race, Archer said. Dumb sumbucks dont know they are the race.

By the time they reached the foot of the stone palisades the hounds had already driven the dogs out of the rocks and they could hear them in a running fight and then a long howling chase up through the broken scree and boulders. It was by now gray light and they trotted the horses singlefile along the base of the cliffs, following a trail that wound among the fallen traprock. Travis put his horse alongside John Grady. He reached and put his hand on the horse's neck and John Grady slowed.

Listen, said Travis.

They halted and sat the horses and listened. Billy rode up.

Build your loops, boys, Travis said.

Think you all can see to rope?

We're fixin to find out.

They pulled the ties on their catchropes. Let's dont get in a hurry, said Travis. They're fixin to break out up here. Let em get out in the clear. Be careful now. Let's not rope our own dogs.

They ran their loops and nudged their horses forward.

Keep em small, said Travis. Keep em small. They'll go through one like a dose of salts through a cat.

The hounds' cries were suddenly just above them where the trail turned and angled up behind some large fallen boulders. They saw three shapes leaping from rock to rock. Then two more. John Grady was riding Watson's blue dun horse and he put his heels to the horse's ribs and the horse squatted and bolted. Billy was right behind him.

The trailing hounds came out of the rocks above them in full cry and John Grady reined off to the right. Both he and Billy were sitting up high in the saddle in an effort to see the running dogs. When they came out onto the upper trail John Grady looked back. Billy was whipping over and under with the small toy loop of his catchrope. A hundred feet behind him among the rocks several of Travis's appaloosa-colored dogs were coming hard. He leaned low over the horse's neck to talk it on and then raised up again to see. Three yellowlooking dogs were loping dead ahead in tandem before him up a long gravel wash. He leaned and spoke again to the horse but the horse had already seen them. He glanced back to check for Billy and when he looked ahead again the hindmost dog had broken away from the other two. He put the horse down the slope and went pounding out over the flat after it.

The loop being so small had no weight to it and he doubled it and swung it over his head and then caught it and doubled it again. When the horse saw the rope loft past its left ear it laid back its ears and came hauling down upon the running cur with its mouth open like some terrible vengeance.

The dog had no experience as quarry. It did not check or swerve but ran on and John Grady cranked the loop and leaned over the pommel of the saddle. He looked for the dog to cut back but the dog seemed to think it could outrun the horse. The coiled rope sailed out and the loop swiveled out of its turnings. The dun horse tossed up its head and set its forefeet in the gravel and squatted and John Grady dallied the home end of the rope about the polished leather of the pommel and the rope popped taut and the dog snapped into the air mutely. It cartwheeled soundlessly and landed on the gravel with a soft dead whump.

By now three more dogs had started across the plain with Travis and Joaquín after them. They passed a hundred feet out riding hard and John Grady punched the dun forward and set out after them with the yellow dog bouncing behind over the rocks and through the creosote at the end of the thirty-five foot maguey rope. Other hounds and riders had come out of the rocks to the west and were lined out upon the floodplain and he rode on dragging the dog a ways and then hauled the horse up short and jumped down and ran back to get his rope off of the dog. The dog was limp and bloody and it lay in the gravels grinning with its eyes half started from their sockets. He stood on it with his boot and pulled off the loop and trotted back to the waiting horse coiling the rope as he went.

By this time it was good daylight and there were already four riders out on the plain before him riding in a long sweep and he mounted up and slung the coiled rope over his shoulder and set out after them at a handgallop.

When he passed Joaquín the Mexican shouted something after him but he couldnt hear what it was. He quirted the horse on with the loop end of the rope, following Travis and JC and Travis's hounds. He almost ran over one of the outlaw dogs. It had crawled up and hidden in a clump of greasewood and he would have ridden past it had it not lost its nerve at the last moment and bolted. He reined the horse around so hard he nearly lost a stirrup. Billy came up on his right and passed him and the dog cut back and tried to cross in front of his horse and as it did so Billy rode it down and leaned and roped it and the horse squatted and slid to a stop in a boil of dust and the dog went sailing and bounced and skidded and then scrambled up and stood looking about. Billy turned his horse and pulled the dog down but it got up again and began to run at the end of the rope. When John Grady went past the dog was standing and twisting and pawing at the rope but Billy put his heels to the horse and the dog was snatched away. Out on the floodplain Joaquín was sawing his horse about and whooping and the dogs were scattered and baying and fighting. Travis rode up swinging his loop and John Grady reined to one side but the dog he was after cut in front of the horse and suddenly appeared in front of him. He put the horse after it and the dog tried to cut back but he swung his loop and dallied and reined the horse to the right. The dog spun in the air and landed and rose running and turned and was snatched up again. John Grady spurred the dun forward and the dog went bouncing and slamming mutely in a wide arc and then went dragging through the brush and gravel behind him.

He came back trailing the empty rope, paying it up and recoiling it as he rode. Travis and Joaquín and Billy were sitting the horses and letting them blow. The second cast of hounds were now tracking the dogs along the lower end of the floodplain, running them down among the boulders and scree and fighting and going on again. Joaquín was grinning.

I hogged your all's dog, I reckon, John Grady said.

Plenty of dogs, Joaquín said.

Watch JC, Billy said. Watch him now. He looks like he's fightin bees.

How many of these damn dogs are there?

I dont know. Archer started up a whole other bunch yonder where that big wash comes out.

Have they caught any?

I dont think so. Troy's afoot up in them rocks.

Two hounds appeared out of the chaparral and circled and sniffed the ground and stood uncertainly.

Hyeah, called Travis. Hunt em up.

Well pardner if your horse aint bottomed out completely why dont we ride on down there where the fun's at?

Billy booted his horse forward. You aint waitin on me, he said.

You all go on, said Travis. I'll catch you up.

Dogropers, called Billy. I knew it'd come to this.

Joaquín grinned and pressed his horse into a lope and raised one fist over his head. Adelante, muchachos, he called.

Perreros.

Tonteros.

Travis watched them go. He shook his head and leaned and spat and turned his horse to ride up toward where he'd last seen Archer.

Where they came up off the desert parkland there were great boulders fallen from the mesa above and they rode up the slope among them until John Grady halted his horse and held up his hand. They stopped to listen. John Grady stood in the saddle and scanned the slope above them. Billy rode up.

I think they're headed up towards the top of the mesa.

I do too.

Can they get up there?

I dont know. Probably. They seem to think so.

Can you see them?

No. There was one big yellow son of a bitch and another kindly spotted one. There may be three or four of em.

I guess they've thrown the dogs, aint they?

It looks like it.

You think we can get up there?

I think I might know a way.

Billy squinted up at the stone ramparts. He leaned and spat. I'd hate to get a horse half way up that draw and not be able to go either way.

So would I.

Plus I dont know how much good we're goin to do runnin these varmints without dogs. Do you?

We just need to get up there before they get gone. It's pretty open country up on top.

Well, lead on then.

All right.

Let's not get in too big a hurry.

All right.

Let's just cover the ground in front of us. Let's not get in a jackpot up here.

All right.

He followed John Grady back down the way they'd come and they rode for the better part of a mile and then turned up along the wash. The way grew steep, the path more narrow. They dismounted and led the horses. They crossed gray bands of midden soil from ancient campsites washed down out of the arroyo that carried bits of bone and pottery and they passed under pictographs upon the rimland boulders that bore images of hunter and shaman and meetingfires and desert sheep all picked into the rock a thousand years and more. They passed beneath a band of dancers holding hands like paper figures scissored out by children and stenciled on the stone. Under the caprock was a running shelf and they turned and looked back down over the floodplain and the desert. Troy was riding out toward Travis and JC and Archer and they were crossing toward the truck with most of the dogs in tow. They couldnt see Joaquín anywhere. In the distance they could see the highway through a gap in the low hills fifteen miles away. The horses stood blowing.

Where to now, cowboy? said Billy.

John Grady nodded toward the country above them and set out again leading the horse.

The shelf narrowed upward to a break in the strata of the rock and they led the horses into a defile so narrow that Billy's horse balked and would not follow. It backed and jerked at the bridlereins and skittered dangerously on the shales. Billy looked up the narrow passageway. The sheer rock walls rose up into the blue sky.

Bud are you real sure about this?

John Grady had dropped the reins on the blue horse and he peeled out of his jacket and made his way back to Billy.

Take my horse, he said.

What?

Take my horse. Or Watson's. He's been through here before.

He took the reins from Billy and calmed the horse and tied the jacket by the sleeves over the horse's eyes, leaning against the animal with his whole body. Billy worked his way up to where the dun horse stood and took up the reins and led it on up through the rocks, the horse scrabbling in the shale, the loose spurs clinking off the stone. At the top of the defile the horses lunged and clambered up and out onto the mesa and stood trembling and blowing. John Grady pulled the jacket off the horse's head and the horse blew and looked about. A mile away on the mesa three of the dogs were loping and looking back.

You want to ride that good horse? said John Grady.

Let me ride this good horse.

Well yonder they go.

They set off across the open tableland with their ropes popping and loud cries, leaning low in the saddle, riding neck and neck. In a mile they'd halved the dogs' lead. The dogs kept to the mesa and the mesa widened before them. If they'd kept to the rim they might have found a place to go down again where the horses could not follow but they seemed to think they could outrun anything that cared to follow and run they did, two of them side by side and the third behind, their long dogshadows beside them in the sun racing brokenly over the sparse taupe grass of the tableland.

Billy overhauled them on the dun horse before they could separate and leaned and roped the hindmost dog. He didnt even dally the rope but just caught two turns about his wrist and gave a yank and snatched the dog from the ground and rode on dragging it behind the horse with the rope in one hand.

He overtook the dogs again and rode past so as to head them. The running dogs looked up, their eyes lost, their tongues lolling. Their dead companion came sliding up beside them at the end of the trailing rope. Billy looked back and reined the horse to the right and dragged the dead dog in front of them and headed them in a long running arc. John Grady was coming hard across the mesa and Billy brought the dun horse to a halt in a series of hops and jumped down and freed his noose from the dog and rewound it on the run and mounted up again.

He reached the dogs first and snapped his loop around the big yellow dog in the lead. The speckled dog cut back almost under the horse's legs and headed toward the rim. The yellow dog rolled and bounced and got up again and continued running with the noose about its neck. John Grady came riding up behind Billy and swung his rope and heeled the yellow dog and quirted the horse on with the doubled rope end and then dallied. The slack of Billy's catchrope hissed along the ground and stopped and the big yellow dog rose suddenly from the ground in headlong flight taut between the two ropes and the ropes resonated a single brief dull note and then the dog exploded.

The sun was not an hour up and in the flat traverse of the light on the mesa the blood that burst in the air before them was as bright and unexpected as an apparition. Something evoked out of nothing and wholly unaccountable. The dog's head went cartwheeling, the ropes recoiled in the air, the dog's body slammed to the ground with a dull thud.

Goddamn, said Billy.

There was a long whoop from down the mesa. Joaquín was riding toward them with three of the blueticks. He'd seen them heel and head the dog and he waved his hat laughing. The hounds loped beside the horse. They still hadnt seen the spotted dog making for the rim of the mesa.

Ayeee muchachos, called Joaquín. He whooped and laughed

and leaned and hazed his hat at the heeling dogs.

Damn, said Billy. I didnt know you was goin to do that.

I didnt either.

Son of a bitch. He hauled his rope toward him, coiling it as it came. John Grady rode out to where the dog's headless body lay in the bloodstained grass and dismounted and freed his rope from the animal's hindquarters and mounted up again. The hounds came up circling the carcass and sniffing at the blood with their hackles up. One of them circled John Grady's horse and then backed and stood baying him but he paid it no mind. He coiled his rope and turned and dug his heels into the horse's flanks and set out across the mesa after the lone remaining dog. Joaquín by now had also seen the dog and he came riding after it, quirting his horse with the doubled rope and shouting to the dogs. Billy sat watching them go. He coiled the rope and tied it and wiped the blood from his hands on the leg of his jeans and then sat watching the race head out along the edge of the mesa. The spotted dog seemed to see no way down from the table-land and it looked to be tiring as it loped along the rim. When it heard the hounds it turned upcountry again and crossed behind Joaquín and Joaquín brought his horse around and in a flat race overtook it and roped it in less than a mile of ground. Billy rode out to the rimrock and dismounted and lit a cigarette and sat looking out over the country to the south.

They came riding back across the mesa with the hounds at the horses' heels. Joaquín trailed the dead dog through the grass at the end of his rope. The dog was bloody and half raw and its eyes were glazed and its lolling tongue was stuck with chaff and grass. They rode up to the rimrock and Joaquín dismounted and retrieved his rope from the dead dog.

Got some pups here somewhere, he said.

Billy walked up and stood looking at the dog. It was a bitch with swollen teats. He walked over and got his horse and mounted up and looked back at John Grady.

Let's take that long way back. Crawlin through them rocks gives me the fidgets.

John Grady had taken off his hat and set it in the fork of the saddle before him. His face was streaked with blood and there was blood on his shirt. He passed the back of his sleeve across his forehead and picked up his hat and put it on again. That's all right by me, he said. Joaquín?

Sure, said Joaquín. He eyed the sun. We'll be back for dinner.

You think we got em all?

Hard to say.

I'd say we broke a few of em of their habits.

I'd say we did too.

How many of Archer's dogs come up here with you?

Three.

Well we aint got but two.

They turned in their saddles and scanned the mesa.

Where do you reckon he's got to?

I dont know, said Joaquín.

He could of gone down the far side yonder.

Joaquín leaned and spat and turned his horse. Let's go, he said. He could be anywheres. There's always one that dont want to go home.

IT WAS STILL DARK in the morning when John Grady woke him. He groaned and turned and put the pillow over his head.

Wake up, cowboy.

What the hell time is it?

Five-thirty.

What's wrong with you?

You want to see if we can find them dogs?

Dogs? What dogs? What the hell are you talkin about?

Them pups.

Shit, said Billy.

John Grady sat in the doorway and propped one boot against the frame. Billy? he said.

What, damn it.

We could ride up there and take a look around.

He rolled over and looked at John Grady sitting sideways in the door in the dark. You're makin me completely crazy, he said.

Cut for sign. I guarantee you we could find em.

You couldnt find em.

We could get a couple of dogs from Travis.

Travis wont loan his dogs. We done been through all that.

I know about where that den's at.

Why wont you let me sleep?

We could be back by dinnertime. I guarantee you.

I'm beggin you to leave me alone, son. Beggin you. I dont want to have to shoot you. I'd never hear the end of it from Mac.

Where the dogs struck that first time just below that big slide of gravel? I'll bet we rode within fifty feet of that den. You know they're in those big rocks.

THEY RODE OUT carrying across the pommels of their saddles a longhanded spade, a mattock, a fourfoot iron prybar. Socorro had come to her door in wrapper and hairpapers while they were finding something to eat and shooed them to the table while she cooked eggs and sausage and made coffee. She packed their lunch while they ate.

Billy looked out the window to where the horses stood saddled at the kitchen door. Let's eat and get gone, he said. And do not tell her where we're goin.

All right.

I dont want to have to listen to it.

They crossed into the Valenciana pasture before the sun was up and rode past the old well. The cattle moved off before them in the gray half-light. Billy rode with the spade over his shoulder. I'll tell you one thing, he said.

What's that.

There's places up in them rocks where if they are denned you damn sure wont dig em out.

Yeah. I know it.

When they reached the trail along the western edge of the floodplain the sun was up behind the mesa and the light that overshot the plain crossed to the rocks above them so that they rode out the remnant night in a deep blue sink with the new day falling slowly down about them. They rode to the upper end and came back slowly, Billy in the lead studying the ground at either side of the horse, leaning with his forearm across the horse's withers.

Are you a tracker? said John Grady.

I'm a trackin fool. I can track lowflyin birds.

What do you see?

Not a damn thing.

The sun came down the rocks and over the broken ground toward them. They sat the horses.

They been runnin these cowtracks, Billy said. Or did run. I dont think they were all denned together. I think there was two separate bunches.

That could be.

Any close place like that right yonder?

Yeah?

There's doghair on ever rock. Let's just circle up here and keep our eyes open.

They came back up the valley close under the wall among the boulders and scree. They circled among the rocks and studied the ground. It was weeks since the last rain and what dogtracks had been printed in the clay trails below them had long since been trodden out by the cattle and in the dry ground the dogs made no track at all.

Let's go back up here, said Billy.

They rode along the upper slope close under the rock bluffs. They crossed the gravel slide and rode under the old shamans and the ledgerless arcana inscribed upon those outsize tablets.

I know where they're at, Billy said.

He turned the horse on the narrow trail and rode back down through the rocks. John Grady followed. Billy halted and dropped the reins and stood down. He passed afoot through a narrow place in the rocks and then he came back out again and pointed down the hill.

They've come in here from three sides, he said. Down yonder the cows have come right up to the rocks but they cant get in. See that tall grass?

I see it.

Reason it's tall is the cows couldnt get in there to eat it.

John Grady dismounted and followed him into the rocks. They walked up and back and they studied the ground. The horses stood looking in.

Let's just set a while, said Billy.

They sat. Within the rocks it was cool. The ground was cold. Billy smoked.

I hear em, John Grady said.

I do too.

They rose and stood listening. The mewling stopped. Then it began again.

The den was in a corner of the rocks and it angled back under a boulder. They lay on their bellies in the grass and listened.

I can smell em, Billy said.

I can too.

They listened.

How are we goin to get em out?

Billy looked at him. You aint, he said.

Maybe they'll come out.

What for?

We could get some milk and set it out for them.

I dont think they'll come out. Listen at how young they are. I'll bet their eyes aint open. What do you want with em anyway? he said.

I dont know. I hate leavin em down there.

We might could twist em out. Get a ocotillo long enough.

John Grady lay peering into the darkness under the rock. Let me have your cigarette, he said.

Billy handed it across.

There's another entrance, John Grady said. There's air blowin out of this one. See the smoke?

Billy reached and took the cigarette. Yeah, he said. But the den is still under that rock and the rock's the size of Mac's kitchen.

A kid could crawl down in there.

Where you goin to get a kid at? And suppose he got stuck down in there?

You could tie a rope to his legs.

They'd tie one to your neck if anything happened to him. Let me have your knife.

John Grady handed him his pocketknife and he rose and went off and after a while he came back with an ocotillo branch. It was a good ten feet long and he sat and trimmed the thorns off the lower couple of feet for a handhold and then they lay and took turns for the next half hour with the ocotillo down in the hole turning it in an effort to twist up the fur of the pups in the thorns.

We dont even know if this is long enough, Billy said.

I think what it is is that the hole's too big down there. You'd have to run the end of it underneath them some way to do any good and that would just be luck.

I aint heard one of em squeal for a while.

They might of moved back in a corner or somethin.

Billy sat up and pulled the ocotillo out of the hole and examined the end of it.

Is there any hair on it?

Yeah. Some. But there probably aint no shortage of hair down there.

What do you think that rock weighs?

Shit, said Billy.

All we'd have to do is tip it over.

I'll bet that damn rock weighs five tons. How in the hell are you goin to tip it over?

I dont believe it would be all that hard.

And where you goin to tip it to?

We could tip it this way.

Then it'd be layin over the hole.

So what? The pups are at the back.

What makes you so bullheaded? You cant get the horses in here and if you could they'd pull the damn rock over on top of theirselves.

They wouldnt have to be in here. They could be outside.

The ropes wont reach.

They will if we tie em end to end.

They still wont. It'd take near one just to go around the rock.

I think I can make it reach.

You got a ropestretcher in your saddlebags? Anyway, no two horses could tip that rock over.

They could with some leverage.

Bullheaded, Billy said. Worst case I believe I ever saw.

There's some fairsized saplin trees at the upper end of the wash. If we could cut one of em with the mattock we could use it for a prypole. Then we could tie the rope to the end of it and that would save havin to tie it around the rock. We'd be killin two birds with one stone.

Two horses and two cowboys is more like it.

We should of brought a axe.

You let me know when you're ready to go back. I'm goin to see if I can catch me a little nap.

All right.

John Grady rode up to the wash with the mattock across the saddle in front of him. Billy stretched out and crossed his boots one over the top of the other and pulled his hat over his face. It was totally silent in the basin. No wind, no bird. No call of cattle. He was almost asleep when he heard the first dull chock of the mattock blade. He smiled into the darkness of his hatcrown and slept.

When John Grady came back he was dragging behind the horse a cottonwood sapling he'd topped out and limbed. It was about eighteen feet long and close to six inches in diameter at the base and the weight of it hanging by the loop of rope from the saddlehorn was pulling his saddle over. He rode half standing in the offside stirrup with his left leg hanging over the sapling trunk and the horse was walking on eggshells. When he reached the rocks he stepped down and unlooped the rope and let the pole down on the ground and walked in and kicked Billy's bootsole.

Wake up and piss, he said. The world's on fire.

Let the son of a bitch burn.

Come on and give me a hand.

Billy shoved the hat back from his face and looked up. All right, he said.

They tied John Grady's catchrope to the end of the pole and stood it up behind the rock and made a cairn of rocks to bridge between the butt of it and the next ledge of rock up the slope. Then John Grady joined the home ends of the two reatas with a running splice and looped a broad Y in the end of Billy's rope that would afford loops for both pommels. They stood the horses side by side and dropped the loops over the horns and looked up at the rope bellying down from the end of the pole and they looked at each other and then they untracted the horses and walked them forward by the cheekstraps. The rope stretched taut. The pole bowed. They talked the horses forward and the horses leaned into their work. Billy looked up at the rope. If that sumbuck breaks, he said, we're goin to be huntin a hole.

The pole sawed suddenly sideways and stopped again and stood quivering.

Shit, said Billy.

I hear you. If that thing comes out of there you'll be huntin more than a hole.

We'll be huntin a undertaker.

What do you want to do?

It's your show, cowboy.

John Grady walked around and checked the pole and came back. Let's head the horses a little bit more to the left, he said.

All right.

They eased the horses forward. The rope stretched and began to unwind slowly on its axis. They looked at the rope and they looked at the horses. They looked at each other. Then the rock moved. It began to rear haltingly up out of its resting place these thousand years and it tilted and tottered and fell forward into the little grotto with a thud they could feel through their bootsoles. The pole clattered among the rocks, the horses recovered and stood.

Kiss my ass, said Billy.

They set to digging in the bare sunless earth that the rock had vacated and in twenty minutes they'd uncovered the den. The pups were back in the farthest corner huddled in a pile. John Grady lay on his stomach and reached down and back and brought one out and held it to the light. It just filled the palm of his hand and it was fat and it swung its small muzzle about and whined and blinked its pale blue eyes.

Hold him.

How many are they?

I dont know.

He ran his arm down the hole again and reached back and brought out another. Billy sat and piled the dogs together in the crook of his knee as they came. There were four of them. I'll bet these little shits are hungry, he said. Is that all of em?

John Grady lay with his cheek in the dirt. I think that's them, he said.

The dogs were trying to hide under Billy's knee. He held one up by its small nape. It hung like a sock, glaring bleakly at the world with its watery eyes.

Listen a minute, said John Grady.

They sat listening.

There's anothern.

He ran his arm down the hole and lay on the ground feeling

about in the dark beneath them. He closed his eyes. I got him, he said.

The dog he brought up was dead.

Yonder's your runt, Billy said.

The little dog was curled and stiff, its paws before its face. He put it down and pushed his shoulder deeper into the hole.

Can you find him?

No.

Billy stood. Let me try, he said. My arm's longern yours.

All right.

Billy lay in the dirt and ran his arm down into the hole. Come here you little turd, he said.

Have you got him?

Yeah. Damn if I dont think he's offerin to bite me.

The dog came up mewling and twisting in his hand.

This aint no runt, he said.

Let me see him.

He's fat as a butterball.

John Grady took the little dog and held it in his cupped hand.

Wonder what was he doin off back there by himself?

Maybe he was with the one that died.

John Grady held the dog up and looked into its small wrinkled face. I think I got me a dog, he said.

HE WORKED all through the month of December at the cabin. He carried tools horseback up the Bell Springs trail and he left a mattock and a spade beside the road and worked on the roadway by hand in the evenings when it was cool, filling the washes and cutting brush and ditching and filling in the gullies and squatting and eyeing the terrain for the way the water would run. In three weeks' time he had the worst of the trash hauled or burned and he had painted the stove and patched the roof and driven the truck for the first time up the old road all the way to the cabin with the new lengths of blue sheetmetal stovepipe in the truckbed and the cans of paint and whitewash and new pine shelving for the kitchen.

At the wreckingyard out on Alameda he went up and down the aisles of old stacked windowsash with a steel tape measuring by height and width and checking figures against those he'd jotted on the notepad in his shirtpocket. He dragged the windows he wanted out into the aisle and got the truck and backed it to the door and he and the yardman loaded the windows in the truck. The man sold him some panes of glass to replace the broken ones and showed him how to score and break them with a glasscutter and then gave him the glasscutter.

He bought an old Mennonite kitchen table made of pine and the man helped him carry it out and set it in the bed of the truck and the man told him to take the drawer out and stand it in the bed.

You go around a curve it'll come out of there.

Yessir.

Liable to go plumb overboard.

Yessir.

And take that glass and put it up there in the cab with you if you dont want it broke.

All right.

I'll see you.

Yessir.

He worked long into the nights and he'd come in and unsaddle the horse and brush it in the partial darkness of the barn bay and walk across to the kitchen and get his supper out of the warmer and sit and eat alone at the table by the shaded light of the lamp and listen to the faultless chronicling of the ancient clockworks in the hallway and the ancient silence of the desert in the darkness about. There were times he'd fall asleep in the chair and wake at some strange hour and stagger up and cross the yard to the barn and get the pup and take it and put it in its box on the floor beside his bunk and lie face down with his arm over the side of the bunk and his hand in the box so that it would not cry and then fall asleep in his clothes.

Christmas came and went. In the afternoon of the first Sunday in January Billy rode up and crossed the little creek and halloed the house and stood down. John Grady came to the door.

What are you doin? Billy said.

Paintin windowsash.

Billy nodded. He looked about. You aint goin to ask me in?

John Grady passed his sleeve along the side of his nose. He had a paintbrush in one hand and his hands were blue. I didnt know I had to, he said. Come on in.

Billy came in and stood. He took a cigarette from his pocket and lit it and looked around. He walked into the other room and he came back. The adobe brick walls had been whitewashed and the inside of the little house was bright and monastically austere. The clay floors were swept and slaked and he'd beaten them down with a homemade maul contrived from a fencepost with a section of board nailed to the bottom.

The old place dont look half bad. You aim to get you a santo to put in the corner yonder?

I might.

Billy nodded.

I'll take all the help I can get, John Grady said.

I hear you, said Billy. He looked at the bright blue of the sash of the windows. Did they not have any blue paint? he said.

They said this was about as close as they could get.

You fixin to paint the door the same color?

Yep.

You got another brush?

Yeah. I got one.

Billy took off his hat and hung it on one of the pegs by the door. Well, he said. Where's it at?

John Grady poured paint from his paintcan into an empty one and Billy squatted on one knee and stirred the brush into the paint. He passed the flat of the brush carefully across the rim of the can and painted a bright blue band down the center stile. He looked across his shoulder.

How come you to have a extra brush?

Just in case some fool showed up wantin to paint, I reckon.

They quit before dark. A cool wind was coming down from the gap in the Jarillas. They stood by the truck and Billy smoked and they watched the running fire deepening to darkness over the mountains to the west.

It's goin to be cold up here in the wintertime, pardner, Billy said.

I know it.

Cold and lonely.

It wont be lonely.

I'm talkin about her.

Mac says she can come down and work with Socorro whenever she wants.

Well that's good. I dont expect there'll be a lot of empty chairs at the table on them days.

John Grady smiled. I expect you're right.

When have you seen her?

Not for a while.

How long a while?

I dont know. Three weeks.

Billy shook his head.

She's still there, John Grady said.

You got a lot of confidence in her.

Yes I do.

What do you think is goin to happen when her and Socorro get their heads together?

She dont tell everthing she knows.

Her or Socorro?

Either one.

I hope you're right.

They aint goin to run her off, Billy. There's more to her than just she's good lookin.

Billy flipped the cigarette out across the yard. We better get on back.

You can take the truck if you want.

That's all right.

Go on. I'll ride that old crowbait of yours.

Billy nodded. Ride him blind through the brush tryin to beat me back. Get him snakebit and I dont know what all.

Go on. I'll ride behind the truck.

Horse like that it takes a special hand to ride him in the dark.

I'll bet it does.

A rider that can instill confidence in a animal.

John Grady smiled and shook his head.

A rider that's accustomed to the ways and the needs of the nighthorse. Ride the bedgrounds slow. Ride left to right. Sing to them snuffies. Dont pop no matches.

I hear you.

Did your grandaddy used to talk about goin up the trail?

Some. Yeah.

You think you'll ever go back to that country?

I doubt it.

You will. One of these days. Or I say you will. If you live.

You want to take the truck back?

Naw. Go on. I'll be along.

All right.

Dont eat my dessert.

All right. I appreciate you comin up.

I didnt have nothin else to do.

Well.

If I had I'd of done it.

I'll see you at the house.

See you at the house.

JOSEFINA WAS STANDING in the door watching. In the room the criada turned, one hand lofting the weight of the girl's dark hair for her to see.

Bueno, said Josefina. Muy bonita.

The criada smiled thinly, her mouth bristling with hairpins. Josefina looked back down the hall and then leaned in the door.

Él viene, she whispered. Then she turned and padded away down the corridor. The criada turned the girl quickly and studied her and touched her hair and stood back. She passed her thumb across her lips gathering the pins. Eres la china poblana perfecta, she said. Perfecta.

Es bella la china poblana? the girl said.

The criada arched her brows in surprise. The wrinkled lid fluttered over the pale blind eye. Sí, she said. Sí. Por supuesto. Todo el mundo lo sabe.

Eduardo stood in the doorway. The criada saw the girl's eyes and turned. He jerked his chin at her and she went to the dresser and laid down the hairbrush and put the pins in a china tray and went past him and out the door.

He came in and shut the door behind him. The girl stood quietly in the center of the room.

Voltéate, he said. He made a stirring motion with his forefinger.

She turned.

Ven aquí.

She came slowly forward and stood. He took her jaw in the palm of his hand and raised her face and looked into her painted eyes. When she lowered it again he put his hand into the gathered hair at her neck and pulled her head back. She turned her eyes up toward the ceiling. Her pale throat exposed. The visible bloodpulse in the thick arteries at either side of her neck and the small tic at the corner of her mouth. He told her to look at him and she did but she seemed to have power to cause those dark and hooded eyes of hers to go opaque. So that the visible depth in them was lost or shrouded. So that they hid the world within. He recaught his grip in her hair and the smooth skin tautened over her cheekbones and her eyes widened. He commanded again that she look at him but she was already looking at him and she did not answer.

A quién le rezas? he hissed.

A Dios.

Quién responde?

Nadie.

Nadie, he said.

That night she felt the cold pneuma come upon her as she lay naked in the bed. She turned and called to the cliente standing in the room.

I'm bein as quick as I can, he said.

By the time he'd slid into the bed beside her she'd cried out and gone rigid and her eyes white. In the muted light he could not see her but he placed his hand on her body and felt her bowed and trembling under his palm and taut as a snaredrum. He felt the tremor of her like the hum of a current running in her bones.

What is it? he said. What is it?

He came out into the hallway half dressed and pulling on his clothes. Tiburcio appeared from nowhere. He pushed the man aside and knelt in the girl's bed and unbuckled his belt and whipped it from about his waist and caught it and folded it and seized the girl's jaw and forced the leather between her teeth. The cliente watched from the doorway. I didnt do nothin, he said. I never even touched her.

Tiburcio rose and strode toward the door.

She just went that way, the cliente said.

Speak to no one, Tiburcio said. You understand me?

You got it, old buddy. Just you let me get my shoes.

The alcahuete shut the door after him. The girl was breathing harshly through the belt. He sat and pulled back the covers. He studied her without expression. He bent over her slightly in his black silk. The soft false whisper of it. A morbid voyeur, a mortician. An incubus of uncertain proclivity or perhaps just a dark dandy happened in from off the neon streets who aped imperfectly with his pale and tapered hands those ministrations of the healing arts that he had seen or heard of or as he imagined them to be. What are you? he said. You are nothing.

WHEN HE STEPPED OUT onto the porch and let the screen-door to behind him Mr Johnson was sitting on the edge of the porch with his elbows propped on his knees watching the sunset where it deepened and flared over the Franklins to the west. Distant flocks of geese were moving downriver along the jornada. They looked no more than bits of string against the raucous red of the sky and they were far too distant to be heard.

Where are you off to? said the old man.

John Grady walked to the edge of the porch and stood picking his teeth and looking out across the country along with him. What makes you think I'm off to somewhere?

Hair all slicked back like a muskrat. Boots.

He sat on the boards beside the old man. Goin to town, he said.

The old man nodded. Well, he said. I reckon it's still there.

Yessir.

You couldnt prove it by me.

When was the last time you were in El Paso?

I dont know. Been a year, I'd say. Maybe longer.

You dont get tired bein out here all the time?

I do. At times.

You dont ever want to make a run in to sort of see what's goin on?

I dont believe it would help. I dont believe there's anything goin on.

Did you used to go over to Juárez?

Yes I did. Back when I was a drinkin man. The last time I was in Juárez Mexico was in nineteen and twenty-nine. I seen a man shot in a bar. He was standin at the bar drinkin a beer and this man come in and walked up behind him and pulled a government forty-five out of his belt and shot him in the back of the head with it. Stuck the gun back in his breeches and turned and walked out again. He wasnt even in a hurry about it.

Shot him dead?

Yes. He was dead standin there. Thing I remember is how quick he fell down. Just dead weight. The movies dont ever get that part right neither.

Where were you?

I was standin almost next to him. I seen it in the bar mirror. I'm partially deaf to this day in this one ear on account of it. His head just damn near come off. Blood everwhere. Brains. I had on a brand new Stradivarius gabardine shirt and a pretty good Stetson hat and I burned everthing I had on save the boots. I bet I took nine baths handrunnin.

He looked out across the country to the west where the sky was darkening. Tales of the old west, he said.

Yessir.

Lot of people shot and killed.

Why were they?

Mr Johnson passed the tips of his fingers across his jaw. Well, he said. I think these people mostly come from Tennessee and Kentucky. Edgefield district in South Carolina. Southern Missouri. They were mountain people. They come from mountain people in the old country. They always would shoot you. It wasnt just here. They kept comin west and about the time they got here was about the time Sam Colt invented the sixshooter and it was the first time these people could afford a gun you could carry around in your belt. That's all there ever was to it. It had nothin to do with the country at all. The west. They'd of been the same it dont matter where they might of wound up. I've thought about it and that's the only conclusion I could ever come to.

How bad of a drinkin man did you used to be, Mr Johnson? If you dont care for me to ask.

Pretty bad. Maybe not as bad as some might like to remember it. But it was more than a passin acquaintance.

Yessir.

You can ask whatever you want.

Yessir.

You get my age you kindly get weaned off standin on ceremony. I think it embarrasses Mac at times. But dont worry about askin me stuff.

Yessir. Was that when you quit drinkin?

No. I was more dedicated than that. I quit and took it up again. Quit and took it up. Finally got around to quittin all together. Maybe I just got too old for it. There wasnt any virtue in it.

The drinkin or the quittin?

Either one. There aint no virtue in quittin what you aint able any longer to do in the first place. That's pretty, aint it.

He nodded toward the sunset. Deep laminar red. The cool of the coming dark was in it and it was all around them.

Yessir, said John Grady. It is.

The old man took his cigarettes from his shirtpocket. John Grady smiled. I see you aint quit smokin, he said.

I intend to be buried with a pack in my pocket.

You think you'll need em on the other side?

Not really. A man can hope though.

He watched the sky. Where do bats go in the wintertime? They got to eat.

I think maybe they migrate.

I hope so.

Do you think I ought to get married?

Hell, son. How would I know?

You never did.

That dont mean I didnt try.

What happened?

She wouldnt have me.

Why not?

I was too broke for her. Or maybe for her daddy. I dont know.

What happened to her?

It was a peculiar thing. She went on and married another old boy and she died in childbirth. It was not uncommon in them days. She was a awful pretty girl. Woman. I dont think she'd turned twenty. I think about her yet.

The last of the colors died in the west. The sky was dark and blue. Then just dark. The kitchen windowlights lay across the porch boards beside them where they sat.

I miss knowin whatever become of certain people. Where they're livin at and how they're gettin on or where they died at if they did die. I think about old Bill Reed. Sometimes I'll say to myself, I'll say: I wonder whatever happened to old Bill Reed? I dont reckon I'll ever know. Me and him was good friends, too.

What else?

What else what?

What else do you miss?

The old man shook his head. You dont want to get me started.

A lot?

Not all of it. I dont miss pullin a tooth with a pair of shoein tongs and nothin but cold wellwater to numb it. But I miss the old range life. I went up the trail four times. Best times of my life. The best. Bein out. Seein new country. There's nothin like it in the world. There never will be. Settin around the fire of the evenin with the herd bedded down good and no wind. Get you some coffee. Listen to the old waddies tell their stories. Good stories, too. Roll you a smoke. Sleep. There's no sleep like it. None.

He flipped the cigarette out into the dark. Socorro opened the door and looked out. Mr Johnson, she said, you ought to come in. It is too cold for you.

I'll be in directly.

I better go on I guess, John Grady said.

Dont keep one waitin, the old man said. They wont tolerate it.

Yessir.

Go on then.

He rose. Socorro had gone back in. He looked down at the old man. Still you dont think it's all that good a idea, do you?

What dont I think?

About gettin married.

I never said that.

Do you think it?

I think you ought to follow your heart, the old man said.
That's all I ever thought about anything.

Going up Juárez Avenue among the crowds of tourists he
saw the shineboy at his corner and waved a hand to him.

I guess you're on your way to see your girl, the boy said.

No. I'm goin to see a friend of mine.

Is she still your novia?

Yes she is.

When you gettin married?

Pretty soon.

Did you ask her?

Yes.

She said yes?

She did.

The boy grinned. Otro más de los perdidos, he said.

Otro más.

Ándale pues, the boy said. I cant help you now.

He entered the Moderno and took off his hat and hung it
among the hats and instruments along the long wallrack by the
door and he took a table next to the one reserved for the maestro. The barman nodded to him across the room and raised one
hand. Buenas tardes, he called.

Buenas tardes, said John Grady. He folded his hands before
him on the tabletop. Two of the ancient musicians in their dull
black stage suits were sitting at a table in the corner and they
nodded to him politely who was a friend to the maestro and he
nodded back and the waiter came across the concrete floor in
his white apron and greeted him. He ordered a tequila and the
waiter bowed. As if the decision were a grave one well taken.
From outside in the street came the cries of children, the calls
of vendors. A square shaft of light fell slant from the barred
streetwindow above him and terminated out on the floor in a

pale trapezoid. In the center of it like a thing displayed in a bent and veering cage sat a large lemoncolored housecat washing itself. It shook its head and yawned. It turned and looked at him. The waiter brought the tequila.

He wet the top of his fist with his tongue and poured on salt from a tableshaker and he sipped the tequila and took a wedge of sliced lemon from the dish and crushed it between his teeth and laid it back in the dish and licked the salt from his fist. Then he took another sip of the tequila. The musicians watched him, sitting quietly.

He drank the tequila and ordered another. The cat was gone. The cage of light moved across the floor. After a while it started up the wall. The waiter had turned on the lights in the other room and a third musician had come in and joined the first two. Then the maestro entered with his daughter.

The waiter came over and helped him with his coat and held the chair. They spoke briefly and the waiter nodded and smiled at the girl and carried away the maestro's coat and hung it up. The girl turned slightly in her chair and looked at John Grady.

Cómo estás? she said.

Bien. Y tú?

Bien, gracias.

The blind man had tilted archly in his chair listening. Good evening, he said. Will you join us please?

Thank you. Yes. I would like to.

Then you must.

He pushed back his chair and rose. The maestro smiled at his approach and held out his hand into the darkness.

How are you?

Fine, thank you.

The blind man spoke to the girl in spanish. He shook his head. María is shy, he said. Por qué no hablas inglés con nuestro amigo? You see. She will not. It is of no use. Where is the waiter? What will you have please?

The waiter brought the drinks and the maestro ordered for

his guest. He put his hand on the girl's arm for her to wait till all were served. When the waiter had gone he turned. Now, he said. What has happened?

I asked her to marry me.

She has refused? Tell me.

No. She accepted.

But so solemn. You gave us a scare.

The girl rolled up her eyes and looked away. John Grady had no idea what it meant.

I came to ask you a favor.

Of course, said the maestro. By all means.

She has no family. No sponsor. I would like for you to be her padrino.

Ah, said the maestro. He put his folded hands to his chin and then placed them on the table again. They waited.

I am honored of course. But this is a serious matter. You understand.

Yes. I understand.

You will be living in America.

Yes.

America, the maestro said. Yes.

They sat. The blind man in his silence was twice silent. Even the three musicians in the corner were watching him. They could not hear what he was saying but they seemed to be waiting also for him to continue.

The office of the padrino is not a mere ceremony, he said. It is not some gesture of kinship or some way to bind friends.

Yes. I understand.

It is a serious matter and it is no insult that a man should refuse to accept it if his reasons are honorable.

Yessir.

One needs to be logical in these matters.

The maestro raised one hand before him and spread his fingers and he held it there. Like an evocation perhaps, or a gesture of fending away. Had he not been blind he would simply have been studying his nails. My health is poor, he said. But even were that not so this girl will be making a new life and she should have counsel in her new country. Dont you think this would be best?

I dont know. I feel like she needs all the help she can get.

Yes. Of course.

Is it because of your sight?

The blind man lowered his hand. No, he said. It is not a matter of sight.

He waited for the blind man to continue but he did not.

Is there something you cant say in front of the girl?

The girl? said the maestro. He smiled his blind smile, he shook his head. Oh my, he said. No no. We have no secrets. An old blind father with secrets? No, that would never do.

We dont have padrinos in America, John Grady said.

The waiter came and set John Grady's drink in front of him and the maestro thanked the waiter and slid his fingers across the wood of the table until they touched his own glass.

I drink to the boda, he said.

Gracias.

They drank. The girl bent down the straw in her bottle of refresco and leaned and sipped.

If a person could be found, said the maestro, of intelligence and heart, then perhaps the office could be explained to him. What do you think?

I think you are that person.

The blind man sipped his wine and set the glass back in the very ring upon the table it had vacated and folded his hands in thought.

Let me say this to you, he said.

Yessir.

In a matter such as this, once one is asked he is already responsible. Even should he refuse.

I'm just thinking about her.

I too.

She doesnt have anyone else. She has no friends.

But the padrino does not need to be a friend.

He has to be something.

He has to be a man of character who is willing to undertake certain duties. That is all. He could be a friend or not. He could be a rival from another house. He could be one to reunite families distanced by intrigue or bad blood or politics. You understand. He could be one with little connection to the family even. He could even be an enemy.

An enemy?

Yes. I know of such a case. In this very city.

Why would a man want an enemy for a padrino?

For the best of reasons. Or the worst. This man of whom we speak was a dying man when his lastborn came into the world. A son. His only son. So what did he do? He called upon that man who once had been a friend to him but now was his sworn enemy and he asked that man to be padrino to his son. The man refused of course. What? Are you mad? He must have been surprised. It had been years since last they spoke and their enemistad was a deep and bitter thing. Perhaps they had become enemies for the same reason they had once been friends. Which often happens in the world. But this man persisted. And he had the—how do you say—el naipe? En su manga.

The ace.

Yes. The ace up his sleeve. He told his enemy that he was dying. There was the naipe. Upon the table. The man could not refuse. All choosing was taken from his hands.

The blind man raised one hand into the smoky air in a thin upward slicing motion. Now comes the talk, he said. No end to it. Some say that the dying man wished to mend their friendship. Others that he had done this man some great injustice and wished to make amends before leaving this world forever. Others said other things. There is more than meets the eye. I say this: This man who was dying was not a man given to sentimentality. He also had lost friends to death. He was not a man given to illusions. He knew that those things we most desire to hold in our hearts are often taken from us while that which we would put away seems often by that very wish to become endowed with unsuspected powers of endurance. He knew how frail is the memory of loved ones. How we close our eyes and speak to them. How we long to hear their voices once again, and how those voices and those memories grow faint and faint until what was flesh and blood is no more than echo and shadow. In the end perhaps not even that.

He knew that our enemies by contrast seem always with us. The greater our hatred the more persistent the memory of them so that a truly terrible enemy becomes deathless. So that the man who has done you great injury or injustice makes himself a guest in your house forever. Perhaps only forgiveness can dislodge him.

Such then was this man's thinking. If we may believe the best of him. To bind the padrino to his cause with the strongest bonds he knew. And there was more. For in this appointment he also posted the world as his sentinel. The duties of a friend would come under no great scrutiny. But an enemy? You can see how nicely he has caught him in the net he has contrived. For this enemy was in fact a man of conscience. A worthy enemy. And this enemy-padrino now must carry the dying man in his heart forever. Must suffer the eyes of the world eternally on him. Such a man can scarce be said to author any longer his own path.

The father dies as die he must. The enemy become padrino now becomes the father of the child. The world is watching. It stands in for the dead man. Who by his audacity has pressed it into his service. For the world does have a conscience, however men dispute it. And while that conscience may be thought of as the sum of consciences of men there is another view, which is that it may stand alone and each man's share be but some small imperfect part of it. The man who died favored this view. As I do myself. Men may believe the world to be—what is the word? Voluble.

Fickle.

Fickle? I dont know. Voluble then. But the world is not voluble. The world is always the same. The man appointed the world as his witness that he might secure his enemy to his service. That this enemy would be faithful to his duties. That is what he did. Or that was my belief. At times I believe it yet.

How did it turn out?

Quite strangely.

The blind man reached for his glass. He drank and held the glass before him as if studying it and then he set it on the table before him once again.

Quite strangely. For the circumstance of his appointment came to elevate this man's padrinazgo to the central role of his life. It brought out what was best in him. More than best. Virtues long neglected began almost at once to blossom forth. He abandoned every vice. He even began to attend Mass. His new office seemed to have called forth from the deepest parts of his character honor and loyalty and courage and devotion. What he gained can scarcely be put into words. Who would have foreseen such a thing?

What happened? said John Grady.

The blind man smiled his pained blind smile. You smell the rat, he said.

Yes.

Quite so. It was no happy ending. Perhaps there is a moral to the tale. Perhaps not. I leave it to you.

What happened?

This man whose life was changed forever by the dying request of his enemy was ultimately ruined. The child became his life. More than his life. To say that he doted upon the child says nothing. And yet all turned out badly. Again, I believe that the intentions of the dying man were for the best. But there is another view. It would not be the first time that a father sacrificed a son.

The godchild grew up wild and restless. He became a criminal. A petty thief. A gambler. And other things. Finally, in the winter of nineteen and seven, in the town of Ojinaga, he killed a man. He was nineteen years of age. Close to your own, perhaps.

The same.

Yes. Perhaps this was his destiny. Perhaps no padrino could have saved him from himself. No father. The padrino squandered all he owned in bribes and fees. To no avail. Such a road once undertaken has no end and he died alone and poor. He was never bitter. He scarcely seemed even to consider whether he had been betrayed. He once had been a strong and even a ruthless man, but love makes men foolish. I speak as a victim myself. We are taken out of our own care and it then remains to be seen only if fate will show to us some share of mercy. Or little. Or none.

Men speak of blind destiny, a thing without scheme or purpose. But what sort of destiny is that? Each act in this world from which there can be no turning back has before it another, and it another yet. In a vast and endless net. Men imagine that the choices before them are theirs to make. But we are free to act only upon what is given. Choice is lost in the maze of generations and each act in that maze is itself an enslavement for it voids every alternative and binds one ever more tightly into the constraints that make a life. If the dead man could have forgiven his enemy for whatever wrong was done to him all would have been otherwise. Did the son set out to avenge his father? Did the dead man sacrifice his son? Our plans are predicated upon a future unknown to us. The world takes its form hourly by a weighing of things at hand, and while we may seek to puzzle out that form we have no way to do so. We have only God's law, and the wisdom to follow it if we will.

The maestro leaned forward and composed his hands before him. The wineglass stood empty and he took it up. Those who cannot see, he said, must rely upon what has gone before. If I do not wish to appear so foolish as to drink from an empty glass I must remember whether I have drained it or not. This man who became padrino. I speak of him as if he died old but he did not. He was younger than I am now. I speak as if his conscience or the world's eyes or both led him to such rigor in his duties. But those considerations quickly fell to nothing. It was for love of the child that he came to grief, if grief it was. What do you make of that?

I dont know.

Nor I. I only know that every act which has no heart will be found out in the end. Every gesture.

They sat in silence. The room was quiet about them. John Grady watched the water beading upon his glass where it sat untouched before him. The blind man set his own glass back upon the table and pushed it from him.

How well do you love this girl?

I would die for her.

The alcahuete is in love with her.

Tiburcio?

No. The grand alcahuete.

Eduardo.

Yes.

They sat quietly. In the outer hall the musicians had arrived and were assembling their instruments. John Grady sat staring at the floor. After a while he looked up.

Can the old woman be trusted?

La Tuerta?

Yes.

Oh my, said the blind man softly.

The old woman tells her that she will be married.

The old woman is Tiburcio's mother.

John Grady leaned back in his chair. He sat very quietly. He looked at the blind man's daughter. She watched him. Quiet. Kind. Inscrutable.

You did not know.

No. Does she know? Yes, of course she knows.

Yes.

Does she know that Eduardo is in love with her?

Yes.

The musicians struck up a light baroque partita. Aging dancers moved onto the floor. The blind man sat, his hands before him on the table.

She believes that Eduardo will kill her, John Grady said.

The blind man nodded.

Do you believe he will kill her?

Yes, said the maestro. I believe he will kill her.

Is that why you wont be her godfather?

Yes. That is why.

It would make you responsible.

Yes.

The dancers moved with their stiff formality over the swept and polished concrete floor. They danced with an antique grace, like figures from a film.

What do you think I should do?

I cannot advise you.

You will not.

No. I will not.

I'd give her up if I thought I could not protect her.

Perhaps.

You dont think I could.

I think the difficulties might be greater than you imagine.

What should I do.

The blind man sat. After a while he said: You must understand. I have no certainty. And it is a grave matter.

He passed his hand across the top of the table. As if he were making smooth something unseen before him. You wish for me to tell you some secret of the grand alcahuete. Betray to you some weakness. But the girl herself is the weakness.

What do you think I should do?

Pray to God.

Yes.

Will you?

No.

Why not?

I dont know.

You dont believe in Him?

It's not that.

It is that the girl is a mujerzuela.

I dont know. Maybe.

The blind man sat. They are dancing, he said.

Yes.

That is not the reason.

What's not?

That she is a whore.

No.

Would you give her up? Truly?

I dont know.

Then you would not know what to pray for.

No. I wouldnt know what to ask.

The blind man nodded. He leaned forward. He placed one elbow on the table and rested his forehead against his thumb like a confessor. He seemed to be listening to the music. You knew her before she came to the White Lake, he said.

I saw her. Yes.

At La Venada.

Yes.

As did he.

Yes. I suppose.

That is where it began.

Yes.

He is a cuchillero. A filero, as they say here. A man of a certain rigor. A serious man.

I am serious myself.

Of course. If you were not there would be no problem.

John Grady studied that passive face. Closed to the world even as the world was closed to him.

What are you telling me?

I have nothing to tell.

He is in love with her.

Yes.

But he would kill her.

Yes.

I see.

Perhaps. Let me tell you only this. Your love has no friends. You think that it does but it does not. None. Perhaps not even God.

And you?

I do not count myself. If I could see what lies ahead I would tell you. But I cannot.

You think I'm a fool.

No. I do not.

You would not say so if you did.

No, but I would not lie. I dont think it. I never did. A man is always right to pursue the thing he loves.

No matter even if it kills him?

I think so. Yes. No matter even that.

HE WHEELED the last barrowload of trash from the kitchen yard out to the trashfire and tipped it and stood back and watched the deep orange fire gasping in the dark chuffs of smoke that rose against the twilight sky. He passed his forearm across his brow and bent and took up the handles of the wheelbarrow again and trundled it out to where the pickup was parked and loaded it and raised and latched the tailgate and went back into the house. Héctor was backing across the floor sweeping with the broom. They carried the kitchen table in from the other room and then brought in the chairs. Héctor brought the lamp from the sideboard and set it on the table and lifted away the glass chimney and lit the wick. He blew out the match and set back the chimney and adjusted the flame with the brass knob. Where is the santo? he said.

It's still in the truck. I'll get it.

He went out and brought in the rest of the things from the cab of the truck. He set the crude wooden figure of the saint on the dresser and unwrapped the sheets and set about making the bed. Héctor stood in the doorway.

You want me to help you?

No. Thanks.

He leaned against the doorjamb smoking. John Grady smoothed the sheets and unfolded the pillowcases and stuffed the feather pillows into them and then unfolded the pieced quilt that Socorro had given him. Héctor stuck the cigarette in his mouth and came around to the other side of the bed and they spread the quilt and stood back.

I think we're done, John Grady said.

They went back into the kitchen and John Grady leaned and cupped his hand at the top of the lamp chimney and blew out the flame and they went out and shut the door behind them. They walked out in the yard and John Grady turned and looked back toward the cabin. The night was overcast. Dark, cloudy, cold. They walked down to the truck.

Will they wait supper on you?

Yeah, said Héctor. Sure.

You can eat at the house if you want.

That's all right.

They climbed in and pulled the truck doors shut. John Grady started the engine.

Can she ride a horse? said Héctor.

Yeah. She can ride.

They pulled out down the rutted road, the tools sliding and clanking behind them in the truckbed. En qué piensas? said John Grady.

Nada.

They jostled on, the truck in second gear, the headlights rocking. When they rounded the first turn in the road the lights of the city appeared out on the plain below them thirty miles away.

It gets cold up here, Héctor said.

Yep.

You spent the night up here yet?

I was up here a couple of nights till past midnight.

He looked at Héctor. Héctor took his makings from his shirtpocket and sat rolling a cigarette.

Tienes tus dudas.

He shrugged. He popped a match with the nail of his thumb and lit the cigarette and blew the match out. Hombre de precaución, he said.

Yo?

Yo.

Two owls crouching in the dust of the road turned their pale and heartshaped faces in the trucklights and blinked and rose on their white wings as silent as two souls ascending and vanished in the darkness overhead.

Buhos, said John Grady.

Lechuzas.

Tecolotes.

Héctor smiled. He took a drag on the cigarette. His dark face glowed in the dark glass. Quizás, he said.

Pueda ser.

Pueda ser. Sí.

WHEN HE WALKED into the kitchen Oren was still at the table. He hung up his hat and went to the sink and washed and got his coffee. Socorro came out of her room and shooed him away from the stove and he took his coffee to the table and sat. Oren looked up from his paper.

What's the news, Oren?

You want the good or the bad?

I dont know. Just pick out somethin in the middle.

They dont have nothin like that in here. It wouldnt be news.

I guess not.

McGregor girl's been picked to be the Sun Carnival Queen. You ever see her?

No.

Sweet girl. How's your place comin?

Okay.

Socorro set his plate before him together with a plate of biscuits covered with a cloth.

She aint no city gal is she?

No.

That's good.

Yeah. It is.

Parham tells me she's pretty as a speckled pup.

He thinks I'm crazy.

Well. You might be a little crazy. He might be a little jealous.

He watched the boy eat. He sipped his coffee.

When I got married my buddies all told me I was crazy. Said I'd regret it.

Did you?

No. It didnt work out. But I didnt regret it. It wasnt her fault.

What happened?

I dont know. A lot of things. Mostly I couldnt get along with her folks. The mother was just a goddamned awful woman. I thought I'd seen awful but I hadnt. If the old man would of lived we might of had a chance. But he had a bad heart. I seen the whole thing comin. When I inquired after his health it was more than just idle curiosity. He finally up and died and here she come. Bag and baggage. That was pretty much the end of it.

He took his cigarettes from the table and lit one. He blew smoke thoughtfully out across the room. He watched the boy.

We was together three years almost to the day. She used to bathe me, if you can believe that. I liked her real well. She'd of been a orphan we'd be married yet.

I'm sorry to hear it.

A man gets married he dont know what's liable to happen. He may think he does, but he dont.

Probably right.

If you sincerely want to hear all about what is wrong with you and what you ought to do to rectify it all you need to do is let them inlaws on the place. You'll get a complete rundown on the subject and I guarantee it.

She aint got no family.

That's good, said Oren. That's your smartest move yet.

After Oren had gone he sat over his coffee a long time. Through the window far to the south he could see the thin white adderstongues of lightning licking silently along the rim of the sky in the darkness over Mexico. The only sound was the clock ticking in the hallway.

When he entered the barn Billy's light was still on. He went down to the stall where he kept the pup and gathered it up all twisting and whimpering in the crook of his arm and brought it back to his bunkroom. He stood at the door and looked back.

Goodnight, he called.

He pushed aside the curtain and felt overhead in the dark for the lightswitch chain.

Goodnight, called Billy.

He smiled. He let go the chain and sat on his bunk in the darkness rubbing the pup's belly. He could smell the horses. The wind was gusting up and a piece of loose roofingtin at the far end of the barn rattled and the wind passed on. It was cold in the room and he thought to light the little kerosene heater but after a while he just pulled off his boots and trousers and put the pup in his box and crawled under the blankets. The wind outside and the cold in the room were like those winter nights on the north Texas plains when he was a child in his grandfather's house. When the storms blew down from the north and the prairie land about the house stood white in the sudden lightning and the house shook in the thunderclaps. On just such nights and just such mornings in the year he'd gotten his first colt he'd wrap himself in his blanket and go out and cross to the barn, leaning into the wind, the first drops of rain slapping at him hard as pebbles, moving down the long barn bay like some shrouded refugee among the sudden slats of light that stood staccato out of the parted board walls, moving through those serried and electric prosceniums where they flared white and fugitive across the barn row on row until he reached the stall where the little horse stood waiting and unlatched the door and sat in the straw with his arms around its neck till it stopped trembling. He would be there all night and he would be there in the morning when Arturo came to the barn to feed. Arturo would walk with him back to the house before anyone else was awake, brushing the straw from his blanket as he walked beside him, not saying a word. As if he were a young lord. As if he were never to be disinherited by war and war's machinery. All his early dreams were the same. Something was afraid and he had come to comfort it. He dreamed it yet. And this: standing in the room in the black suit tying the new black tie he wore to his grandfather's funeral on the cold and windy day of it. And standing in his cubicle in Mac McGovern's horsebarn on another such day in the cold dawn before work in another such suit, the two halves of the box it came in lying on the bunk with the crepe tissue spilling out and the cut string lying beside it on the bunk together with the knife he'd cut it with that had belonged to his father and Billy standing in the doorway watching him. He buttoned the coat and stood. His hands crossed at the wrist in front of him. His face pale in the glass of the little mirror he'd propped on one of the two by fours that braced the rough stud wall of the room. Pale in the light of the winter that was on the country. Billy leaned and spat in the chaff and turned and went out down the barn bay and crossed to the house for breakfast.

THE LAST TIME he was to see her was in the same corner room on the second floor of the Dos Mundos. He watched from the window and saw her pay the driver and he went to the door so that he could watch her come up the stairs. He held her hands while she sat half breathless on the edge of the bed.

Estás bien? he said.

Sí, she said. Creo que sí.

He asked was she sure she had not changed her mind.

No, she said. Y tú?

Nunca.

Me quieres?

Para siempre. Y tú?

Hasta el fin de mi vida.

Pues eso es todo.

She said that she had tried to pray for them but that she could not.

Porqué no?

No sé. Creí que Dios no me oiría.

El oirá. Reza el domingo. Dile que es importante.

They made love and lay with her curled against him and not moving but breathing very quietly against his side. He did not know if she was awake but he told her the things about his life that he had not told her. He told her about working for the hacendado at Cuatro Ciénegas and about the man's daughter and the last time he saw her and about being in the prison in Saltillo and about the scar on his face that he had promised to tell her about and never had. He told her about seeing his mother on stage at the Majestic Theatre in San Antonio Texas and about the times that he and his father used to ride in the hills north of San Angelo and about his grandfather and the ranch and the Comanche trail that ran through the western sections and how he would ride that trail in the moonlight in the fall of the year when he was a boy and the ghosts of the Comanches would pass all about him on their way to the other world again and again for a thing once set in motion has no ending in this world until the last witness has passed.

The shadows were long in the room before they left. He told her that the driver Gutiérrez would pick her up at the cafe in la Calle de Noche Triste and take her to the other side. He would have with him the documents necessary for her to cross.

Todo está arreglado, he said.

She held his hands more tightly. Her dark eyes studied him. He told her that there was nothing to fear. He said that Ramón was their friend and that the papers were arranged and that no harm would come to her.

Él te recogerá a las siete por la mañana. Tienes que estar allí en punto.

Estaré allí.

Quédate adentro hasta que él llegue.

Sí, sí.

No le digas nada a nadie.

No. Nadie.

No puedes traer nada contigo.

Nada?

Nada.

Tengo miedo, she said.

He held her. Dont be afraid, he said.

They sat very quietly. Down in the street the vendors had begun to call. She pressed her face against his shoulder.

Hablan los sacerdotes español? she said.

Sí. Ellos hablan español.

Quiero saber, she said, si crees hay perdón de pecados.

He opened his mouth to speak but she put her hand to his lips. Lo que crees en tu corazón, she said.

He stared past her dark and shining hair toward the deepening dusk in the streets of the city. He thought about what he believed and what he did not believe. After a while he said that he believed in God even if he was doubtful of men's claims to know God's mind. But that a God unable to forgive was no God at all.

Cualquier pecado?

Cualquier. Sí.

Sin excepción de nada? She pushed her hand against his lips a second time. He kissed her fingers and took her hand away.

Con la excepción de desesperación, he said. Para eso no hay remedio.

Lastly she asked if he would love her all his life and she'd have touched her fingers to his mouth but he held her hand. No tengo que pensarlo, he said. Sí. Para todo mi vida.

She took his face in her hands and kissed him. Te amo, she said. Y seré tu esposa.

She rose and turned and held his hands. Debo irme, she said. He stood and put his arms around her and kissed her there in the darkening room. He would have walked her down the hallway to the head of the stairs but she stopped him at the door and kissed him and said goodbye. He listened to her steps in the stairwell. He went to the window to watch for her but she must have gone along the street beneath him because he could not see her. He sat on the bed in the empty room and listened to the sounds of all that alien commerce in the world outside. He sat a long time and he thought about his life and how little of it he could ever have foreseen and he wondered for all his will and all his intent how much of it was his own doing. The room was dark and the neon hotel sign had come on outside and after a while he rose and took his hat from the chair by the bed and put it on and went out and down the stairs.

AT THE INTERSECTION the cab stopped. A small man with a black crape armband stepped into the street and raised his hand and the cabdriver took off his hat and set it on the dashboard. The girl leaned forward to see. She could hear trumpets muted in the street, the clop of hooves.

The musicians who appeared were old men in suits of dusty black. Behind them came the pallbearers carrying upon their shoulders a flowerstrewn pallet. Wreathed among those flowers the pale face of a young man newly dead. His hands lay at his sides and he jostled woodenly on his coolingboard there astride the shoulders of his bearers and the wild notes from the dented gypsy horns carried back from the glass of the storefronts they passed and back from the old mud or stuccoed facades and a clutch of women in black rebozos passed weeping and children and men in black or with black armbands and among them led by the girl the blind maestro shuffling with his small steps and look of pained wonder. Behind them came two mismatched horses drawing to a weathered wooden cart and in the bed of it unswept of its straw and chaff a wooden coffinbox of handplaned boards pinned with wooden trunnels and no nails to it like some sephardic box of old and the wood blacked by scorching it and the blacking sealed with beeswax and lampoil so that save for the faint wood grain of it it looked a thing of burnished iron. Behind the cart came a man bearing the coffinlid and he carried it upon his back like death's penitent and his clothes and he were blackened with it wax or no. The cabdriver crossed himself silently. The girl crossed herself and kissed the tips of her fingers. The cart rattled past and the spoked wheels diced slowly the farther streetside and the solemn watchers there, a cardfan of sorted faces under the shopfronts and the long skeins of light in the street broken in the turning spokes and the shadows of the horses tramping upright and oblique before the oblong shadows of the wheels shaping over the stones and turning and turning.

She put up her hands and pressed her face into the musty back of the cabseat. She sat back, one hand over her eyes and her face averted into her shoulder. Then she sat bolt upright with her arms beside her and cried out and the driver wrenched himself around in the seat. Señorita? he said. Señorita?

THE CEILING of the room was of concrete and bore the impression of the boards used to form it, the concrete knots and nailheads and the fossil arc of the circlesaw's blade from some mountain sawmill. There was a single sooty bulb that burned there with a grudging orange light and a millermoth that patrolled it in random clockwise orbits.

She lay strapped to a steel table. The steel was cold against her back through the short white shift she wore. She looked at the light. She turned her head and looked at the room. After a while a nurse came in through the gray metal door and she turned her stained and dirty face toward her. Por favor, she whispered. Por favor.

The nurse loosed the straps and smoothed her hair back from her face and said she would return with something for her to drink, but when the door closed she sat upright on the table and climbed down. She looked for some place where they might have put her clothes but save for a second steel table against the far wall the room was empty. The door when she opened it led to a long green corridor dimly lit and stretching away to a closed door at the end. She went down the corridor and tried the door. It opened onto a flight of concrete steps, a rail of metal pipe. She descended three flights and exited into the darkened street.

She did not know where she was. At the corner she asked a man for directions to el centro and he stared at her breasts and continued to do so even as he spoke. She set out along the broken sidewalk. She watched the paving for glass or stones. The carlights that passed fetched her slight figure up onto the walls in enormous dark transparency with the shift burned away and the bones all but showing and then passing cast her reeling backwards to vanish once more into the dark. A man pulled up in a car and drove beside her and talked to her in low obscenities. He pulled ahead and waited. She turned into a dirt alley between two buildings and crouched shivering behind some battered steel oildrums. She waited a long time. It was very cold. When she went out again the car was gone and she went on. She passed a lot where a dog lunged at her silently along a fence and then stood in the fencecorner shrouded in its own breath silently watching her go. She passed a darkened house and a yard where an old man also in nightclothes stood urinating against a mud wall and these two nodded silently to each other across the darkened space like figures met in a dream. The sidewalk gave out and she walked on in the cold sand along the roadside and stopped from time to time to stand tottering while she picked the little goathead burrs from the soles of her bleeding feet. She kept the haze of light from the city before her and she walked a long time. When she crossed the Boulevard 16 de Septiembre she kept her arms folded tightly at her bosom and her eyes lowered in the glare of the headlights, crossing half naked in a hooting of carhorns like some tattered phantom routed out of the ordinal dark and hounded briefly through the visible world to vanish again into the history of men's dreams.

She went on through the barrios north of the city, along the old mud walls and the tin sides of warehouses where the sand streets were lit only by the stars. Someone was singing on the road a song from her own childhood and she soon passed a woman walking toward the city. They spoke good evening each to each and passed on but the woman stopped and turned and called after her.

Adónde va? she called.

A mi casa.

The woman stood quietly. The girl asked do I know you but the woman said that she did not. She asked the girl if this were her barrio and the girl said that it was and the woman then asked her how it could be that she did not know her. When she did not answer the woman came slowly back down the road toward her.

Qué pasó? she said.

Nada.

Nada, the woman said. She walked in a half circle around her where she stood shivering with her arms crossed over her breasts. As if to find some favored inclination in the blue light of the desert stars by which she would stand revealed for who she truly was.

Eres del White Lake, she said.

The girl nodded.

Y regresas?

Sí.

Por qué?

No sé.

No sabes.

No.

Quieres ir conmigo?

No puedo.

Porqué no?

She didnt know. The woman asked her again. She said that she could come with her and live in her house where she lived with her children.

The girl whispered that she did not know her.

Te gusta tu vida por allá? the woman said.

No.

Ven conmigo.

She stood shivering. She shook her head no. The sun was coming soon. In the dark above them a star fell and in the cold wind before the dawn papers loped and clutched and rattled briefly in the spines of the roadside growth and loped on again. The woman looked toward the desert sky to the east. She looked at the girl. She asked the girl if she was cold and she said that she was. She asked her again: Quieres ir conmigo?

She said that she could not. She said that in three days' time the boy she loved would come to marry her. She thanked her for her kindness.

The woman raised the girl's face in her hand and looked at her. The girl waited for her to speak but she only looked into her face as if to remember her. Perhaps to read at second hand the shapes of the roads that had led her to this place. What was lost or what was ruined. Whom bereft. Or what remained.

Cómo se llama? the girl said, but the woman did not answer. She touched the girl's face and took away her hand and turned and went on along the dark of the road out of the darkened barrio and did not look back.

Eduardo's car was gone. She crept shivering along the alley under the warehouse wall and tried the door but it was locked. She tapped and waited and tapped again. She waited a long time. After a while she went back out to the street. Her breath pluming in the light along the corrugated wall. She looked back down the alley again and then went around to the front of the building and through the gate and up the walkway.

The portress with her painted face seemed unsurprised to

see her standing there clutching herself in the stenciled shift. She stepped back and held the door and the girl entered and thanked her and went on through the salon. Two men standing at the bar turned to watch her. Pale and dirty waif drifted by mischance in from the outer cold to cross the room with eyes cast down and arms crossed at her breasts. Leaving bloody footprints in the carpet as if a penitent had passed.

HE SEEMED to have dressed with care for the occasion although it may have been that he had business elsewhere in the city. He slid back the goldlinked cuff of his shirt to consult his watch. His suit was of light gray silk shantung and he wore a silk tie of the same color. His shirt was a pale lemon yellow and he wore a yellow silk handkerchief in the breastpocket of the suit and the lowcut black boots with the zippers up the inner sides were freshly polished for he left his shoes outside his door several pair at a time as if the whorehouse hallway were a pullman car.

She sat in the saffroncolored robe he'd given her. Upon the antique bed where her feet did not quite reach the floor. She sat with her head bowed so that her hair cascaded over her thighs and she sat with her hands placed on the bed at either side of her as if she might be afraid of falling.

He spoke in reasoned tones the words of a reasonable man. The more reasonably he spoke the colder the wind in the hollow of her heart. At each juncture in her case he paused to give her space in which to speak but she did not speak and her silence only led inexorably to the next succeeding charge until that structure which was composed of nothing but the spoken word and which should have passed on in its very utterance and left no trace or residue or shadow in the living world, that bodiless structure stood in the room a ponderable being and within its phantom corpus was contained her life.

When he was done he stood watching her. He asked her what she had to say. She shook her head.

Nada? he said.

No, she said. Nada.

Qué crees que eres?

Nada.

Nada. Sí. Pero piensas que has traido una dispensa especial a esta casa? Que Dios te ha escogido?

Nunca creí tal cosa.

He turned and stood looking out the small barred window. Along the limits of the city where the roads died in the desert in sand washes and garbage dumps, out to the white perimeters at midday where smoke from the trashfires burned along the horizon like the signature of vandal hordes come in off the inscrutable wastes beyond. He spoke without turning. He said that she had been spoiled in this house. Because of her youth. He said that her illness was illness only and that she was a fool to believe in the superstitions of the women of the house. He said that she was twice a fool to trust them for they would eat her flesh if they thought it would protect them from disease or secure for them the affections of the lover of whom they dreamt or cleanse their souls in the sight of the bloody and bar-barous god to whom they prayed. He said that her illness was illness only and that it would so prove itself when at last it killed her as it soon would do.

He turned to study her. The slope of her shoulders and their movement with the rise and fall of her breath. The bloodbeat in the artery of her neck. When she looked up and saw his face she knew that he had seen into her heart. What was so and what was false. He smiled his hardlipped smile. Your lover does not know, he said. You have not told him.

Mande?

Tu amado no lo sabe.

No, she whispered. Él no lo sabe.

HE SET OUT the pieces loosely on the board and swiveled it about. I'll go you one more, he said.

Mac shook his head. He held the cigar and blew smoke slowly over the table and then picked up his cup and drained the last of his coffee.

I'm done, he said.

Yessir. You played a good game.

I didnt believe you'd sacrifice a bishop.

That was one of Schönberger's gambits.

You read a lot of chess books?

No sir. Not a lot. I read his.

You told me you played poker.

Some. Yessir.

Why do I think that means somethin else.

I never played that much poker. My daddy was a poker player. He always said that the problem with poker was you played with two kinds of money. What you won was gravy but what you lost was hard come by.

Was he a good poker player?

Yessir. He was one of the best, I reckon. He cautioned me away from it though. He said it was not any kind of a life.

Why did he do it if he thought that?

It was the only other thing he was good at.

What was the first thing?

He was a cowboy.

I take it he was pretty good at that.

Yessir. I've heard of some that was supposed to be better and I'm sure there were some better. I just never did see any of em.

He was on the death march, wasnt he?

Yessir.

There was a lot of boys from this part of the country was on it. Quite a few of em Mexicans.

Yessir. There was.

Mac pulled at his cigar and blew the smoke toward the window. Has Billy come around or are you and him still on the outs?

He's all right.

Is he still goin to stand up for you?

Yessir.

Mac nodded. She aint got nobody to stand on her side?

No sir. Socorro is bringin her family.

That's good. I aint been in my suit in three years. I'd better make a dry run in it, I reckon.

John Grady put the last of the pieces in the box and fitted and slid shut the wooden lid.

Might need Socorro to let out the britches for me.

They sat. Mac smoked. You aint Catholic are you? he said.

No sir.

I wont need to make no disclaimers or nothin?

No sir.

So Tuesday's the day.

Yessir. February seventeenth. It's the last day before Lent. Or I guess next to last. After that you cant get married till Easter.

Is that cuttin it kindly close?

It'll be all right.

Mac nodded. He put the cigar in his teeth and pushed back the chair. Wait here a minute, he said.

John Grady listened to him going down the hall to his room. When he came back he sat down and placed a gold ring on the table.

That's been in my dresser drawer for three years. It aint doin nobody any good there and it never will. We talked about everthing and we talked about that ring. She didnt want it put in the ground. I want you to take it.

Sir I dont think I can do that.

Yes you can. I've already thought of everthing you could possibly say on the subject so rather than go over it item by item let's just save the aggravation and you put it in your pocket and come Tuesday you put it on that girl's finger. You might need to get it resized. The woman that wore it was a beautiful woman. You can ask anybody, it wasnt just my opinion. But what you saw wouldnt hold a candle to what was on the inside. We would like to of had children but we didnt. It damn sure wasnt from not tryin. She was a woman with a awful lot of common sense. I thought she just wanted me to keep that ring for a remembrance but she said I'd know what to do with it when the time come and of course she was right. She was right about everthing. And there's no pride in it when I tell you that she set more store by that ring and what it meant than anything else she ever owned. And that includes some pretty damn fine horses. So take it and put it in your pocket and dont be arguin with me about everthing.

Yessir.

And now I'm goin to bed.

Yessir.

Goodnight.

Goodnight.

FROM THE PASS in the upper range of the Jarillas they could see the green of the benchland below the springs and they could see the thin standing spire of smoke from the fire in the stove rising vertically in the still blue morning air. They sat their horses. Billy nodded at the scene.

When I was a kid growin up in the bootheel me and my brother used to stop where we topped out on this bench south of the ranch goin up into the mountains and we'd look back down at the house. It would be snowin sometimes or snow on the ground in the winter and there was always a fire in the stove and you could see the smoke from the chimney and it was a long ways away and it looked different from up there. Always looked different. It was different. We'd be gone up in the mountains sometimes all day throwin them spooky cattle out of the draws and bringin em down to the feedstation where we'd put out cake. I dont think there was ever a time we didnt stop and look back thataway before we rode up into that country. From where we'd stop we were not a hour away and the coffee was still hot on the stove down there but it was worlds away. Worlds away.

In the distance they could see the thin straight line of the highway and a toysized truck running silently upon it. Beyond that the green line of the river breaks and range on range the distant mountains of Mexico. Billy watched him.

You think you'll ever go back there?

Where?

Mexico.

I dont know. I'd like to. You?

I dont think so. I think I'm done.

I came out of there on the run. Ridin at night. Afraid to make a fire.

Been shot.

Been shot. Those people would take you in. Hide you out. Lie for you. No one ever asked me what it was I'd done.

Billy sat with his hands crossed palm down on the pommel of his saddle. He leaned and spat. I went down there three separate trips. I never once come back with what I started after.

John Grady nodded. What would you do if you couldnt be a cowboy?

I dont know. I reckon I'd think of somethin. You?

I dont know what it would be I'd think of.

Well we may all have to think of somethin.

Yeah.

You think you could live in Mexico?

Yeah. Probably.

Billy nodded. You know what a vaquero makes in the way of wages.

Yep.

You might luck up on a job as foreman or somethin. But sooner or later they're goin to run all the white people out of that country. Even the Babícora wont survive.

I know it.

You'd go to veterinary school if you had the money I reckon. Wouldnt you?

Yep. I would.

You ever write to your mother?

What's my mother got to do with anything?

Nothin. I just wonder if you even know what a outlaw you are.

Why?

Why do I wonder it?

Why am I a outlaw.

I dont know. You just got a outlaw heart. I've seen it before.

Because I said I could live in Mexico?

It aint just that.

Dont you think if there's anything left of this life it's down there?

Maybe.

You like it too.

Yeah? I dont even know what this life is. I damn sure dont know what Mexico is. I think it's in your head. Mexico. I rode a lot of ground down there. The first ranchera you hear sung you understand the whole country. By the time you've heard a hundred you dont know nothin. You never will. I concluded my business down there a long time ago.

He hooked his leg over the pommel of the saddle and sat rolling a cigarette. They'd dropped the reins and the horses leaned and picked bleakly at the sparse tufts of grass trembling in the wind coming through the gap. He bent with his back to the wind and popped a match with his thumbnail and lit the cigarette and turned back.

I aint the only one. It's another world. Everbody I ever knew that ever went back was goin after somethin. Or thought they was.

Yeah.

There's a difference between quittin and knowin when you're beat.

John Grady nodded.

I guess you dont believe that. Do you?

John Grady studied the distant mountains. No, he said. I guess I dont.

They sat for a long time. The wind blew. Billy had long since finished his cigarette and stubbed it out on the sole of his boot.

He unfolded his leg back over the horn of the saddle and slid his boot into the stirrup and leaned down and took up the reins. The horses stepped and stood.

My daddy once told me that some of the most miserable people he ever knew were the ones that finally got what they'd always wanted.

Well, said John Grady. I'm willin to risk it. I've damn sure tried it the other way.

Yeah.

You cant tell anybody anything, bud. Hell, it's really just a way of tellin yourself. And you cant even do that. You just try and use your best judgment and that's about it.

Yeah. Well. The world dont know nothin about your judgment.

I know it. It's worse than that, even. It dont care.

QUINQUAGESIMA SUNDAY in the predawn dark she lit a candle and set the candledish on the floor beside the bureau where the light would not show beneath the doorway to the outer hall. She washed herself at the sink with soap and cloth and she leaned and let her black hair fall before her and passed the wet cloth the length of it a half a hundred times and brushed it as many more. She poured a frugal few drops of scent into her palm and pressed her palms together and scented her hair and the nape of her neck. Then she gathered her hair and twisted it into a rope and coiled and pinned it up.

She dressed with care in one of the three street dresses she owned and stood regarding herself in the dimly lit mirror. The dress was navy blue with white bands at the collar and sleeves and she turned in the mirror and reached over her shoulder and fastened the topmost buttons and turned again. She sat in the chair and pulled on the black pump shoes and stood and went to the bureau and got her purse and put into it the few toilet articles it would hold. No coja nada, she whispered. She folded in her clean underwear and her brush and combs and forced the catch shut. No coja nada. She took her sweater from the back of the chair and pulled it over her shoulders and turned to look at the room she would never see again. The crude carved santo stood as before. Holding his staff so crookedly glued. She took a towel from the rack by the washstand and she wrapped the santo in the towel and then she sat in the chair with the santo in her lap and the purse hanging from her shoulder and waited.

She waited a long time. She had no watch. She listened for the bells to toll in the distant town but sometimes when the wind was coming in off the desert you could not hear them. By and by she heard a rooster call. Finally she heard the slippered steps of the criada along the corridor and she rose as the door opened and the old woman looked in on her and turned and looked back down the hallway and then entered with her hand fanned before her and one finger to her lips and pressed the door shut silently behind her.

Lista? she hissed.

Sí. Lista.

Bueno. Vámonos.

The old woman gave a hitch of her shoulder and a sort of half jaunty cock of her head. Some powdered stepdam from a storybook. Some ragged conspiratress gesturing upon the boards. The girl clutched her purse and stood and put the santo under her arm and the old woman opened the door and peered out and then urged her forward with her hand and they stepped out into the hallway.

Her shoes clicked on the tiles. The old woman looked down and the girl bent slightly and raised her feet each in turn and slipped off the shoes and tucked them under her arm along with the santo.

The old woman shut the door behind them and they moved down the hallway, the crone holding her hand like a child's and tugging at her apron to sort forth her keys where they hung by their thong from the piece of broomhandle.

At the outer door she stood and put her shoes on again while the old woman muffled the heavy latch with her rebozo and turned it with her key. Then the door opened onto the cold and the dark.

They stood facing one another. Rápido, rápido, whispered the old woman and the girl pressed the money that she had promised into her hands and then threw her arms around her neck and kissed her dry and leather cheek and turned and stepped through the door. On the step she turned to take the old woman's blessing but the criada was too distraught to respond and before she could step away from out of the doorway light the old woman had reached and seized her arm.

No te vayas, she hissed. No te vayas.

The girl tore her arm away from the old woman's grip. The sleeve of her dress ripped loose along the shoulder seam. No, she whispered, backing away. No.

The old woman held out one hand. She called hoarsely after her. No te vayas, she called. Me equivoqué.

The girl clutched her santo and her purse and went down the alleyway. Before she reached the end she turned and looked back a last time. La Tuerta was still standing in the door watching her. Holding the clutch of pesos to her breast. Then her eye blinked slowly in the light and the door closed and the key turned and the bolt ran forever on that world.

She went down the alleyway to the road and turned toward the town. Dogs were barking and the air was smoky from the charcoal fires in the low mud hovels of the colonias. She walked along the sandy desert road. The stars in flood above her. The lower edges of the firmament sawed out into the black shapes of the mountains and the lights of the cities burning on the plain like stars pooled in a lake. She sang to herself softly as she went a song from long ago. The dawn was two hours away. The town one.

There were no cars on the road. From a rise she could see to the east across the desert five miles distant the random lights of trucks moving slowly upon the highway that came up from

Chihuahua. The air was still. She could see her breath in the dark. She watched the lights of a car that crossed from left to right somewhere before her and she watched the lights move on. Somewhere out there in the world was Eduardo.

When she reached the crossroads she studied the distance in either direction for any sign of approaching carlights before she crossed. She kept to the narrow streets down through the barrios in the outlying precincts of the city. Already there were windows lit with oil-lamps behind the walls of ocotillo or woven brush. She began to come upon occasional workmen with their lunches in lardcans they carried by the bail, whistling softly as they set forth in the early morning cold. Her feet were bleeding again in her shoes and she could feel the wet blood and the coldness of it.

The cafe held the only light along the Calle de Noche Triste. In the darkened window of the adjacent shoestore a cat sat silently among the footwear watching the empty street. It turned its head to regard her as she passed. She pushed open the steamed glass door of the cafe and entered.

Two men at a table by the window looked up when she came in and followed her with their eyes as she went by. She went to the rear and sat at one of the little wooden tables and put her purse and her parcel in the chair beside her and took up the menu from the chrome wire stand and sat looking at it. The waiter came over. She ordered a cafecito and he nodded and went back to the counter. It was warm in the cafe and after a while she took off the sweater and laid it in the chair. The men were still watching her. The waiter brought the coffee and set it before her with spoon and napkin. She was surprised to hear him ask where she was from.

Mande? she said.

De dónde viene?

She told him she was from Chiapas and he stood for a moment studying her as if to see how such people might be different from those he knew. He said that he'd been told to ask by one of the men. When she turned and looked at them they smiled but there was no joy in it. She looked at the waiter. Estoy esperando a un amigo, she said.

Por supuesto, said the waiter.

She sat over the coffee a long time. The street outside grew gray in the February dawn. The two men at the front of the cafe had long since finished their coffee and left and others had come to take their place. The shops remained closed. A few trucks passed in the street and people were coming in out of the cold and a waitress was now going from table to table.

Shortly after seven a blue taxi pulled up at the door and the driver got out and came in and canvassed the tables with his eyes. He came to the rear of the cafe and looked down at her.

Lista? he said.

Dónde está Ramón?

He stood picking at his teeth reflectively. He said that Ramón could not come.

She looked toward the front of the cafe. The cab stood in the street with the engine running in the cold.

Está bien, said the driver. Vámonos. Debemos darnos prisa.

She asked him if he knew John Grady and he nodded and waved the toothpick. Sí, sí, he said. He said that he knew everyone. She looked again at the cab smoking in the street.

He had stepped back to allow her to rise. He looked down at the chair where she'd put her purse. The santo wrapped in the whorehouse towel. She placed her hand over these things. Which he might wish to carry for her. She asked him who it was who had paid him.

He put the toothpick back in his mouth and stood looking at her. Finally he said that he had not been paid. He said that he was cousin to Ramón and that Ramón had been paid forty dollars. He put his hand on the back of the empty chair and stood looking down at her. Her shoulders were rising and falling with her breath. Like someone about to attempt a feat of strength. She said that she did not know.

He leaned down. Mire, he said. Su novio. Él tiene una cicatriz aquí. He passed his forefinger across his cheek to trace the path of the knife that had made the scar her lover carried from the fight three years ago in the comedor of the cárcel at Cuellar in the city of Saltillo. Verdad? he said.

Sí, she whispered. Es verdad. Y tiene mi tarjeta verde?

Sí. He took the greencard from his pocket and placed it on the table. On the card was printed her name.

Está satisfecha? he said.

Sí, she whispered. Estoy satisfecha. And rose and gathered up her things and left money on the table to pay for the coffee and followed him out into the street.

In the cold dawn all that halfsordid world was coming to light again and as she rode in silence in the rear of the cab through the waking streets she clutched the illcarved wooden relic and said a silent goodbye to everything she knew and to each thing she would not see again. She said goodbye to an old woman in a black rebozo come to a door to see what sort of day it was and she said goodbye to three girls her age stepping with care around the water standing in the street from the recent rains who were on their way to Mass and she said goodbye to dogs and to old men at streetcorners and to vendors pushing their carts through the street to commence their day and to shopkeepers opening their doors and to the women who knelt with pail and rag to wash the walkway tiles. She said goodbye to the small birds strung shoulder to shoulder along the lightwires overhead who had slept and were waking and whose name she would never know.

They passed through the outskirts of the city and she could see the river to the left through the river trees and the tall buildings of the city beyond that were in another country and the barren mountains where the sun would soon fall upon the rocks. They passed the old abandoned municipal buildings. Rusted watertanks in a yard strewn with trashpapers the wind had left. The sudden thin iron palings of a fence that ratcheted silently past the window from right to left and which in their passing and in the period of their passing began to evoke the dormant sorcerer within before she could tear her gaze away. She put her hands to her eyes, breathing deeply. In the darkness inside the cups of her palms she saw herself on a cold white table in a cold white room. The glass of the doors and the windows to that room were meshed with heavy wire and clamoring there were whores and whores' handmaids many in number and all crying out to her. She sat upright on the table and threw back her head as if she would cry out or as if she would sing. Like some young diva remanded to a madhouse. No sound came. The cold pneuma passed. She should have called it back. When she opened her eyes the cab had turned off the road and was jostling over a bare dirt track and the driver was watching her in the mirror. She looked out but she could not see the bridge. She could see the river through the trees and the mist coming off the river and the raw rock mountains beyond but she could not see the city. She saw a figure moving among the trees by the river. She asked the driver if they were to cross here to the other side and he said yes. He said that she would be going to the other side now. Then the cab pulled into the clearing and came to a stop and when she looked what she saw coming toward her across the clearing in the earliest light of morning was the smiling Tiburcio.

HE'D LEFT THE RANCH around five and driven to the darkened front of the bar where he could see the dimly lit face of the clock within. He backed the truck around on the gravel apron so that he could watch the road and he tried not to turn around to look at the clock every few minutes but he did.

Few cars passed. Shortly after six oclock a set of headlights slowed and he sat upright over the steering wheel and cleared the glass with the forearm of his jacket but the lights went past and the car was not a taxi but a sheriff's prowlcar. He thought they might come back and ask him what he was doing there but they didnt. It was very cold sitting in the truck and after a while he got out and walked around and flailed at himself with his arms and stamped his boots. Then he got back in the truck. The bar clock said six-thirty. When he looked to the east he could see the gray shape of the landscape.

The lights of the gas station a half mile down the highway went out. A truck went down the highway. He wondered if he could drive down there and get a cup of coffee before the cab arrived. By eight-thirty he'd decided that if that was what it would take to make the cab arrive then that's what he would do and he started the engine. Then he shut it off again.

A half hour later he saw Travis's truck go by on the highway. In a few minutes it came back and slowed and pulled into the parking lot. John Grady rolled down the truck window. Travis pulled up and sat looking at him. He leaned and spat.

What'd they do, give you your time?

Not yet.

I thought maybe the truck was stole. You ain't broke down are you?

No. I was just waitin on somebody.

How long you been here?

I been here a while.

Has that thing got a heater in it?

Not much of a one.

Travis shook his head. He looked toward the highway. John Grady leaned and cleared the glass again with his sleeve. I better get on, he said.

Are you in some kind of trouble?

Yeah. Maybe.

Over a girl, I reckon.

Yeah.

They aint worth it, son.

I've heard that.

Well. Dont do nothin dumb.

It's probably too late.

It aint too late if you aint done it.

I'm all right.

He reached and turned the key and pushed the starter button. He turned and looked at Travis. I'll see you, he said.

He pulled out of the parking lot and headed back up the highway. Travis sat watching the truck until it was out of sight.

IV

W HEN HE got to the cafe in the Calle de Noche
Triste the place was full and the girl was hurrying
back and forth with orders of eggs and baskets of
tortillas. She didnt know anything. She'd only come to work an
hour ago. He followed her into the kitchen. The cook looked
up from the stove and looked at the girl. Quién es? he said. The
girl shrugged. She looked at John Grady. She balanced plates
up her arm and pushed back out through the door. The cook
didnt know anything. He said the waiter's name was Felipe but
he wasnt here. He wouldnt be back until late afternoon. John
Grady watched him for a few minutes while he turned the tortillas on the grill with his fingers. Then he pushed open the
door and went back out through the restaurant.

He followed the trail of the cabdriver through the various
sidestreet bars where he plied his trade. Bars where patrons
from the prior night clutched their drinks and squinted in the
light from the opening door like suspects under interrogation.
He narrowly avoided two fights for refusing to accept a drink.
He went to the Venada and knocked at the door but no one
came. He stood outside the Moderno peering into the interior
but all was closed and dark.

He went to the poolhall in Mariscal Street that was fre-
quented by the musicians and where their instruments hung
along the wall, guitars and mandolins and horns of brass or ger-
man silver. A mexican harp. He asked after the maestro but
none had seen him. By noon he had nowhere else to go but to
the White Lake. He sat in a cafe over a cup of black coffee. He

sat for a long time. There was another place to go but he didnt want to go there either.

A dwarf of a man in a white coat led him down a corridor. The building smelled of damp concrete. Outside he could hear street traffic, a jackhammer.

The man pushed through a door at the end of the corridor and held the door and nodded him through and then reached and threw the lightswitch. The boy took off his hat. They stood in a room where the recent dead four in number lay on their coolingboards. The boards were trestled up on legs made from plumbing pipe and the dead lay upon them with their hands at their sides and their eyes closed and their necks in dark stained wooden chocks. None were covered over but all lay in their clothes as death had found them. They had the look of rumpled travelers resting in an anteroom. He walked along slowly past the tables. The overhead ceiling lights were covered with small wire baskets. The walls were painted green. In the floor a brass drain. Bits of gray mopstring twisted about the castered wheels under the tables.

The girl to whom he'd sworn his love forever lay on the last table. She lay as the rushcutters had found her that morning in the shallows under the shore willows with the mist rising off the river. Her hair damp and matted. So black. Hung with strands of dead brown weed. Her face so pale. The severed throat gaping bloodlessly. Her good blue dress was twisted about on her body and her stockings were torn. She'd lost her shoes.

There was no blood for it had all washed away. He reached and touched her cheek. Oh God, he said.

La conoce? said the orderly.

Oh God.

La conoce?

He leaned on the table, crushing his hat. He put his hand across his eyes, gripping his skull. Had he the strength he'd have crushed out all it held. What lay before him now and all else it might hold forever.

Señor, said the orderly, but the boy turned and pushed past him and stumbled out. The man called after him. He stood in the door and called down the hallway. He said that if he knew this girl he must make an identification. He said that there were papers to be filled out.

THE CATTLE in the long Cedar Springs Draw up through which he rode studied him as they stood chewing and then lowered their heads again. The rider knew they could tell his intentions by the attitude of the horse he rode. He passed on and rode up into the hills and crested out on the mesa and rode slowly along the rim. He sat the horse facing into the wind and watched the train going up the valley fifteen miles away. To the south the thin green line of the river lay like a child's crayon mark across that mauve and bistre waste. Beyond that the mountains of Mexico in paling blues and grays washing out in the distance. The grass along the mesa underfoot twisted in the wind. A dark head of weather was making up to the north. The little horse dipped its head and he pulled it about and rode on. The horse seemed uncertain and looked off to the west. As if to remember the way. The boy booted him forward. You dont need to worry about it, he said.

He crossed the highway and crossed through the westernmost section of the McGregor ranch. He rode through country he'd not seen before. In the early afternoon he came upon a rider sitting his horse with his hands crossed loosely over the pommel of his saddle. The horse was a goodlooking black gelding with a savvy look to its eye. It was ochred to the knees from the dust of that country and the rig was an old rimfire outfit with visalia stirrups and a flat saddlehorn the size of a coffeesaucer. The rider was chewing tobacco and he nodded as John Grady rode up. Can I help you? he said.

John Grady leaned and spat. Meanin I aint supposed to be on your land, he said. He looked at the rider. A man a few years older than he. The rider studied him back with his pale blue eyes.

I work for Mac McGovern, John Grady said. I reckon you know him.

Yes, the rider said. I know him. You all got stock drifted up this way?

No. Not that I know of. I just kindly drifted up this way myself.

The rider pushed the brim of his hat back slightly with his thumb. They were met upon a clay floodplain bereft of grass or any growing thing and the only sound the wind made was in their clothes. The dark clouds stood banked in a high wall to the north and a thin and soundless wire of lightning appeared there and quivered and vanished again. The rider leaned and spat and waited.

I was supposed to get married in two days' time, the boy said.

The rider nodded but the boy said no more.

I take it you changed your mind.

The boy didnt answer. The rider looked off to the north and looked back again.

We might get some rain out of that.

We might. It's rained over in town the last two nights.

Have you had your dinner?

No. I guess I aint.

Why dont you come on to the house.

I better get on back.

I reckon she changed hers.

The boy looked away. He didnt answer.

There'll be anothern along directly. You'll see.

No there wont.

Why dont you come on to the house and take dinner with us.

I appreciate it. I need to get back.

You remind me some of myself. Get somethin on your mind and just ride.

John Grady sat loosely holding the reins. He looked a long

time out at the running country before he spoke. When he did speak the rider had to lean to catch his words. I wish I could ride, he said. I wish I could.

The rider wiped the corners of his mouth with the heel of his thumb. Maybe you'd better ought not to go back just yet, he said. Maybe you ought to just wait a little while.

I'd ride and I'd never look back. I'd ride to where I couldnt find a single day I ever knew. Even if I was to turn back and ride over ever foot of that ground. Then I'd ride some more.

I've been thataway, said the rider.

I better get on.

You sure you wont change your mind? We feed pretty good.

No. I thank you.

Well.

I hope you get that rain up here.

I appreciate it.

He turned the horse and set out south down the broad flood-plain. The rider turned his own horse and started back upcountry but he stopped before he'd gone far. He sat the horse and watched the boy riding out down the broad valley and he watched him for a long time. When he could see him no more he raised himself slightly in the stirrups. As if he might call after him. The boy never looked back. When he was gone the rider stayed a while yet. He'd dropped the reins and he sat with one leg crossed over the fork of the saddle and he pushed back his hat and leaned and spat and studied the country. As if it ought to have something to tell him for that figure having passed through it.

IT WAS LATE EVENING and almost dark when he rode the horse through the ford and dismounted under the cottonwoods in the glade at the far side. He let drop the reins and crossed to the cabin and pushed open the door. Inside it was dark and he stood in the doorway and looked back out at the evening. The darkening land. The sky to the west blood red where the sun had gone and the small dark birds blowing down before the storm. The wind in the flue moaned with a long dry sound. He went into the bedroom and stood. He got a match and lit the lamp and turned down the wick and put back the glass chimney and sat on the bed with his hands between his knees. The carved wooden santo leered from the shadows. His own shadow from the lamp rose up the wall behind him. A hulking shape which looked no description of him at all. After a while he took off his hat and let it drop to the floor and lowered his face into his hands.

When he rode out again it was dark and windy and starless and cold and the sacaton grass along the creek thrashed in the wind and the small bare trees he passed hummed like wires. The horse quivered and stepped and raised the flues of its nose to the wind. As if to sort what there might be in the coming storm that was not storm alone. They crossed the creek and set out down the old road. He thought he heard a fox bark and he looked for it along the rimrock skylined above the road to the left. Evenings in Mexico he used to see them come out and walk the traprock dikes above the plains for the vantage of the view there. To spy out what smaller life might venture forth in the dusk. Or they would simply sit upon those godlaid walls in silhouette like icons out of Egypt, silent and still against the deepening sky, sufficient to all that might be asked of them.

He'd left the lamp burning in the cabin and the softly lit window looked warm and inviting. Or it would have to other eyes. For himself he was done with all that and after he'd crossed the creek and taken the road he had to take he did not look back again.

When he rode into the yard it was raining lightly and he could see them all at supper through the rainbleared glass of the kitchen window. He rode on toward the barn and then halted the horse and looked back. He thought it was like seeing these people in some other time before he'd ever come to the ranch. Or they were like people in some other house of whose lives and histories he knew nothing. Mostly they all just seemed to be waiting for things to be a way they'd never be again.

He rode into the barn and dismounted and left the horse standing there and went to his room. The horses looked out over the stall doors and watched him as he passed. He did not turn on the light. He got his flashlight from the shelf and knelt and opened the footlocker and rummaged out his slicker and a dry shirt and he got the huntingknife that had belonged to his father from the bottom of the locker and the brown envelope that held his money and laid them on the bed. Then he stripped out of his shirt and put on the dry shirt and pulled on the slicker and put the huntingknife in the slicker pocket. He took some bills from the envelope and put the envelope back in the locker and closed the lid. Then he switched off the flashlight and set it back on the shelf and went out again.

When he reached the end of the road he dismounted and tied the reins together over the saddlehorn and led the horse a ways back up the road sliding in the mud and then let go the cheekstrap and stepped away and slapped the horse on the rump and stood watching as it trotted off up the road in the heavy muck to disappear in the rain and the dark.

The first lights that picked him up standing by the side of the highway slowed and stopped. He opened the car door and looked in.

My boots are awful muddy, he said.

Get in here, the man said. You cant hurt this thing.

He climbed in and pulled the door shut. The driver put the car in gear and leaned forward and squinted out at the road. I cant see at night worth a damn, he said. What are you doin out in the rain like this?

You mean aside from gettin wet?

Aside from gettin wet.

I just needed to get to town.

The driver looked at him. He was an old rancher, lean and rawboned. He wore the crown of his hat round the way some old men used to do. Damn, son, he said. You a desperate case.

It aint nothin like that. I just got some business to attend to.

Well I reckon it must be somethin that wont keep or you wouldnt be out here, would you?

No sir. I wouldnt.

Well I wouldnt either. It's a half hour past my bedtime right now.

Yessir.

Errand of mercy.

Sir?

Errand of mercy. I got a animal down.

He was bent over the wheel and the car was astraddle of the white center line. He looked at the boy. I'll get over if anything comes, he said. I know how to drive. I just cant see.

Yessir.

Who you work for?

Mac McGovern.

Old Mac. He's one of the good'ns. Aint he?

Yessir. He is.

You'd wear out a Ford pickup truck findin a better.

Yessir. I believe I would.

Got a mare down. Young mare. Tryin to foal.

You leave anybody with her?

My wife's at the house. At the barn, I should say.

They drove. The rain slashed over the road in the lights and the wipers rocked back and forth over the glass.

We'll be married sixty years April twenty-second.

That's a long time.

Yes it is. It dont seem like it, but it is. She come out here with her family from Oklahoma in a covered wagon. Got married we was both seventeen. We went to Dallas to the exposition on our honeymoon. They didnt want to rent us a room. Didnt neither one of us look old enough to be married. There aint been a day passed in sixty years I aint thanked God for that woman. I never done nothin to deserve her, I can tell you that. I dont know what you could do.

BILLY PAID HIS TOLL at the booth and walked across the bridge. The boys along the river beneath the bridge held up their buckets on poles and called out for money. He walked down Juárez Avenue among the tourists, past the bars and curioshops, the shills calling to him from the doorways. He went into the Florida and ordered a whiskey and drank it and paid and went out again.

He walked up Tlaxcala to the Moderno but it was closed. He tapped and waited under the green and yellow tiled arch. He walked around the side of the building and looked in through a broken corner in one of the barred windows. He could see the small light over the bar at the rear of the building. He stood in the rain looking out down the street where it lay in a narrow corridor of shops and bars and lowbuilt houses. The air smelled of dieselsmoke and woodfires.

He went back to Juárez Avenue and got a cab. The driver looked at him in the mirror.

Conoce el White Lake?

Sí. Claro.

Bueno. Vámonos.

The driver nodded and they pulled away. Billy sat back in the cab and watched the bleak streets of the bordertown pass in the rainy afternoon light. They left the paved road and went out through the mud roads of the outlying barrios. Vendors' burros piled high with cordwood turned away their heads as the taxi passed splashing through the potholes. Everything was covered with mud.

When they pulled up in front of the White Lake Billy got out and lit a cigarette and took his billfold from the hip pocket of his jeans.

I can wait for you, the driver said.

That's all right.

I can come in and wait.

I might be a while. What do I owe you?

Three dollars. You dont want me to wait for you?

No.

The driver shrugged and took the money and rolled the window back up and pulled away. Billy put the cigarette in his mouth and looked at the building there at the edge of the barrio between the mud and cratewood hovels and the pleated sheetiron walls of the warehouse.

He walked on to the rear of the place and turned up the alley past the warehouse and knocked at the first of two doors and waited. He flipped the butt of the cigarette into the mud. He'd reached to knock at the door again when it opened and the old criada looked out. As soon as she saw him she tried to shut the door but he shoved it back open and she turned and went scuttling down the hallway with one hand atop her head crying out. He shut the door behind him and looked down the hall. Whores' heads in curlingpapers ducked out and ducked back like chickens. Doors closed. He'd not gone ten feet along the hallway when a man in black with a thin and weaselshaped face stepped out and tried to take his arm. Excuse me, the man said. Excuse me.

Billy jerked his arm away. Where's Eduardo? he said.

Excuse me, the man said. He tried to take Billy's arm again. Mistake. Billy took him by the front of his shirt and slammed him against the wall. He was so light. There was nothing to him at all. He put up no resistance but seemed to be merely reaching about him as if he'd lost something and Billy turned loose of the handful of black silk knotted up in his fist just in time. The thin blade of the knife snickered past his belt and he leapt back and raised up his arms. Tiburcio crouched and feinted with the knife before him.

You little son of a bitch, said Billy. He hit the Mexican squarely in the mouth and the Mexican slammed back against the wall and sat down on the floor. The knife went spinning and clattering down the hallway. The old woman at the end of the hall was watching with her fingers in her teeth. Her eye closed and opened again in a huge and obscene wink. He turned to the pimp and was surprised to see him struggling to his feet holding a small silver penknife still fastened to the chain draped across the front of his pegged black trousers. Billy hit him in the side of the head and heard bone crack. The pimp's head spun away and he slid several feet down the hallway and lay in a twisted black pile in the floor like a dead bird. The old woman came down the hall at a tottering run crying out. He caught her as she went past and pulled her around. She threw up her hands and closed her good eye. Aiee, she cried. Aiee. He gripped her wrists and shook her. Dónde está mi compañero? he said.

Aiee, she cried. She tried to pull away to go to the pimp lying in the floor.

Dígame. Dónde está mi cuate?

No sé. No sé. Por Dios, no sé nada.

Dónde está la muchacha? Magdalena? Dónde está Magdalena?

Jesús María y José ten compasión no está. No está.

Dónde está Eduardo?

No está. No está.

Aint a damn soul está, is there?

He turned her loose and she threw herself on the fallen pimp and raised his face to her breast. Billy shook his head in disgust and went down the hall and picked up the knife and stuck the blade between the door and the jamb and snapped the blade off and slung the handle away and turned and came back. The criada cowered and held up one hand over her head but he reached down past her and snatched away the silver chain from the pimp's waistcoat and broke off the blade of the penknife also.

Has this son of a bitch got any more knives on him?

Aiee, moaned the criada, rocking back and forth with the pimp's oiled head in her bosom. The pimp had come awake and was looking up at him with one walled eye through the woman's stringy hair. One arm flailed about loosely. Billy reached down and got him by the hair and pulled his face up.

Dónde está Eduardo?

The criada was moaning and blubbering and sat trying to
unclamp Billy's fingers from the pimp's hair.

En su oficina, wheezed the pimp.

He turned him loose and straightened up and wiped his oily
hand on the leg of his jeans and walked down the hallway to the
far end. Eduardo's foilcovered door had no doorknob to it and
he stood looking at it for a minute and then raised one boot and
kicked it in. It came completely off the hinges in a great
splintering of wood and turned slightly sideways and fell into
the room. Eduardo sat at his desk. He seemed strangely un-
alarmed.

Where is he? said Billy.

The mysterious friend.

His name is John Cole and if you've harmed a hair on his
head you're a dead son of a bitch.

Eduardo leaned back. He opened the drawer of his desk.

You better have a shoebox full of pistols in there, said Billy.

Eduardo took a cigar from the desk drawer and closed it and
took his gold cigarcutter from his pocket and held up the cigar
and clipped it and put the cigar in his mouth and the cutter
back in his pocket.

Why would I need a pistol?

I'm fixin to point out several reasons if I dont get some sense
out of you.

The door was not locked.

What?

The door was not locked.

I aint studyin your damn door.

Eduardo nodded. He'd taken his lighter from his pocket and
was wafting the flame across the end of the cigar and rotating
the cigar in his mouth slowly with his fingers. He looked at
Billy. Then he looked past Billy. When Billy turned the alcahuete was standing in the door, one hand on the splintered
jamb, breathing slowly and evenly. One eye was swelled half
shut and his mouth was puffed and bleeding and his shirt was

torn. Eduardo gestured him away with a small toss of his chin.

Surely, he said, you dont believe that we are unable to protect ourselves from the riffraff and drunks that come here?

He put the lighter in his pocket and looked up. Tiburcio was still standing in the doorway. Ándale pues, he said. Tiburcio looked at Billy for a moment with no more expression than a pitviper and then turned and went back down the hall.

Your friend is being sought by the police, said Eduardo. The girl is dead. Her body was found in the river this morning.

Damn you to hell.

Eduardo studied the cigar. He looked up at Billy. You see what has come to pass.

You couldnt just cut her loose, could you.

You remember our conversation when last we met.

Yeah. I remember it.

You did not believe me.

I believed you.

You spoke to your friend?

Yeah. I spoke to him.

But your words carried no weight with him.

No. They didnt.

And now I cannot help you. You see.

I didnt come here for your help.

You might wish to consider the question of your own implication in this matter.

I got nothin to answer for.

Eduardo drew deeply on the cigar and blew the smoke slowly into the uninhabited center of the room. You present an odd picture, he said. In spite of whatever views you may hold everything that has come to pass has been the result of your friend's coveting of another man's property and his willful determination to convert that property to his own use without regard for the consequences. But of course this does not make the consequences go away. Does it? And now I find you before me breathless and half wild having wrecked my place of business and maimed my help. And having almost certainly colluded in enticing away one of the girls in my charge in a manner that has led to her death. And yet you appear to be asking me to help you to resolve your difficulties for you. Why?

Billy looked at his right hand. It was already badly swollen. He looked at the pimp seated sideways at the desk. The expensive boots crossed before him.

You think I got no recourse, dont you?

I dont know what you have or do not have.

I know this country too.

No one knows this country.

Billy turned. He stood in the doorway and looked down the corridor. Then he looked at the pimp again. Damn you to hell, he said. You and all your kind.

HE SAT IN A STEEL CHAIR in an empty room with his hat on his knee. When the door finally opened again the officer looked at him and motioned him forward with the tips of his fingers. He rose and followed the man down the corridor. A prisoner was mopping the worn linoleum and as they passed he stepped back and waited and then went to mopping again.

The officer knocked at the captain's door with one knuckle and then opened the door and gestured for Billy to enter. He stepped in and the door closed behind him. The captain sat at his desk writing. He glanced up. Then he went on writing. After a while he gestured slightly with his chin toward two chairs to his left. Please, he said. Be seated.

Billy sat in one of the chairs and set his hat in the chair beside him. Then he picked it up again and held it. The captain laid his pen aside and stood the papers and tapped and edged them square and set them aside and looked at him.

How may I help you? he said.

I come to see you about a girl that was found dead in the river this mornin. I think I can identify her.

We know who she is, the captain said. He leaned back in his chair. She was a friend of yours?

No. I seen her one time is all.

She was a prostitute.

Yessir.

The captain sat with his hands pressed together. He leaned forward and took from an oakwood tray at the corner of his desk a large and glossy photo and handed it across.

Is that the girl?

Billy took the photo and turned it and looked at it. He looked up at the captain. I dont know, he said. It's kindly hard to tell.

The girl in the photo looked made of wax. She'd been turned so as to afford the best view of her severed throat. Billy held the photo gingerly. He looked up at the captain again.

I expect that's probably her.

The captain reached and took the photo and returned it to the tray face down. You have a friend, he said.

Yessir.

What was his relationship with this girl?

He was goin to marry her.

Marry her.

Yessir.

The captain picked up his pen and unscrewed the cap. What is his name?

John Grady Cole.

The captain wrote. Where is your friend? he said.

I dont know.

You know him well?

Yes. I do.

Did he kill the girl?

No.

The captain screwed the cap back onto the pen and leaned back. All right, he said.

All right what.

You are free to go.

I was free to go when I come in here.

Did he send you?

No he didnt send me.

All right.

Is that all you got to say?

The captain put his hands together again. He tapped at his teeth with the tips of his fingers. Outside the sound of people talking in the corridor. Beyond that the traffic in the street.

How do you say your name?

Sir?

How do you say your name.

Parham. You say Parham.

Parham.

You aint goin to write it down?

No.

You've already got it writ.

Yes.

Well.

You are not going to tell me anything. Are you?

Billy looked down into his hat. He looked up at the captain. You know that pimp killed her.

The captain tapped his teeth. We would like to talk to your friend, he said.

You'd like to talk to him but not to the pimp.

The pimp we have already talked to.

Yeah. And I know what talks, too.

The captain shook his head wearily. He looked at the name on the pad. He looked up at Billy.

Mr Parham, he said. Every male in my family for three generations has been killed in defense of this republic. Grandfathers, fathers, uncles, brothers. Eleven men in all. Any beliefs they may have had now reside in me. Any hopes. This is a sobering thought to me. You understand? I pray to these men. Their blood ran in the streets and gutters and in the arroyos and among the desert stones. They are my Mexico and I pray to them and I answer to them and to them alone. I do not answer elsewhere. I do not answer to pimps.

If that's true then I take back what I said.

The captain inclined his head.

Billy nodded toward the photo in the box. What have they done with her? The body.

The captain raised one hand and let it fall again. He has already made his visit. This morning.

He saw that?

Yes. Before we knew the identity of the girl. The—how do you call him? The practicante. The practicante told my lieutenant that he spoke excellent spanish. He has a cicatriz. A scar. Here.

That dont make him a bad person.

Is he a bad person?

He's as good a boy as I ever knew. He's the best.

You dont know where he is.

No sir. I dont.

The captain sat for a moment. Then he stood up and held out his hand. I thank you for coming, he said.

Billy rose and they shook hands and Billy put on his hat. At the door he turned.

He dont own the White Lake, does he? Eduardo.

No.

I dont reckon you'd tell me who does.

It is not important. A businessman. He has nothing to do with any of this.

You dont consider him to be a pimp, I reckon.

The captain studied him. Billy waited.

Yes, the captain said. I do so consider him.

I'm glad to hear it, Billy said. I'm the same way.

The captain nodded.

I dont know what happened, Billy said. But I know why it happened.

Tell me then.

He fell in love with her.

Your friend.

No. Eduardo.

The captain drummed his fingers lightly on the edge of his desk. Yes? he said.

Yes.

The captain shook his head. I dont see how a man could run such a place if he fell in love with the girls.

I dont either.

Yes. Why this girl?

I dont know.

You told me you only saw her once.

I did.

You think your friend was not such a fool.

I told him to his face he was. I might of been wrong.

The captain nodded. I'm not a fool either, Mr Parham. I know you would not bring him to me. Even if his hands were dripping. Especially not then.

Billy nodded. You take care, he said.

He walked out up the street and went into the first bar he came to and ordered a shot of whiskey and carried it to the pay-phone on the back wall. Socorro answered and he told her what had happened and asked for Mac but Mac was already on the phone.

I guess you'll tell me what all this is about.

Yessir. I will. If he shows up there dont let him leave if you can help it.

Maybe you'll let me know how you propose to keep him someplace he dont want to be kept.

I'll be there quick as I can get there. I'm just goin to check a few places.

I knew there was somethin about this that didnt rattle right.

Yessir.

Do you know where he's at?

No sir. I dont.

You call me back as quick as you know somethin. You hear?

Yessir.

You call me back anyways. Dont leave me settin here all evenin.

Yessir. I will.

He hung the phone up and drank the shot and carried the empty tumbler to the bar and set it down. Otra vez, he said. The barman poured. The place was empty save for a single drunk. He drank the second shot and laid a quarter on the bar and went out. Walking up Juárez Avenue the cabdrivers kept calling out to him to go and see the show. To go and see the girls.

JOHN GRADY drank one whiskey neat at the Kentucky Club and paid and went out and nodded to the cabman standing at the corner. They got in and the cabdriver turned and looked at him.

Where are you going my friend?

The White Lake.

He turned and started the engine and they pulled away into the street. The rain had settled into a steady light drizzle but the streets were flooded and the cab moved out slowly and went up Juárez Avenue like a boat with the garish lights reflected in the black water dishing and wobbling and righting themselves again in its wake.

Eduardo's car was parked in the alley under the dark of the warehouse wall and he crossed to where it stood and tried the door. Then he raised his boot and kicked in the doorglass. The glass was laminated and it spidered whitely in the light and sagged inward. He put his boot to it again and it caved down into the seat and he reached in and laid the heel of his hand on the horn and blew it three times and stepped back. The sound echoed in the alley and died. He took off his slicker and took the knife out of the pocket and he squatted and tucked his jeans into his boottops and stuck the knife and sheath down into his left boot. Then he laid the slicker across the hood of the car and blew the horn again. The echo had barely died when the door at the rear of the building opened and Eduardo stepped out and stood back against the wall away from the light.

John Grady walked out from the side of the car. A match flared and Eduardo's face leaned in the flame with one of his little cigarillos in his teeth. The dying match arced out into the alley.

The suitor, he said.

He stepped forward into the light and leaned on the iron railing. He smoked and looked out at the night. He looked down at the boy.

You could have just knocked at my door.

John Grady had taken the slicker from the hood of the car and he stood in the alley with it folded under his arm. Eduardo smoked.

You have come to pay me the money you owe me, I suppose.

I come to kill you.

The pimp drew slowly on the cigarillo. He tilted his head slightly and blew the smoke upward in a thin stream from his thin lips.

I dont think so, he said.

He turned and slowly descended the three steps into the alley. John Grady moved out to the left and stood waiting.

I think you do not even know why you are here, Eduardo said. Which is very sad. Perhaps I can teach you. Perhaps there is still time to learn. He drew again on the cigarillo and then dropped it and twisted it out with his boot.

John Grady never even saw him reach for the knife. Perhaps he'd palmed it in his hand the while. There was a sharp little click and a wink of light off the blade. And then the wink again. As if he were turning it in his hand. John Grady drew his knife from the top of his boot and wrapped the slicker around his right forearm and caught the loose end in his fist. Eduardo walked out into the alley so as to have the light behind him. He stepped carefully to avoid the pools of rainwater. His pale silk shirt rippled in the light. He turned and looked at the boy.

Change your mind, he said. Go back. Choose life. You are young.

I come to kill you or be killed.

Ah, said Eduardo.

I didnt come to talk.

It is only a formality. Because of your youth.

You dont need to worry about my youth.

The pimp stood in the alleyway. His shirt open at the neck. His sleek oiled head blue in the light. Holding the thin switchblade knife loosely in one hand. I wanted you to know that I was still willing to forgive you, he said.

He had come forward by steps almost imperceptible. He stood. His head slightly cocked to one side. Waiting.

I will give you every advantage. Perhaps you have not been in so many fights. I think you will find that often in a fight the last one to speak is the loser.

He put two fingers to his lips to caution silence. Then he cupped his hand and gestured the boy forward. Come, he said. We must make a beginning. It is like a first kiss.

He did. He stepped forward and feinted and passed the knife sideways at the pimp and stepped back. Eduardo arched his back like a cat and held his elbows up that the blade pass beneath them. His shadow on the wall of the warehouse looked like some dark conductor raising his baton to commence. He smiled and circled. His sleek head shone. When he moved in it was very low and from left to right and the knife passed before him three times too fast to follow and almost too fast to see. John Grady fended the blade away with his wrapped right arm and stumbled back and recovered but Eduardo was circling again, smiling.

You think we have not seen your kind before? I have seen your kind before. Many and many. You think I dont know America? I know America. How old do you think I am?

He stopped and crouched and feinted and moved on, circling. I am forty years old, he said. An old man, no? Deserving respect, no? Not this fighting in alleys with knives.

He moved in again and when he stepped back his arm was cut just below the elbow and the yellow silk shirt was dark with blood. He seemed not to notice.

Not this fighting with suitors. With farmboys. Of whom there can be no end.

He stopped in his tracks and turned and started back the other way. He looked like an actor pacing a stage. At times he hardly seemed to notice the boy.

They drift down out of your leprous paradise seeking a thing now extinct among them. A thing for which perhaps they no longer even have a name. Being farmboys of course the first place they think to look is in a whorehouse.

The blood dripped from his sleeve. The slow dark gouts vanished in the dark sand underfoot. He swung the knife back and forth before him on his slow clockwise walk. Like a man hacking randomly at weeds.

By now of course longing has clouded their minds. Such minds as they may possess. The simplest truths are obscured. They cannot seem to see that the most elementary fact concerning whores—

He was suddenly very low before John Grady. Almost kneeling. Almost like a supplicant. The boy could not say how he got there but when he stepped away and commenced his circling again the boy's thigh was laid open in a deep gash and the warm blood was running down his leg.

Is that they are whores, said Eduardo.

He crouched and feinted and circled again. Then he stepped in and with the knife backhand made another cut no more than an inch above the first.

Do you think she did not beg me to come to her? Should I tell you the things she wished me to do? Things beyond a farmboy's imagining, I can assure you.

You're a liar.

The suitor speaks.

He lunged with his knife but Eduardo stepped aside and drew himself up so small and narrow and turned his head away in disdain in the manner of toreros. They circled.

Before I name you completely to myself I will give you even yet a last chance to save yourself. I will let you walk, suitor. If walk you will.

The boy moved sideways, watching. The blood had gone cold on his leg. He passed the sleeve of his knifehand across his nose. Save yourself, he said. If you can. Save yourself, whoremaster.

He calls me names.

They circled.

He is deaf to reason. To his friends. The blind maestro. All. He wishes nothing so fondly as to throw himself into the grave of a dead whore. And he calls me names.

He had turned his face upward. He held out one hand as if to display the vanity of counsel and he seemed to address some unseen witness.

This is quite a farmboy, he said. This is some farmboy.

He feinted to the left and cut John Grady a third time across the thigh.

I will tell you what I am doing. What in fact I have already done. For even knowing you will have no power to stop it. Do you wish me to tell you?

He says nothing, the suitor. Very well. Here is my plan. A medical transplant. To put the suitor's mind inside his thigh. What do you think of that?

He circled. The knife wafted slowly back and forth. I think it may be there already. And how is such a man to think? Whose mind has undergone such a relocation. He still hopes to live. Of course. But he is becoming weaker. The sand is drinking his blood. What do you think, suitor? Will you speak?

He feinted again with the switchblade and stepped away and continued his circling.

He says nothing. Yet how many times was he warned? And then to try to buy the girl? From that moment to this all was certain as dark and day.

John Grady feinted and slashed twice with the knife. Eduardo twisted like a falling cat. They circled.

You are like the whores from the campo, farmboy. To believe that craziness is sacred. A special grace. A special touch. A partaking of the godhead.

He held the knife before him at the level of his waist and passed it slowly back and forth.

But what does this say of God?

They moved simultaneously. The boy tried to grab his arm. They grappled, hacking. The pimp pushed him away and backed, circling. His shirt was sliced open at the front and there was a red slash across his stomach. The boy stood with his hands low, the palms down, waiting. His arm was laid open and he'd dropped the knife in the sand. He did not take his eyes off the pimp. He was cut twice across his stomach and he was reeking blood. The slicker had come unraveled and hung from his forearm and he slowly wound it up again and caught the end of it in his fist and stood.

The suitor seems to have lost his knife. Not so good, eh?

He turned, he circled back. He looked down at the knife.

What are we going to do now?

The boy didnt answer.

What will you give me for the knife?

The boy watched him.

Make me an offer, said Eduardo. What would you give at this point to have the knife back?

The boy turned his head and spat. Eduardo turned and paced slowly back.

Will you give me an eye?

The boy feinted to bend and reach for the knife but Eduardo warned him away and stood on the blade with his thin black boot.

If you let me pry one eye from your head I will give you your knife, he said. Otherwise I will simply cut your throat.

The boy said nothing. He watched.

Think about it, said Eduardo. With one eye in your head you still might kill me. A careless slip. A lucky thrust. Who knows? Anything is possible. What do you say?

He paced away slightly to the left and returned. The knife lay crushed into its mold in the sand.

Nothing, eh? I'll tell you what. I'll make you a better offer. Give me one ear. What about that?

The boy lunged and grabbed for his arm. He spun away and passed the blade twice more across the boy's belly. The boy made a lunge for the fallen knife but Eduardo was already standing over it and he backed away, holding his stomach, the warm blood running between his fingers.

You are going to see your guts before you die, said Eduardo. He stepped away. Pick it up, he said.

The boy watched him.

Pick it up. Did you think I was serious? Pick it up.

He bent and picked up the knife and wiped the blade on the side of his jeans. They circled. Eduardo's blade had severed the fascia of his stomach muscles and he felt hot and sick and his hand was sticky with blood but he was afraid to turn loose holding himself. The slicker had come unwound again and he shook it free and let it fall behind him. They circled.

Lessons are hard, said Eduardo. I think you must agree. But at this point the future is not so uncertain. What do you see? As one cuchillero to another. One filero to another.

He feinted with the switchblade. He smiled. They circled.

What does he see, the suitor. Does he still hope for some miracle? Perhaps he will see the truth at last in his own intestines. As do the old brujos of the campo.

He stepped in with his knife and feinted at the boy's face and then the blade dropped in a vanishing arc of falling light and connected the three bars by a vertical cut to form the letter E in the flesh of his thigh.

He circled to the left. He flung back his oiled hair with a toss of his head.

Do you know what my name is, farmboy? Do you know my name?

He turned his back on the boy and walked slowly away. He addressed the night.

In his dying perhaps the suitor will see that it was his hunger for mysteries that has undone him. Whores. Superstition. Finally death. For that is what has brought you here. That is what you were seeking.

He turned back. He passed the blade again before him in that slow scythelike gesture and he looked questioningly at the boy. As if he might answer at last.

That is what has brought you here and what will always bring you here. Your kind cannot bear that the world be ordinary. That it contain nothing save what stands before one. But the Mexican world is a world of adornment only and underneath it is very plain indeed. While your world—he passed the blade back and forth like a shuttle through a loom—your world totters upon an unspoken labyrinth of questions. And we will devour you, my friend. You and all your pale empire.

When he moved again the boy made no effort to defend himself. He simply slashed away with his knife and when Eduardo stepped back he had fresh cuts on his arm and across his chest. He flung back his head again to clear his lank black locks from before his face. The boy stood stolidly, following him with his eyes. He was drenched in blood.

Dont be afraid, said Eduardo. It doesnt hurt so bad. It would hurt tomorrow. But there will be no tomorrow.

John Grady stood holding himself. His hand was slick with blood and he could feel something bulging through into his palm. They met again and Eduardo laid open the back of his arm but he held himself and would not move the arm. They turned. His boots made a soft sloshing sound.

For a whore, the pimp said. For a whore.

They closed again and John Grady lowered his knife arm.

He felt Eduardo's blade slip from his rib and cross his upper stomach and pass on. It took his breath away. He made no effort to step or to parry. He brought his knife up underhand from the knee and slammed it home and staggered back. He heard the clack of the Mexican's teeth as his jaw clapped shut. Eduardo's knife dropped with a light splash into the small pool of standing water at his feet and he turned away. Then he looked back. The way a man might look getting on a train. The handle of the huntingknife jutted from the underside of his jaw. He reached and touched it. His mouth was clenched in a grimace. His jaw was nailed to his upper skull and he held the handle in both hands as if he would withdraw it but he did not. He walked away and turned and leaned against the warehouse wall. Then he sat down. He drew his knees up to him and sat breathing harshly through his teeth. He put his hands down at either side of him and he looked at John Grady and then after a while he leaned slowly over and lay slumped in the alleyway against the wall of the building and he did not move again.

John Grady was leaning against the wall on the opposite side of the alley, holding himself with both hands. Dont sit down, he said. Dont sit down.

He steadied himself and blew and got his breath and looked down. His shirt hung in bloody tatters. A gray tube of gut pushed through his fingers. He gritted his teeth and took hold of it and pushed it back and put his hand over it. He walked over and picked up Eduardo's knife out of the water and he crossed the alley and still holding himself he cut away the silk shirt from his dead enemy with one hand and leaning against the wall with the knife in his teeth he tied the shirt around himself and bound it tight. Then he let the knife fall in the sand and turned and wobbled slowly down the alleyway and out into the road.

He tried to keep off the main streets. The wash of the lights from the city by which he steered his course hung over the desert like a dawn eternally to come. His boots were filling up with blood and he left bloody tracks in the sand streets of the barrios and dogs came into the street behind him to take his scent and raise their hackles and growl and slink away. He talked to himself as he went. He took to counting his steps. He could hear sirens in the distance and at every step he felt the warm blood ooze between his clutched fingers.

By the time he reached the Calle de Noche Triste he was lightheaded and his feet were reeling beneath him. He leaned against a wall and gathered himself to cross the street. No cars passed.

You didnt eat, he said. That's where you were smart.

He pushed himself off the wall. He stood at the streetcurb and felt before him with one foot and he tried to hurry in case a car should come but he was afraid he'd fall and he didnt know if he could get up again.

A little later he remembered crossing the street but it seemed a long while ago. He'd seen lights ahead. They turned out to be from a tortilla factory. A clanking of old chaindriven machinery, a few workers in flourdusted aprons talking under a yellow lightbulb. He lurched on. Past dark houses. Empty lots. Old slumped mud walls half buried in wind-driven trash. He slowed, he stood teetering. Dont sit down, he said.

But he did. What woke him was someone going through his bloodsoaked pockets. He seized a thin and bony wrist and looked up into the face of a young boy. The boy flailed and kicked and tried to pull away. He called out to his friends but they were on the run across the empty lot. They'd all thought he was dead.

He pulled the boy close. Mira, he said. Está bien. No te molestaré.

Déjame, said the boy.

Está bien. Está bien.

The boy wrenched about. He looked after his friends but they'd vanished in the darkness. Déjame, he said. He was close to tears.

John Grady talked to him the way he'd talk to a horse and after a while the boy stopped pulling and stood. He told him that he was a great filero and that he had just killed an evil man and that he needed the boy's help. He said that the police would be looking for him and that he needed to hide from them. He spoke for a long time. He told the boy of his exploits as a knifefighter and he reached with great difficulty to his hip pocket and got his billfold and gave it to the boy. He told him that the money in it was his to keep and then he told him what he must do. Then he had the boy repeat it back. Then he turned loose of the boy's wrist and waited. The boy stepped back. He stood holding the bloodstained wallet. Then he squatted and looked into the man's eyes. His arms clutching his bony knees. Puede andar? he said.

Un poquito. No mucho.

Es peligroso aquí.

Sí. Tienes razón.

The boy got him up and he leaned on that narrow shoulder while they made their way to the farther corner of the lot where behind the wall was a clubhouse made from packingcrates. The boy knelt and pulled back a drapery of sacking and helped him to crawl in. He said that there was a candle there and matches but the wounded filero said that it was safer in the dark. He'd started to bleed all over again. He could feel it under his hand. Vete, he said. Vete. The boy let drop the curtain.

The cushions he lay on were damp from the rain and they stank. He was very thirsty. He tried not to think. He heard a car pass in the street. He heard a dog bark. He lay with the yellow silk of his enemy's shirt wrapped about him like a ceremonial sash gone dark with blood and he held his bloodied claw of a hand over the severed wall of his stomach. Holding himself close that he not escape from himself for he felt it over and over, that lightness that he took for his soul and which stood so tentatively at the door of his corporeal self. Like some light-footed animal that stood testing the air at the open door of a cage. He heard the distant toll of bells from the cathedral in the city and he heard his own breath soft and uncertain in the cold and the dark of the child's playhouse in that alien land where he lay in his blood. Help me, he said. If you think I'm worth it. Amen.

WHEN HE FOUND the horse standing saddled in the bay of the barn he led it out and mounted up and rode out in the dark up the old road toward John Grady's little adobe house. He hoped the horse would tell him something. When he reached the house and saw the light in the window he put the horse forward at a trot and went splashing through the little creek and into the yard where he pulled up and dismounted and halloed the house.

He pushed open the door. Bud? he said. Bud?

He walked into the bedroom.

Bud?

There was no one there. He went out and called and waited and called again. He went back in and opened the stove door. A fire was laid with stovechunks and kindling and newsprint. He shut the door and went out. He called but no one answered. He mounted up and gave the horse its head and kneed it forward but it only wanted to set out across the creek and back down the road again.

He turned and rode back and waited at the little house for an hour but no one came. By the time he got back to the ranch it was almost midnight.

He lay on his bunk and tried to sleep. He thought he heard the whistle of a train in the distance, thin and lost. He must have been sleeping because he had a dream in which the dead girl came to him hiding her throat with her hand. She was covered in blood and she tried to speak but she could not. He opened his eyes. Very faintly he had heard the phone ring in the house.

When he got to the kitchen Socorro was on the phone in her robe. She gestured wildly at Billy. Sí, sí, she said. Sí, joven. Espérate.

HE WOKE COLD and sweating and raging with thirst. He knew that it was the new day because he was in agony. When he moved the crusted blood in his clothes cracked about him like ice. Then he heard Billy's voice.

Bud, he said. Bud.

He opened his eyes. Billy was kneeling over him. Behind him the boy was holding back the cloth and outside the world was cold and gray. Billy turned to the boy. Ándale, he said. Rápido. Rápido.

The curtain fell. Billy struck a match and held it. You daggone fool, he said. You daggone fool.

He reached down the stub of a candle in its saucer from the shelf nailed to the crate and lit the candle and held it close. Aw shit, he said. You daggone fool. Can you walk?

Dont move me.

I got to.

You couldnt get me across the border noway.

The hell I cant.

He killed her, bud. The son of a bitch killed her.

I know.

The police are huntin me.

JC's bringin the truck. We'll run the goddamn gate if we have to.

Dont move me, bud. I aint goin.

The hell you aint.

I cant make it. I thought there for a while I could. But I cant.

Just take it easy now. I aint listenin to that shit. Hell, I've had worse scratches than that on my eyeball.

I'm cut all to pieces Billy.

We'll get you back. Dont quit on me now, goddamn it.

Billy. Listen. It's all right. I know I aint goin to make it. I done told you.

No. Listen. Whew. You dont know what I'd give for a cool drink of water.

I'll get it.

He started to set the candle by but John Grady took hold of his arm. Dont go, he said. Maybe when the boy gets back.

All right.

He said it wouldnt hurt. The lyin son of a bitch. Whew. It's gettin daylight, aint it?

Yeah.

I seen her, bud. They had her laid out and it didnt look like her but it was. They found her in the river. He cut her throat, bud.

I know.

I just wanted him. Bud, I wanted him.

You should of told me. You didnt have no business comin down here by yourself.

I just wanted him.

Just take it easy. They'll be here directly. You just hang on.

It's okay. Hurts like a sumbitch, Billy. Whew. It's okay.

You want me to get that water?

No. Stay here. She was so goddamned pretty, bud.

Yes she was.

I worried about her all day. You know we talked about where people go when they die. I just believe you go someplace and I seen her layin there and I thought maybe she wouldnt go to heaven because, you know, I thought she wouldnt and I thought about God forgivin people and I thought about if I could ask God to forgive me for killin that son of a bitch because you and me both know I aint sorry for it and I reckon this sounds ignorant but I didnt want to be forgiven if she wasnt. I didnt want to do or be nothin that she wasnt like goin to heaven or anything like that. I know that sounds crazy. Bud when I seen her layin there I didnt care to live no more. I knew my life was over. It come almost as a relief to me.

Hush now. They aint nothin over.

She wanted to do the right thing. That's got to count for somethin dont it? It did with me.

It does with me too.

There's a pawnshop ticket in the top of my footlocker. If you wanted to you could get my gun out and keep it.

We'll get it out.

There's thirty dollars owin on it. There's some money in there too. In a brown envelope.

Dont worry about nothin now. Just take it easy.

Mac's ring is in that little tin box. You see he gets it back. Whew. Like a sumbitch, bud.

You just hang on.

We got the little house lookin good, didnt we?

Yes we did.

You reckon you could keep that pup and kindly look after him?

You'll be there. Dont you worry now.

Hurts, bud. Like a sumbitch.

I know it. You just hang on.

I think maybe I'm goin to need that sup of water.

You just hang on. I'll get it. I wont be a minute either.

He set the candlestub in its saucer of grease on the shelf and backed out and let the curtain fall. As he trotted out across the vacant lot he looked back. The square of yellow light that shone through the sacking looked like some haven of promise out there on the shore of the breaking world but his heart misgave him.

Midblock there was a small cafe just opening. The girl setting up the little tin tables started when she saw him there, wild and sleepless, the knees of his breeches red with blood where he'd knelt in the bloodsoaked mat.

Agua, he said. Necesito agua.

She made her way to the counter without taking her eyes off him. She took down a tumbler and filled it from a bottle and set it on the counter and stepped back.

No hay un vaso más grande? he said.

She stared at him dumbly.

Dame dos, he said. Dos.

She got another glass and filled it and set it out. He put a dollar bill on the counter and took the glasses and left. It was gray dawn. The stars had dimmed out and the dark shapes of the mountains stood along the sky. He carried the glasses carefully one in each hand and crossed the street.

When he got to the packingcrate the candle was still burning and he took the glasses both in one hand and pushed back the sacking and crouched on his knees.

Here you go, bud, he said.

But he had already seen. He set the waterglasses slowly down. Bud, he said. Bud?

The boy lay with his face turned away from the light. His eyes were open. Billy called to him. As if he could not have gone far. Bud, he said. Bud? Aw goddamn. Bud?

Aint that pitiful, he said. Aint that the most goddamn pitiful thing? Aint it? Oh God. Bud. Oh goddamn.

When he had him gathered in his arms he rose and turned. Goddamn whores, he said. He was crying and the tears ran on his angry face and he called out to the broken day against them all and he called out to God to see what was before his eyes. Look at this, he called. Do you see? Do you see?

The Sabbath had passed and in the gray Monday dawn a procession of schoolchildren dressed in blue uniforms all alike were being led along the gritty walkway. The woman had stepped from the curb to take them across at the intersection when she saw the man coming up the street all dark with blood bearing in his arms the dead body of his friend. She held up her hand and the children stopped and huddled with their books at their breasts. He passed. They could not take their eyes from him. The dead boy in his arms hung with his head back and those partly opened eyes beheld nothing at all out of that passing landscape of street or wall or paling sky or the figures of the children who stood blessing themselves in the gray light. This man and his burden passed on forever out of that nameless crossroads and the woman stepped once more into the street and the children followed and all continued on to their appointed places which as some believe were chosen long ago even to the beginning of the world.

EPILOGUE

H<small>E LEFT</small> three days later, he and the dog. A cold and windy day. The pup shivering and whining until he took it up in the bow of the saddle with him. He'd settled up with Mac the evening before. Socorro would not look at him. She set his plate before him and he sat looking at it and then rose and walked down the hallway leaving it untouched on the table. It was still there when he went out through the kitchen again ten minutes later for the last time and she was still there at the stove, bearing on her forehead in ash the thumbprint of the priest placed there that morning to remind her of her mortality. As if she had any thought other. Mac paid him and he folded the money and put it in his shirt-pocket and buttoned it.

When are you leavin?

In the mornin.

You dont have to go.

I dont have to do nothin but die.

You wont change your mind?

No sir.

Well. Nothin's forever.

Some things are.

Yeah. Some things are.

I'm sorry Mr Mac.

I am too, Billy.

I should of looked after him better.

We all should of.

Yessir.

That cousin of his got here about a hour ago. Thatcher Cole.

Called from town. He said they finally got hold of his mother.

What did she have to say?

He didnt say. He said they hadnt heard from him in three years. What do you make of that?

I dont know.

I dont either.

Are you goin to San Angelo?

No. Maybe I ought to. But I aint.

Yessir. Well.

Let it go, son.

I'd like to. I think it's goin to be a while.

I think so too.

Yessir.

Mac nodded toward his blue and swollen hand. You dont think you ought to get somebody to look at that?

It's all right.

You've always got a job here. The army's goin to take this place, but we'll find somethin to do.

I appreciate that.

What time will you be leavin?

Early of the mornin.

You told Oren?

No sir. Not yet.

I reckon you'll see him at breakfast.

Yessir.

But he didnt. He rode out in the dark long before daylight and he rode the sun up and he rode it down again. In the oncoming years a terrible drought struck west Texas. He moved on. There was no work in that country anywhere. Pasture gates stood open and sand drifted in the roads and after a few years it was rare to see stock of any kind and he rode on. Days of the world. Years of the world. Till he was old.

In the spring of the second year of the new millennium he was living in the Gardner Hotel in El Paso Texas and working as an extra in a movie. When the work came to an end he stayed in his room. There was a television set in the lobby and men his age and younger sat in the lobby in the evening in the old chairs and watched the television but he cared little for it and the men had little to say to him or he to them. His money ran out. Three weeks later he was evicted. He'd long since sold his saddle and he set forth into the street with just his AWOL bag and his blanketroll.

There was a shoe repair place a few blocks up the street and he stopped in to see if he could get his boot fixed. The shoeman looked at it and shook his head. The sole was paper thin and the stitching had pulled through the leather. He took it to the rear and sewed it on his machine and returned and stood it on the counter. He wouldnt take any money for it. He said it wouldnt hold and it didnt.

A week later he was somewhere in central Arizona. A rain had come down from the north and the weather turned cool. He sat beneath a concrete overpass and watched the gusts of rain blowing across the fields. The overland trucks passed shrouded in rain with the clearance lights burning and the big wheels spinning like turbines. The east-west traffic passed overhead with a muted rumble. He wrapped himself in his blanket and tried to sleep on the cold concrete but sleep was a long time coming. His bones hurt. He was seventy-eight years old. The heart that should have killed him long ago by what the army's recruiting doctors had said still rattled on in his chest, no will of his. He pulled the blankets about him and after a while he did sleep.

In the night he dreamt of his sister dead seventy years and buried near Fort Sumner. He saw her so clearly. Nothing had changed, nothing faded. She was walking slowly along the dirt road past the house. She wore the white dress her grandmother had sewn for her from sheeting and in her grandmother's hands the dress had taken on a shirred bodice and borders of tatting threaded with blue ribbon. That's what she wore. That and the straw hat she'd gotten for Easter. When she passed the house he knew that she would never enter there again nor would he see her ever again and in his sleep he called out to her but she did not turn or answer him but only passed on down that empty road in infinite sadness and infinite loss.

He woke and lay in the dark and the cold and he thought of her and he thought of his brother dead in Mexico. In everything that he'd ever thought about the world and about his life in it he'd been wrong.

Toward the small hours of the morning the traffic on the freeway slacked and the rain stopped. He sat up shivering and hitched the blanket about his shoulders. He'd put some crackers from a roadside diner in the pocket of his coat and he sat eating them and watching the gray light flush out the raw wet fields beyond the roadway. He thought he heard the distant cries of cranes where they would be headed north to their summering grounds in Canada and he thought of them asleep in a flooded field in Mexico in a dawn long ago, standing singlefooted in the wetlands with their bills tucked, gray figures aligned in rows like hooded monks at prayer. When he looked across the overpass to the far side of the turnpike he saw another such as he sitting also solitary and alone.

The man raised his hand in greeting. He raised his back.

Buenos días, the man called.

Buenos días.

Qué tiene de comer?

Unas galletas, nada más.

The man nodded. He looked away.

Podemos compartirlas.

Bueno, called the man. Gracias.

Allí voy.

But the man stood. I will come to you, he called.

He descended the concrete batterwall and crossed the roadway and climbed over the guardrail and crossed the median between the round concrete pillars and crossed the northbound lanes and climbed up to where Billy was sitting and squatted and looked at him.

It aint much, Billy said. He pulled the remaining few packages of crackers from his pocket and held them out.

Muy amable, the man said.

Está bien. I thought at first you might be somebody else.

The man sat and stretched out his legs before him and crossed his feet. He tore open a package of the crackers with his eyetooth and took one out and held it up and looked at it and then bit it in two and sat chewing. He wore a wispy moustache, his skin was smooth and brown. He was of no determinable age.

Who did you think I might be? he said.

Just somebody. Somebody I sort of been expectin. I thought I caught a glimpse of him once or twice these past few days. I aint never got all that good a look at him.

What does he look like?

I dont know. I guess more and more he looks like a friend.

You thought I was death.

I considered the possibility.

The man nodded. He chewed. Billy watched him.

You aint are you?

No.

They sat eating the dry crackers.

Adónde vas? Billy said.

Al sur. Y tú?

Al norte.

The man nodded. He smiled. Qué clase de hombre comparta sus galletas con la muerte?

Billy shrugged. What kind of death would eat them?

What kind indeed, said the man.

I wasnt tryin to figure anything out. De todos modos el compartir es la ley del camino, verdad?

De veras.

At least that's the way I was raised.

The man nodded. In Mexico on certain days of the calendar it is the custom to set a place at the table for death. But perhaps you know this.

Yes.

He has a big appetite.

Yes he does.

Perhaps a few crackers would be taken as an insult.

Perhaps he's got to take what he can get. Like the rest of us.

The man nodded. Yes, he said. That could be.

Traffic had picked up on the turnpike. The sun was up. The man opened the second package of crackers. He said that perhaps death took a larger view. That perhaps in his egalitarian way death weighed the gifts of men by their own lights and that in death's eyes the offerings of the poor were the equal of any.

Like God.

Yes. Like God.

Nadie puede sobornar a la muerte, Billy said.

De veras. Nadie.

Nor God.

Nor God.

Billy watched the light bring up the shapes of the water standing in the fields beyond the roadway. Where do we go when we die? he said.

I dont know, the man said. Where are we now?

The sun rose over the plain behind them. The man handed him back the last remaining packet of crackers.

You can keep em, Billy said.

No quieres más?

My mouth's too dry.

The man nodded, he pocketed the crackers. Para el camino, he said. I was born in Mexico. I have not been back for many years.

You goin back now?

No.

Billy nodded. The man studied the coming day. In the middle of my life, he said, I drew the path of it upon a map and I studied it a long time. I tried to see the pattern that it made upon the earth because I thought that if I could see that pattern and identify the form of it then I would know better how to continue. I would know what my path must be. I would see into the future of my life.

How did that work out?

Different from what I expected.

How did you know it was the middle of your life?

I had a dream. That was why I drew the map.

What did it look like?

The map?

Yes.

It was interesting. It looked like different things. There were different perspectives one could take. I was surprised.

Could you remember all the places you'd been?

Oh yes. Couldnt you?

I dont know. There's been a bunch of em. Yeah. I suppose. If I put my mind to it. If I was to set down and study about it.

Yes. Of course. That was my method. One thing leads to another. I doubt that our journey can be lost to us. For good or bad.

What sorts of things did it look like? The map.

At first I saw a face but then I turned it and looked at it other ways and when I turned it back the face was gone. Nor could I find it again.

What happened to it?

I dont know.

Did you see it or did you just think you did?

The man smiled. Qué pregunta, he said. What would be the difference?

I dont know. I think there has to be a difference.

So do I. But what is it?

Well. It wouldnt be like a real face.

No. It was a suggestion. Un bosquejo. Un borrador, quizás.

Yes.

In any case it is difficult to stand outside of one's desires and see things of their own volition.

I think you just see whatever's in front of you.

Yes. I dont think that.

What was the dream?

The dream, the man said.

You dont have to tell me.

How do you know?

You dont have to tell me anything.

Perhaps. Nevertheless there was this man who was traveling through the mountains and he came to a place in the mountains where certain pilgrims used to gather in the long ago.

Is this the dream?

Yes.

Ándale pues.

Gracias. Where pilgrims used to gather in the long ago. En tiempos antiguos.

You've told this dream before.

Yes.

Ándale.

En tiempos antiguos. It was a high pass in the mountains that he had come to and here there was a table of rock and the table of rock was very old and it had fallen in the early days of the earth from a high peñasco in the mountains and lay in the floor of the pass with its flat and cloven side to the weather and the sun. And on the face of that rock there were yet to be seen the stains of blood from those who'd been slaughtered upon it to appease the gods. The iron in the blood of these vanished beings had blackened the rock and there it could be seen. Together with the hatching of axemarks or the marks of swords upon the stone to show where the work was done.

Is there such a place?

I dont know. Yes. There are such places. But this was not one of them. This was a dream place.

Ándale.

So the traveler arrived at this place at nightfall when the mountains about were darkening and the wind in the pass was growing cold with night's onset and he put down his burden to rest himself and he removed his hat to cool his brow and then his eyes fell upon this bloodstained altarstone which the weathers of the sierra and the sierra's storms had these millennia been impotent to cleanse. And there he elected to pass the night, such is the recklessness of those whom God has been so good as to shield from their just share of adversity in this world.

Who was the traveler?

I dont know.

Was it you?

I dont think so. But then if we do not know ourselves in the waking world what chance in dreams?

I'd think I'd know if it was me.

Yes. But have you not met people in dreams you never saw before? In dreams or out?

Sure.

And who were they?

I dont know. Dream people.

You think you made them up. In your dream.

I guess. Yeah.

Could you do it waking?

Billy sat with his arms over his knees. No, he said. I guess I couldnt.

No. Anyway I think the self of you in dreams or out is only that which you elect to see. I'm guessing every man is more than he supposes.

Ándale.

So. This traveler was such a man. He laid down his burden and surveyed the darkening scene. In that high pass was naught but rock and scree and as he thought to at least raise himself above the feasible paths of serpents in the night so he came to the altar and placed his hands upon it. He paused, but he did not pause long enough. He unrolled his blanket upon the stone and weighted down the ends with rocks that it not be blown away by the wind before he could remove his boots.

Did he know what kind of stone it was?

No.

Then who knew?

The dreamer knew.

You.

Yes.

Well I reckon you and him had to of been two different people then.

How so?

Because if you were the same then one would know what the other knew.

As in the world.

Yes.

But this is not the world. This is a dream. In the world the question could not occur.

Ándale.

Remove his boots. When he had removed them he climbed onto the stone and rolled himself in his blanket and upon that cold and terrible pallet he composed himself for sleep.

I wish him luck.

Yes. Yet sleep he did.

He fell asleep in your dream.

Yes.

How do you know he was asleep?

I could see him sleeping.

Did he dream?

The man sat looking at his shoes. He uncrossed his legs and recrossed them the other way. Well, he said. I'm not sure how to answer you. Certain events occurred. Some things about them remain unclear. It is difficult to know, for instance, when it was that these events took place.

Why?

The dream I had was on a certain night. And in the dream the traveler appeared. What night was this? In the life of the traveler when was it that he came to spend the night in that rocky posada? He slept and events took place which I will tell you of, but when was this? You can see the problem. Let us say that the events which took place were a dream of this man whose own reality remains conjectural. How assess the world of that conjectural mind? And what with him is sleep and what is waking? How comes he to own a world of night at all? Things need a ground to stand upon. As every soul requires a body. A dream within a dream makes other claims than what a man might suppose.

A dream inside a dream might not be a dream.

You have to consider the possibility.

It just sounds like superstition to me.

And what is that?

Superstition?

Yes.

Well. I guess it's when you believe in things that dont exist.

Such as tomorrow? Or yesterday?

Such as the dreams of somebody you dreamt. Yesterday was here and tomorrow's comin.

Maybe. But anyway the dreams of this man were his own dreams. They were distinct from my dream. In my dream the man was lying on his stone asleep.

You still could of made them up.

En este mundo todo es posible. Vamos a ver.

It's like the picture of your life in that map.

Cómo?

Es un dibujo nada más. It aint your life. A picture aint a thing. It's just a picture.

Well said. But what is your life? Can you see it? It vanishes at its own appearance. Moment by moment. Until it vanishes to appear no more. When you look at the world is there a point in time when the seen becomes the remembered? How are they separate? It is that which we have no way to show. It is that which is missing from our map and from the picture that it makes. And yet it is all we have.

You aint said whether your map was any use to you or not.

The man tapped his lower lip with his forefinger. He looked at Billy. Yes, he said. We will come to that. For now I can only say that I had hoped for a sort of calculus that would sum the convergence of map and life when life was done. For within their limitations there must be a common shape or shared domain between the telling and the told. And if that is so then the picture also in whatever partial form must have a direction to it and if it does then whatever is to come must lie in that path. You say that the life of a man cannot be pictured. But perhaps we mean different things. The picture seeks to seize and immobilize within its own configurations what it never owned. Our map knows nothing of time. It has no power to speak even of the hours implicit in its own existence. Not of those that have passed, not of those to come. Yet in its final shape the map and the life it traces must converge for there time ends.

So if I'm right still it's for the wrong reasons.

Perhaps we should return to the dreamer and his dream.

Ándale.

You might wish to say that the traveler woke and that the events which took place were not a dream at all. But I think to view them as a dream is the wiser course. For if these events were else than a dream he would not wake at all. As you will see.

Ándale.

My own dream is another matter. My traveler sleeps a troubled dream. Shall I wake him? The proprietary claims of the dreamer upon the dreamt have their limits. I cannot rob the traveler of his own autonomy lest he vanish altogether. You see the problem.

I think I'm beginnin to see several problems.

Yes. This traveler also has a life and there is a direction to that life and if he himself did not appear in this dream the dream would be quite otherwise and there could be no talk of him at all. You may say that he has no substance and therefore no history but my view is that whatever he may be or of whatever made he cannot exist without a history. And the ground of that history is not different from yours or mine for it is the predicate life of men that assures us of our own reality and that of all about us. Our privileged view into this one night of this man's history presses upon us the realization that all knowledge is a borrowing and every fact a debt. For each event is revealed to us only at the surrender of every alternate course. For us, the whole of the traveler's life converges at this place and this hour, whatever we may know of that life or out of whatever stuff it may be made. De acuerdo?

Ándale.

So. He composed himself for sleep. And in the night there was a storm in the mountains and the lightning cracked and the wind moaned in the gap and the traveler's rest was a poor rest indeed. The barren peaks about him were hammered out of the blackness again and again by the lightning and in the flare of that lightning he was surprised to see descending down through the rocky arroyos a troupe of men bearing torches in the rain and singing some low chant or prayer as they came. He raised himself up from his stone the better to make them out. He could see little more than their heads and shoulders jostling in the torchlight but they seemed to wear a variety of adornments, primitive headpieces contrived from the feathers of birds or the hides of jungle cats. The fur of marmosets. They wore necklaces of bead or stone or ocean shell and shawls of woven stuff that may have been moss. By the smoky lamps hissing in the rain he could see that they carried upon their shoulders a litter or bier and now he could hear echoing among the rocks the floating notes of a horn and the slow beat of a drum.

When they came into the road he could see them better. In the forefront was a man in a mask made from the carved shell of a seaturtle all inlaid with agate and jasper. He carried a sceptre on the head of which was his own likeness and the likeness carried also such a sceptre in miniature and this sceptre too in what we must imagine to be some unknown infinitude of alternate being and likeness.

Behind him came the drummer with his drum of saltcured rawhide stretched upon a frame of ash and this he beat with a sort of flail made of a hardwood ball tethered to a stick. The drum gave off a low note of great resonance and he struck it with an upward swing of the flail and at each beat he bent his head to listen as perhaps a man might who were tuning a drum.

There followed a man bearing a sheathed sword upon a leather cushion and after him the bearers of torches and then the litter and the men who carried it. The traveler could not tell if the person they carried were alive or if this were not perhaps some sort of funeral procession passing through the mountains in the rain and the night. At the rear of the enfilade came the hornsman bearing an instrument made of cane bound with wrappings of copper wire and hung with tassels. He played it by blowing through a length of tubing and it played three notes which hovered in the shrouded night air above them like a ponderable body itself.

How many of these people were there?

I believe eight.

Go ahead.

They advanced upon the road and the traveler sat up and swung his legs over the side of his altarstone and pulled the blanket about his shoulders and waited. They came on until they were opposite to the place where he sat and here they stopped and here they stood. The traveler watched them. If he was curious he was also afraid.

What about you?

I was only curious.

How did you know he was afraid?

The man studied the empty roadway beneath them. After a while he said: This man was not me. If he may have been some part of me that I do not recognize then so may you. I fall back upon my argument of common histories.

Where were you all this time?

Asleep in my bed.

You were not in the dream.

No.

Billy leaned and spat. Well, he said, I'm seventy-eight years old and in that time I've had a lot of dreams. And as near as I can recollect I was in ever one of em. I dont recall a time that I ever dreamt about other people but what I wasnt around somewheres. My notion is that you pretty much dream about yourself. I even dreamt one time that I was dead. But I was standin there looking at the corpse.

I see, the man said.

What do you see?

I see you've thought a bit about dreams.

I aint thought about em at all. I've just had em.

Can we come back to this question?

You can do whatever you want.

Thank you.

You sure you aint makin all this up.

The man smiled. He looked out across the roadway and the fields and shook his head but he didnt answer.

Or did you want to come back to that?

The problem is that your question is the very question upon which the story hangs.

A tractor-trailer passed overhead and the swallows nesting in the concrete coves flew forth and circled and returned.

Bear with me, the man said. This story like all stories has its beginnings in a question. And those stories which speak to us with the greatest resonance have a way of turning upon the teller and erasing him and his motives from all memory. So the question of who is telling the story is very consiguiente.

Every story is not about some question.

Yes it is. Where all is known no narrative is possible.

Billy leaned and spat again. Ándale, he said.

He was curious and afraid this traveler and he called out to the processional some greeting which echoed among the rocks. He asked them where they were bound but never did they answer back. They stood in the old road through the pass huddled together, these mute and midnight folk with their torches and their instruments and their captive, and they waited. As if he were a mystery to them. Or as if he were expected to say some particular thing which he had yet to say.

He was really asleep.

That is my view.

And if he had of woke?

Then what he saw he would no longer see. Nor I.

Why couldnt you just say it would of vanished or disappeared?

Which?

Which what?

Desaparecer o desvanecerse.

Hay una diferencia?

Sí. Lo que se desvanece es simplemente fuera de la vista. Pero desaparecido? He shrugged. Where do things go? In a case such as that of the traveler and his adventures—where one is on uncertain ground to even say from whence they came at all—there seems little to be said as to where they might be when gone. In such a case one can come upon no footing where even to begin.

Can I say somethin?

Of course.

I think you got a habit of makin things a bit more complicated than what they need to be. Why not just tell the story?

Good advice. Let's see what can be done.

Ándale pues.

Although I should point out to you that you are the one with the questions.

No you shouldnt.

Yes. Of course.

Just get on with it.

Yes.

Mum's the word here.

Cómo?

Nothin. I'll shut up askin questions, that's all.

They were good questions.

You aint goin to tell the story, are you?

So perhaps he struggled to wake. For all that the night was cold and his bed hard stone he could not. In the meantime all was silence. The rain had ceased. The wind. The processioners consulted among themselves and then the bearers came forward and set the litter on the rocky ground. Upon the litter lay a young girl with eyes closed and hands crossed upon her breast as if in death. The dreamer looked at her and he looked at the troupe standing about her. Cold as the night was and colder as it must have been in the windswept reaches from which they had descended they yet were thinly clothed and even the capes and blankets that they wore over their shoulders were of loosely woven stuff. In the light of their torches their faces and their torsos shone with sweat. And strange as was their appearance and the mission they seemed bent upon yet they were also oddly familiar. As if he'd seen all this somewhere before.

Like in a dream.

If you wish.

It aint up to me.

You think you know how this dream ends.

I got a notion or two.

We'll see.

Carry on.

With the troupe was a sort of chemist who carried in a belt at his waist the nostrums of his trade and he and the leader of the group conferred. The leader thumbed back the turtleshell to the top of his head like a welder tipping back his mask but the dreamer could not see his face. The outcome of their conferencing was that three of the halfnaked men from the company detached themselves and approached the altarstone. They carried a flask and a cup and they set the cup upon the stone and poured it full and offered it to the dreamer.

He better think twice.

Too late. He took it in both hands with the same gravity with which it had been offered and raised it to his lips and drank.

What was in it?

I dont know.

What kind of cup?

A cup of horn heated in a fire and shaped so it would stand.

What did it do to him?

It caused him to forget.

What did he forget? Everthing?

He forgot the pain of his life. Nor did he understand the penalty for doing so.

Go ahead.

He drank it down and handed back the cup and almost at once all was taken from him so that he was like a child again and a great peace settled upon him and his fears abated to the point that he would become accomplice in a blood ceremony that was then and is now an affront to God.

Was that the penalty?

No. There was a greater cost even than that.

What was it?

That this too would be forgot.

Would that be such a bad idea?

Wait and see.

Go on.

He drank the cup and gave himself up to the dark mercies of these ancient serranos. And they in turn led him from the stone out into the road and they walked up and back with him. They seemed to be urging him to contemplate his surroundings, the rocks and the mountains, the stars which were belled above them against the eternal blackness of the world's nativity.

What were they sayin?

I dont know.

You couldnt hear them?

The man didnt answer. He sat pondering the forms of the concrete overhead. The nests of the swallows clung in the high corners like colonies of small mud hornos inverted there. The traffic had increased. The boxshaped shadows which the trucks shook off on entering beneath the overpass waited for them where they emerged into the sun again on the far side. He lifted one hand in a slow tossing gesture. There is no way to answer your question. It is not the case that there are small men in your head holding a conversation. There is no sound. So what language is that? In any case this was a deep dream for the dreamer and in such dreams there is a language that is older than the spoken word at all. The idiom is another specie and with it there can be no lie or no dissemblance of the truth.

I thought you said they were talkin.

In my dream of them perhaps they were talking. Or perhaps I was only putting upon it the best construction that I knew. The traveler's dream is another matter.

Go ahead.

The ancient world holds us to account. The world of our fathers . . .

It seems to me if they were talkin in your dream they'd have to be talkin in his. It's the same dream.

It's the same question.

What's the answer?

We're coming to that.

Ándale.

The world of our fathers resides within us. Ten thousand generations and more. A form without a history has no power to perpetuate itself. What has no past can have no future. At the core of our life is the history of which it is composed and in that core are no idioms but only the act of knowing and it is this we share in dreams and out. Before the first man spoke and after the last is silenced forever. Yet in the end he did speak, as we shall see.

All right.

So he walked with his captors until his mind was calm and he knew that his life was now in other hands.

There dont seem to be much fight in him.

You forget the hostage.

The girl.

Yes.

Go on.

It is important to understand that he did not give himself up willingly. The martyr who longs for the flames can be no right candidate for them. Where there is no penalty there can be no prize. You understand.

Go on.

They seemed to be waiting for him to come to some decision. To tell them something perhaps. He studied everything about him that could be studied. The stars and the rocks and the face of the sleeping girl upon her pallet. His captors. Their helmets and their costumes. The torches which they carried that were made of hollow pipes filled with oil and wicks of rope and the flames which were sheltered from the wind by panes of isinglass set into caming and roofed and flued with beaten copper sheet. He tried to see into their eyes but those eyes were dark and they had shadowed them with blacking like men called upon to traverse wastes of snow. Or sand. He tried to see their feet how they were shod but their robes fell over the rocks about them and he could not. What he saw was the strangeness of the world and how little was known and how poorly one could prepare for aught that was to come. He saw that a man's life was little more than an instant and that as time was eternal therefore every man was always and eternally in the middle of his journey, whatever be his years or whatever distance he had come. He thought he saw in the world's silence a great conspiracy and he knew that he himself must then be a part of that conspiracy and that he had already moved beyond his captors and their plans. If he had any revelation it was this: that he was repository to this knowing which he came to solely by his abandonment of every former view. And with this he turned to his captors and he said: I will tell you nothing.

I will tell you nothing. That is what he said and that is all he said. In the next moment they led him to the stone and laid him down upon it and they raised up the girl from her pallet and led her forward. Her bosom was heaving.

Her what?

Her bosom was heaving.

Go ahead.

She leaned and kissed him and stepped away and then the archatron came forward with his sword and raised it in his two hands above him and clove the traveler's head from his body.

I guess that was the end of that.

Not at all.

I suppose you're fixin to tell me he survived havin his head lopped off.

Yes. He woke from his dream and sat shivering with cold and fright. In the selfsame desolate pass. The selfsame barren range of mountains. The selfsame world.

And you?

The narrator smiled wistfully, like a man remembering his childhood. These dreams reveal the world also, he said. We wake remembering the events of which they are composed while often the narrative is fugitive and difficult to recall. Yet it is the narrative that is the life of the dream while the events themselves are often interchangeable. The events of the waking world on the other hand are forced upon us and the narrative is the unguessed axis along which they must be strung. It falls to us to weigh and sort and order these events. It is we who assemble them into the story which is us. Each man is the bard of his own existence. This is how he is joined to the world. For escaping from the world's dream of him this is at once his penalty and his reward. So. I might have woken then myself but as the world neared so did the traveler upon his rock begin to fade and as I was not yet willing to part company with him I called out to him.

Did he have a name?

No. No name.

What did you call?

I simply called upon him to stay and stay he did and so I slept on and the traveler turned to me and waited.

I guess he was surprised to see you.

A good question. He seemed indeed to be surprised and yet in dreams it is often the case that the greatest extravagances seem bereft of their power to astonish and the most improbable chimeras appear commonplace. Our waking life's desire to shape the world to our convenience invites all manner of paradox and difficulty. All in our custody seethes with an inner restlessness. But in dreams we stand in this great democracy of the possible and there we are right pilgrims indeed. There we go forth to meet what we shall meet.

I got another question.

You want to know if the traveler knew that he'd been dreaming. If indeed he had been dreaming.

Like you say, you've told the story before.

Yes.

What's the answer.

You might not like it.

That ought not to stop you.

He asked me the same question.

He wanted to know if he'd been dreaming?

Yes.

What did he say?

He asked me if I had seen them.

Them people with the robes and the candles and all.

Yes.

And.

Well. I had. Of course.

So that's what you told him.

I told him the truth.

Well it would have served as well for a lie wouldnt it?

Because?

If it caused him to believe that what he dreamt was real.

Yes. You see the difficulty.

Billy leaned and spat. He studied the landscape to the north. I better get on, he said. I got a ways to go.

You have people waiting for you?

I hope so. I sure would like to see them.

He wished me to be his witness. But in dreams there can be no witness. You said as much yourself.

It was just a dream. You dreamt him. You can make him do whatever you like.

Where was he before I dreamt him?

You tell me.

My belief is this, and I say it again: His history is the same as yours or mine. That is the stuff he is made of. What stuff other? Had I created him as God makes men how then would I not know what he would say before he ever spoke? Or how he'd move before he did so? In a dream we dont know what's coming. We are surprised.

All right.

So where is it coming from?

I dont know.

Two worlds touch here. You think men have power to call forth what they will? Evoke a world, awake or sleeping? Make it breathe and then set out upon it figures which a glass gives back or which the sun acknowledges? Quicken those figures with one's own joy and one's despair? Can a man be so hid from himself? And if so who is hid? And from whom?

You call forth the world which God has formed and that world only. Nor is this life of yours by which you set such store your doing, however you may choose to tell it. Its shape was forced in the void at the onset and all talk of what might otherwise have been is senseless for there is no otherwise. Of what could it be made? Where be hid? Or how make its appearance? The probability of the actual is absolute. That we have no power to guess it out beforehand makes it no less certain. That we may imagine alternate histories means nothing at all.

So is that the end of the story?

No. The traveler stood at the stone and on the stone visible to see were marks of axe and sword and the dark oxidations of the blood of those who'd died there and which the weathers of the world were powerless to erase. Here the traveler had lain down to sleep with no thought of death and yet when he awoke he'd no thought other. The heavens which he had been invited to scrutinize by his executioners now wore a different look. The order of his life seemed altered in midstride. Some halt-stitch in the workings of things. Those heavens in whose forms men see commensurate destinies cognate to their own now seemed to pulse with a reckless energy. As if in their turning things had come uncottered, uncalendared. He thought that there might even be some timefault in the record. That henceforth there might be no way to log new sightings. Would that matter?

You're askin me.

Yes.

I think it would matter to you. About him I got no idea. What do you think?

The narrator paused thoughtfully. I think, he said, that the dreamer imagined himself at some crossroads. Yet there are no crossroads. Our decisions do not have some alternative. We may contemplate a choice but we pursue one path only. The log of the world is composed of its entries, but it cannot be divided back into them. And at some point this log must outdistance any possible description of it and this I believe is what the dreamer saw. For as the power to speak of the world recedes from us so also must the story of the world lose its thread and therefore its authority. The world to come must be composed of what is past. No other material is at hand. And yet I think he saw the world unraveling at his feet. The procedures which he had adopted for his journey now seemed like an echo from the death of things. I think he saw a terrible darkness looming.

I need to be gettin on.

The man did not answer. He sat contemplating the roadside vegas and the barren lands beyond now shimmering in the newest sun.

This desert about us was once a vast sea, he said. Can such a thing vanish? Of what are seas made? Or I? Or you?

I dont know.

The man stood up and stretched. He stretched mightily, reaching and turning. He looked down at Billy and smiled.

And that's the end of the story, Billy said.

No.

He squatted and held up his hand, palm out.

Hold up your hand, he said. Like this.

Is this a pledge of some kind?

No. You are pledged already. You always were. Hold up your hand.

He held up his hand as the man had asked.

You see the likeness?

Yes.

Yes. It is senseless to claim that things exist in their instancing only. The template for the world and all in it was drawn long ago. Yet the story of the world, which is all the world we know, does not exist outside of the instruments of its execution. Nor can those instruments exist outside of their own history. And so on. This life of yours is not a picture of the world. It is the world itself and it is composed not of bone or dream or time but of worship. Nothing else can contain it. Nothing else be by it contained.

So what happened to the traveler?

Nothing. There is no end to the story. He woke and all was as before. He was free to go.

To other men's dreams.

Perhaps. Of such dreams and of the rituals of them there can also be no end. The thing that is sought is altogether other. However it may be construed within men's dreams or by their acts it will never make a fit. These dreams and these acts are driven by a terrible hunger. They seek to meet a need which they can never satisfy, and for that we must be grateful.

And you were still asleep.

Yes. At the end of the dream we walked out in the dawn and there was an encampment on the plains below from which no smoke rose for all that it was cold and we went down to that place but all was abandoned there. There were huts of skin staked out upon the rocky ground with slagiron pikes and within these huts were remnants of old meals untouched and cold upon cold plates of clay. There were standing stores of primitive and antique arms carved in their metal parts and inlaid with filigree of gold and there were robes sewn up from skins of northern animals and rawhide trunks with latches and corners of hammered copper and these were much scarred from their travels and the years of it and inside of them were old accounts and ledgerbooks and records of the history of that vanished folk, the path they had followed in the world and their reckonings of the cost of that journey. And in a place apart a skeleton of old sepia bones sewn up in a leather shroud.

We walked together through all that desolation and all that abandonment and I asked him if the people were away at some calling but he said that they were not. When I asked him to tell me what had happened he looked at me and he said: I have been here before. So have you. Everything is here for the taking. Touch nothing. Then I woke.

From his dream or yours?

There was only one dream to wake from. I woke from that world to this. Like the traveler, all I had forsaken I would come upon again.

What had you forsaken?

The immappable world of our journey. A pass in the mountains. A bloodstained stone. The marks of steel upon it. Names carved in the corrosible lime among stone fishes and ancient shells. Things dim and dimming. The dry sea floor. The tools of migrant hunters. The dreams enchased upon the blades of them. The peregrine bones of a prophet. The silence. The gradual extinction of rain. The coming of night.

I got to get on.

I wish you well, cuate.

And you.

I hope your friends await you.

And I.

Every man's death is a standing in for every other. And since death comes to all there is no way to abate the fear of it except to love that man who stands for us. We are not waiting for his history to be written. He passed here long ago. That man who is all men and who stands in the dock for us until our own time come and we must stand for him. Do you love him, that man? Will you honor the path he has taken? Will you listen to his tale?

HE SLEPT THAT NIGHT in a concrete tile by the highwayside where a roadcrew had been working. A big yellow Euclid truck was standing out on the mud and the pale and naked concrete pillars of an east-west onramp stood beyond the truck, curving away, clustered and rising without capital or pediment like the ruins of some older order standing in the dusk. In the night a wind blew down from the north that bore the taste of rain but no rain fell. He could smell the wet creosote out on the desert. He tried to sleep. After a while he got up and sat in the round mouth of the tile like a man in a bell and looked out upon the darkness. Out on the desert to the west stood what he took for one of the ancient spanish missions of that country but when he studied it again he saw that it was the round white dome of a radar tracking station. Beyond that and partly overcast also in the moonlight he saw a row of figures struggling and clamoring silently in the wind. They appeared to be dressed in robes and some among them fell down in their struggling and rose to flail again. He thought they must be laboring toward him across the darkened desert yet they made no progress at all. They had the look of inmates in a madhouse palely gowned and pounding mutely at the glass of their keeping. He called to them but his shout was carried away on the wind and in any case they were too far to hear him. After a while he rolled himself again in his blanket on the floor of the tile and after a while he slept. In the morning the storm had passed and what he saw out on the desert in the new day's light were only rags of plastic wrapping hanging from a fence where the wind had blown them.

He made his way east to De Baca County in New Mexico and he looked for the grave of his sister but he could not find it. The people of that country were kind to him and the days warmed and he wanted for little in his life on the road. He stopped to talk to children or to horses. Women fed him in their kitchens and he slept rolled in his blanket under the stars and watched meteorites fall down the sky. He drank one evening from a spring beneath a cottonwood, leaning to bow his mouth and suck from the cold silk top of the water and watch the minnows drift and recover in the current beneath him. There was a tin cup on a stob and he took it down and sat holding it. He'd not seen a cup at a spring in years and he held it in both hands as had thousands before him unknown to him yet joined in sacrament. He dipped the cup into the water and raised it cool and dripping to his mouth.

In the fall of that year when the cold weather came he was taken in by a family just outside of Portales New Mexico and he slept in a shed room off the kitchen that was much like the room he'd slept in as a boy. On the hallway wall hung a framed photograph that had been printed from a glass plate broken into five pieces and in the photograph certain ancestors were puzzled back together in a study that cohered with its own slightly skewed geometry. Apportioning some third or separate meaning to each of the figures seated there. To their faces. To their forms.

The family had a girl twelve and a boy fourteen and their father had bought them a colt they kept stabled in a shed behind the house. It wasnt much of a colt but he went out in the afternoon when they came in off the schoolbus and showed them how to work the colt with rope and halter. The boy liked the colt but the girl was in love with it and she'd go out at night after supper in the cold and sit in the straw floor of the shed and talk to it.

In the evening after supper sometimes the woman would invite him to play cards with them and sometimes he and the children would sit at the kitchen table and he'd tell them about horses and cattle and the old days. Sometimes he'd tell them about Mexico.

One night he dreamt that Boyd was in the room with him but he would not speak for all that he called out to him. When he woke the woman was sitting on his bed with her hand on his shoulder.

Mr Parham are you all right?

Yes mam. I'm sorry. I was dreamin, I reckon.

You sure you okay?

Yes mam.

Did you want me to bring you a sup of water?

No mam. I appreciate it. I'll get back to sleep here directly.

You want me to leave the light on in the kitchen?

If you wouldnt mind.

All right.

I thank you.

Boyd was your brother.

Yes. He's been dead many a year.

You still miss him though.

Yes I do. All the time.

Was he the younger?

He was. By two years.

I see.

He was the best. We run off to Mexico together. When we was kids. When our folks died. We went down there to see about gettin back some horses they'd stole. We was just kids. He was awful good with horses. I always liked to watch him ride. Liked to watch him around horses. I'd give about anything to see him one more time.

You will.

I hope you're right.

You sure you dont want a glass of water?

No mam. I'm all right.

She patted his hand. Gnarled, ropescarred, speckled from the sun and the years of it. The ropy veins that bound them to his heart. There was map enough for men to read. There God's plenty of signs and wonders to make a landscape. To make a world. She rose to go.

Betty, he said.

Yes.

I'm not what you think I am. I aint nothin. I dont know why you put up with me.

Well, Mr Parham, I know who you are. And I do know why. You go to sleep now. I'll see you in the morning.

Yes mam.

DEDICATION

I will be your child to hold
And you be me when I am old
The world grows cold
The heathen rage
The story's told
Turn the page.

A NOTE ON THE TYPE

This book was set in Janson, a typeface long thought to have been made by the Dutchman Anton Janson, who was a practicing typefounder in Leipzig during the years 1668–1687. However, it has been conclusively demonstrated that these types are actually the work of Nicholas Kis (1650–1702), a Hungarian, who most probably learned his trade from the master Dutch typefounder Dirk Voskens. The type is an excellent example of the influential and sturdy Dutch types that prevailed in England up to the time William Caslon (1692–1766) developed his own incomparable designs from them.

Printed and bound by R. R. Donnelley & Sons,
Harrisonburg, Virginia
Designed by Peter A. Andersen